THE BLUE WINDOW

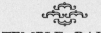

TEMPLE BAILEY

CONTENTS

CHAPTER I

THE WEARING OF BLACK

HILDEGARDE had always known that her mother was different from the others, but she had not known why. She had thought it might be because, before her father died, her mother had had an easy time. And Aunt Catherine and Aunt Olivia had never had an easy time. They had worked hard, as girls, on the farm, and they worked hard now. Aunt Olivia, to be sure, had been married, but she had worked hard for her husband, and when he left her a widow, she made her home with Aunt Catherine and kept on working.

At first, they had all done woman's work, but when the war came on, with labor scarce, the three sisters toiled out of doors, sowing, planting, hoeing, weeding. None of them liked it except Hildegarde's mother. She had explained it to Hildegarde:

" When I plant a seed, I feel that it is an act of creation, as if I had painted a picture or had written a poem — and I love the smell of the fresh earth, with everything bursting into beauty."

Hildegarde's mother had never talked like that to Aunt Catherine and Aunt Olivia. She had kept such thoughts for her child. Now that she was dead, Hildegarde dared not think of the things her mother

had said to her. They tugged at her heart until she
felt it would burst in her breast. It was only by not
remembering that she could go on living.

It was these thoughts of her mother's which had
made her seem so different from the others, and she
was different, too, because she put on gloves when she
worked, to keep her hands smooth, and waved her hair,
and wore her cheap, plain clothes with an air of distinction. Yet these things did not quite explain why
she and her sisters were so unlike. Now and then
their divergence of ideas would create a crisis, as when
the aunts would protest that Hildegarde's manners
were too fine for a farm.

" It makes me nervous to have her stand up when
I come in a room. None of the other boys and girls
do it."

" I don't want her to be like the other boys and
girls," Hildegarde's mother had said.

Yet in spite of that unexplained fineness, her mother
had never shirked the hardest labor. Indeed, it was
whispered that hard work had killed her. Hildegarde
hated that. She knew it was not true. Her mother
had said:

" Work is the most beautiful thing in the world, my
darling. You don't know it yet, but you will some
day. And it holds people from madness."

Her mother had said these things to her, usually,
when they were in their own big room, their two little
white beds side by side, a candle by each bed, and a
book.

Hildegarde's mother had always read late into the
night. Hildegarde would read until half-past nine, and

then blow out her candle and kiss her mother. And her mother would say:

" God bless you, my darling, and keep you safe."

It was this blessing which Hildegarde missed now before she went to sleep. It was, indeed, hard to get to sleep without it. And it was dreadful to have that other little bed empty beside her — dreadful, dreadful, *dreadful* —

She tried to reach out in the dark to that vague thing, her mother's soul. Love never died, her mother had said. It lived on and on until eternity. Hildegarde had always believed in guardian angels — that they were around her, and the saints —

> Matthew, Mark, Luke and John,
> Bless the bed that I lie on —

But now there was no one around her; the angels had fled, and the saints. There was nothing out there in the immeasurable dark; her mother had been caught on the wave of some vast sea of blackness which had swallowed her up.

Hildegarde had kept, however, the awfulness of this feeling to herself. It would have been impossible to talk about it to Aunt Catherine and Aunt Olivia. They were good-hearted, but uncomprehending. There was one person who might have understood, but he was away at the State College. Hildegarde had felt that when he heard of her bereavement he would come to her. But he had not come.

So she had gone to the cemetery in the carriage with her aunts, and had come back to the feast which had been prepared for the relatives and friends who had seen so little of her mother in life, but who had traveled far to do her honor after death.

They all sat around a great table which was loaded with hearty food — boiled beef and baked ham and stacks of bread, pickles and slaw and potato salad, and cakes and pies and preserves. Hildegarde drank a glass of milk and crumbled some bread on her plate. The people around her were solicitous. "You ought to eat," they said. She felt they would have been more solicitous if she had cried at the funeral. She was sure they thought she should have cried. They couldn't, of course, know how numb she had felt. And dazed. She saw their faces now around the table in a blurred line. None of them looked natural; they were either too broad or too tall — as she had seen people in convex and concave mirrors. And they were wabbly, like a reflection in water when the wind blows over it —

She heard some one cry sharply, "Hildegarde," and another voice, "She has fainted."

She came to herself to find that she was on the sofa in the sitting-room, and that a lot of women were bending over her. Aunt Olivia had a glass in her hand which gave out the sweet, spiced aroma of home-made wine.

She learned, when at last she sat up, that her fainting had given her a new place among them. They no longer thought her unfeeling. When the meal was finished, they would not let her help clear the table. They insisted that she lie on the sofa and rest.

Some of the guests went away as soon as they had eaten, but some of the women stayed to help Aunt Catherine and Aunt Olivia wash the dishes, and set the house in order. The men who belonged to these women went out of doors and smoked their pipes and cigars; they talked about their cows and their crops and their little Ford cars.

When the women finished their work, they all came into the sitting-room. It was not late, for they had eaten at twelve. They pulled up the window-shades, restoring the house once more to its normal aspect. The pale October sun streamed in. Hildegarde sat on the high, old horsehair sofa. There was a fire in the tall, iron stove, and the women drew their chairs into a circle around it. The air was chilly — for the sunshine had been excluded, and the windows had been opened to let out the last faint odors of fading flowers and stagnant air.

The women talked about many things, while Hildegarde listened. At last they talked about the wearing of black.

There were, it seemed, two factions — the women who had modern minds and those who hadn't. Mourning, said the modern group, was out of date. One could wear red or blue or green and mourn, and not make the rest of the world unhappy. Quite surprisingly, it seemed to Hildegarde, Aunt Olivia and Aunt Catherine sided with this group.

"It would be foolish," Aunt Catherine said, "for the child to put on black. It would make her gloomy."

And Aunt Catherine supplemented this with, "It would be expensive."

Hildegarde's little white face, under its sweeping cloud of dark hair, was troubled. Her thin hands were clasped tight in her lap. "I want to be gloomy," she said. "And I am going to wear black."

They all turned and looked at her, perched on the

high old sofa, just the tips of her toes touching the carpet. She looked about twelve, but she was eighteen. Nobody had ever thought of Hildegarde as grown-up. Nobody but Crispin Harlowe, and he was at college.

She held to her point, arguing it before them all. " I loved my mother," she said, " and I should hate a red dress or a blue one. I should like to put ashes on my head, and tear my hair — "

" That will do, Hildegarde," her Aunt Olivia said. " You can wear black if you want to, but don't get all worked up about it."

Then Hildegarde fled from them all, and rushed up to her room to cry wildly, calling on her mother, " Darling, darling, *darling* — "

It was nearly three o'clock when at last she rose from her bed and went to the window and looked out. It had been a dry fall, and the trees which lined the driveway had been blown bare by the October winds. There was no wind today, and a sort of amethyst haze enveloped the world. Hildegarde's mother had loved these Indian summer days, with a few grapes still on the vines, a few chrysanthemums still glowing in the garden. Her slight figure seemed to move even now in the midst of that amethystine haze.

The farmhouse stood well back from the road, where there still waited a line of more or less shabby cars. Hildegarde wished that she might get into one of the cars and ride away. She hated to face the loneliness of the house when there was no one left in it but her two aunts and herself. She wondered how she was going to stand it.

Something stirred in her for the first time. Re-

bellion. Anything would be better than this. If her
mother had not left her so suddenly, they might have
planned it.

There was a tap on her door. "Hildegarde."

"Yes, Aunt Catherine."

Her aunt came in. In her hand she held a little
red-lacquered box. "Your mother left it for you,"
she said. "I thought this was the time to give it to
you. It is always hardest after the funeral."

It came to Hildegarde, with a kind of shock, that
Aunt Catherine, too, was unhappy. The plump, flat
face showed signs of weeping. She stood there, bulb-
ous and ungainly in her black dress, a picture of
unattractive woe.

"I don't know how we are going to get along without Bessie," she said. Her features were contorted;
her bosom rose and fell.

Hildegarde had never liked to have them call her
mother "Bessie," but now there seemed something
pathetic in the return to the childish name — there
had been a time when the three sisters had been to
each other "Katie" and "Ollie" and "Bessie." It
had been her mother who had stopped the use of the
diminutives — "Olivia" and "Catherine" and "Elizabeth" were too lovely, she had said, to be spoiled.

Yet now Aunt Catherine had gone back to the little
name, and Hildegarde was moved by it and felt a sense
of nearness and affection for her poor old aunt, and of
compunction that she had wanted to leave her.

"Oh, Aunt Catherine," she said, "why did God do
it?"

Something soft and luminous shone in Aunt Catherine's faded eyes. "Don't blame it on God," she said. "She will be happier."

Hildegarde caught her breath at that. In her youth and egotism, she had not considered her mother's happiness, but her own "I don't believe she could be happy away from me."

"She has never been happy since she lost your father," Aunt Catherine said.

A wild feeling of jealousy assailed Hildegarde. Was that why she couldn't reach her mother out there in the dark? Was she so happy that she had forgotten earth and all that she had left behind? The thought brought desolation.

"I can't bear it," she said tensely, "to be left alone. I don't know what I am going to do with my life."

"None of us does," said Aunt Catherine. "Olivia and I ain't got much to live for."

Again with youth's selfishness Hildegarde felt that it didn't really matter about Aunt Olivia and Aunt Catherine. They were old; the years did not stretch out interminably before them. And they did not suffer, not with the sharp poignancy of youth. She could not know, of course, that Aunt Olivia and Aunt Catherine did not think of themselves as old. Neither of them was fifty. Hildegarde's mother had died at forty-one.

Some one downstairs was calling Aunt Catherine. She handed the box to Hildegarde.

"There is a letter in it from your mother. I expect you'll be surprised when you read what she has to tell you. She told us she was going to do it, and made us promise not to tell you first."

Hildegarde took the box from her; her heart was

beating madly. She waited until Aunt Catherine had gone before she opened the box. The letter lay on top, with her name written on it in her mother's firm script. She was eager to read it, yet half afraid to break the seal. She hardly knew why she was afraid. It was, perhaps, as one holds back a little before crossing the line which leads to undiscovered country.

She read the letter through once. Then read it again. It was astounding. Her father was not dead. He was living somewhere in the East. A divorce had been granted him the year that Hildegarde was born!

That Hildegarde might understand the thing which had happened, her mother rehearsed the history of her early years. Some of it Hildegarde knew, but in the light of the things the letter told, the events of her mother's girlhood gained a new significance.

Elizabeth Musgrove's father had been a country doctor. He had married a plain and pleasant woman, who had been a good housekeeper, but who had not filled his heart. He had died poor, and his wife had soon followed him. He had left the old house and its bit of farm-land to his three daughters. To Elizabeth, his youngest daughter, he had left more than the others, although the thing he had left was not in his will. She had inherited his dreams. Years before, he had told her:

" You will have more than the others, Elizabeth. No matter how hard life may be, you'll always glimpse the Vision Splendid."

Because of this heritage Elizabeth had refused to stagnate on the farm. She had gone back and forth to town to school, driving a little horse in a ramshackle buggy, coming in on winter nights half-frozen but happy, sitting up long after the others were in bed, to read and to study, finding at last a thrilling climax to her ambitions in an appointment to teach school far up in the hills of Colorado.

So she had left the Missouri farm behind her, and it was in Colorado that she had met Louis Carew, who had come out to look after the mining interests of a client. He had fallen in love with her at first sight, and when he had known her only a month he had married her. He was a Baltimorean of good blood and ample means. He had taken Elizabeth back with him, proud of her youth and beauty.

Yet youth and beauty had not been enough. She had found that when she came among her husband's people. She was not like them. And she had found, too, after the first ecstasy had worn from their love-affair, that Louis wanted to make her over to fit the family pattern. His mother and sisters had soft voices and perfect ease of manner. They knew what to do at a dinner-party and what to say. They spoke French fluently, and were much traveled. Compared with them, young Elizabeth was crude, middle-class. She knew only how to be lovely and how to worship her husband.

To please him, she tried to make herself over. She had a dancing teacher and one who taught French. She was manicured and coiffed and cold-creamed. She spent hours in her room trying to change her round, public-school penmanship into something elegant, unshaded, and fashionable. She eliminated her " r's," and her voice was like a murmuring brook.

"Louis' sisters helped me. You must not think they made a Cinderella of me. They really did their best, and I learned much from them that I have tried to pass on to you, my dearest."

Then had come the great tragedy. Just as Elizabeth had begun to hope she might measure up to all that was required of her, and just as she had found, too, that the great joy of motherhood was to be hers, it had been revealed to her that her husband loved another woman.

"It is not necessary to tell you how I found it out. But I knew. They had grown up together, and every one expected he would marry her. And she had expected it. Then he met me and was swept away by a sudden infatuation.

"There was nothing sordid about their — romance. They kept it on a high level. They had simply learned too late that they cared, and their lives were spoiled.

"Well, I adored your father. Even now, I can't think of him without an agony of mind. But I gave him up. I had a sort of sturdy pride which compelled it. He begged me to stay, but I insisted I would go away, and he could get a divorce on the grounds of desertion. I would not take any of his money. If he could not give me love — I would have nothing.

"So I came back here to Catherine and Olivia. Your father does not know he has a daughter. Yet, as the years have passed, I have begun to feel that I have no right to deprive you of the things he might do for you. As long as I live you are mine — but if anything happens to me, I want you to go to him. And I want you to remember this, that he has never wronged you in any way. And what he did to me was a thing he could not help.

"And you are like him, Hildegarde. You look like him and have certain tricks of manner. You have his gaiety, his almost faun-like quality of enjoyment. But I like to think that you are my child in many ways. You have, I am sure, my courage — for it took courage to do the thing I have done — to put from me the love that made my life.

"So, I have said, I want you to go to him and tell him who you are. His wife died several years ago. I could never have asked anything of him for myself, but for you I can ask anything. You may tell him that. I can not bear to think of your future, if you stay here with Catherine and Olivia. They are fine women. You are too much of a child to know that their apparent hardness and harshness is on the surface. But they can never give you what I want you to have. And your father can give it to you if he will. I want him to give, and I want you to take. I have no bitterness in my thought of him. He was always kind, and I loved him. I love him still."

It was on this high note that the letter ended. As she finished, Hildegarde found herself trembling. In the few moments since Aunt Catherine had left her, the world had changed. Out of that dark, immeasurable space her mother's voice had spoken. Yet it was not the rapturous voice of one who would go soaring through eternity with a fore-ordained mate. Out there in that vast space her mother was lonely — a wandering spirit, seeking always the love which has been denied.

There was a picture of her father in the little red box. Hildegarde studied it closely, seeing herself like him in the sweep of dark hair, the gray eyes. Her mother's hair had a copper tint, and her eyes had been blue — such clear blue eyes even at the end of forty years!

There was a ring in the red box and a string of pearls. " The ring is my engagement ring; your father gave me the pearls when we were married. I kept them for you — all the rest I left behind. I wanted none of them."

Chapter II

WILD GEESE AND A WINDY SKY

THERE were steps again on the stairs, Aunt
Olivia this time. It was unusual for Aunt
Olivia or Aunt Catherine to climb the stairs
when they wanted their niece. They had always called
in their high-pitched voices. The extra exertion was
a concession, apparently, to the solemnity of the
occasion.

"Crispin Harlowe is here," Aunt Olivia announced.

Crispin Harlowe was the boy at the State College
who Hildegarde had thought would come when he
heard of her bereavement, and now he had come.

"I'll be down in a moment, Aunt Olivia."

Aunt Olivia looked at the little red box and asked,
"Did you read the letter?"

"Yes." Hildegarde found it hard to speak of the
things that her mother had written. "It was a great
surprise," she said at last.

"Catherine and I sometimes thought she might have
told you sooner. But we didn't advise. It was her
business."

"I am glad she didn't, Aunt Olivia. It wouldn't
have done me any good to know I had a father. I
couldn't have gone to him while she lived."

"No," said Aunt Olivia, "you couldn't."

14

" There'll be a great deal to talk over," Hildegarde
stated, " but we'll have to wait until the others are
gone. Perhaps you'd like to read her letter."

She handed it to her aunt, who stood looking down
at it. " She wrote a prettier hand than Catherine or
I. She learned it after she was married."

Hildegarde, with a heart-breaking vision of
her mother as a young wife striving to fit herself
into her environment, said, " Everything she did was
lovely."

" Yes," Aunt Catherine agreed, " it was." Her voice
was gentle.

They went down together.

There were several people in the room, and Crispin
Harlowe was sitting on the edge of the high sofa. He
rose, as Hildegarde entered, and went up to her.

" I came as soon as I heard."

It was as if he answered in her some accusation of
procrastination.

" I did not hear," he continued, "until this morning."

She had given him her hand, and he still held it.
The eyes of the other people in the room were on them.

" Shall we go for a walk? " he asked in a low tone.
" We can't talk here."

" Presently," she said. " I want to speak to the
Skinners."

The Skinners were distant cousins. They had been
late for the funeral, and for the feast that followed.
Hildegarde had not seen them, so now she sat and
talked to them. Crispin, from across the room,
watched her, and thought he had never seen her lovelier

than now, in her straight black dress, with that smoky cloud of hair framing her white face.

She went out, after a while, wrapped in a black cape which had been her mother's. She wore no hat. In spite of the wind, the air was warm.

Crispin said, as they walked along, " You are beautiful in black."

" They didn't want me to wear it," she told him passionately. " I should have died if I hadn't."

He said he knew how she felt. They were drawn together by his comprehension of her mood. As they passed the garden, he stopped and found a late white rose blooming. She pinned it on her cape. He thought it completed, perfectly, the effect of sorrowing beauty.

As they came to the road, he asked, " Where shall we go? "

" I don't care. Only let it be as far away from people as possible. I have something to tell you — I want to tell you before I talk it over with any one else."

He was touched by her confidence in him, and laid his hand, for a moment, on her arm. He rarely touched her. She was too fine, he felt, for that.

Yet it was not alone her fineness which held him back. It was his own. He belonged to the village and had gone to school with Hildegarde. His father was judge of the county court, and much respected for a certain hearty sense of justice, which made him understand the sinner, but not sentimentalize about his sin.

Crispin was like his father in looks and in his attitude of mind. He was a strong, upstanding fellow. His hair was thick and fair, and gilded by a touch of auburn. His skin had the rich red and brown which belongs to those who live much out of doors.

So they walked along together — she a slender black shadow against the shine and glow of him. They ascended a long hill, going first through a pasture, and then through a wooded grove, coming at last on a bluff which overlooked a wide valley. Below were the farms, with shocks of corn in long, even rows — pale gold and russet — with a line of emerald where the trees along the streams still kept their green. Far off was the village and the church spire, and hanging just above it, the sun, half-shrouded in thin veils of mist, so that its top was arched like the gilded dome of some ethereal Eastern mosque.

They sat down in a place sheltered by a great rock, which loomed up behind them. They faced the south and west. Across the sky was now a rippling, ruddy wave of cloud. Hildegarde, wrapped tight against the wind in her black cape, spoke of it.

" It is like a shining sea," she said. " I like to think that somewhere out there mother is sailing on it."

It seemed as if she could talk of nothing but her mother. Crispin listened patiently enough. But the thing he wished to talk about was Hildegarde.

Presently he came to it. " What are you going to do now that she is gone? "

" That's what I have to tell you."

She was aware of the dramatic qualities of the revelation she was about to make. She was like a little sybil as she sat there speaking — with the black cape drawn tight about her, the wind blowing her hair.

When she had finished, there was silence for a moment, then Crispin said, "How wonderful that she could keep it to herself like that!"

"It changes everything, doesn't it?"

"In what way?"

"To know that I have a father."

He broke out fiercely, "Don't say it as if it were something to be proud of."

Her startled eyes met his. "Isn't it?"

"No. A man like that. To break your mother's heart."

"But you see what she says. He couldn't help it."

"He wasn't true to either of them. He should have found out before he married your mother which one he wanted."

She turned this over in her mind. At last she said, "Still, he's my father."

"And, of course, you'll go?"

"Yes."

"Suppose he doesn't want you?"

"I am not going to find out whether he wants me, but whether I want him."

"Why go at all? Why not stay here and marry me, Hildegarde?"

"Oh," she turned toward him startled, "but I'm not in love with you."

He was eager. "You don't know whether you are or not. You don't know anything about it? But I could teach you." He took her hand, drawing her toward him.

She drew back. "Please —" Then, after a little: "Crispin, I must go to my father. Mother wanted it."

" But you'll come back. I'll make you come. Do you think I'll give you up for all the fathers in the world? "

" I don't want to give you up. But I don't want to think about marriage. Mother used to say that love for a woman is giving; for a man it is taking."

" All men are not like your father."

" How can a woman tell? "

" Well, at least I can tell you this, that there has never one instant been any one else, that however far you may go from me — you will always know that my heart is waiting."

She had no answer ready for him. Darkness was coming fast upon them. Back of them the day was gone. But toward the west and south the clouds had been swept away by a change of wind, and the sky was now one clear, unbroken stretch of chrysoprase.

And out of the sky dropped suddenly a harsh and thrilling cry.

Crispin jumped to his feet. " The wild geese are flying. Look, Hildegarde."

He drew her up beside him. The wind caught her cape, and it billowed out behind her. He swept it down with a strong arm and stood holding her steady. Etched black against the wide green expanse, the geese flew in wedge-like formation, a few laggards trailing in a whipcord behind. Steadily they passed, their strong wings bearing them on, their clamorous voices calling. It was a thing to lift the heart. To feed the soul. Up there in the infinite sky was a faith that carried those feathered things through miles of uncharted flight. Who told them when to go and when to come? Who showed them the way? Who held them thus together? A brave company on a brave adventure?

Crispin, feeling this, said, " When I see them, I want to follow."

It came to Hildegarde that it was wonderful to hear a man speak like that. It was wonderful to be standing there with a strong arm about her in that green light, and with the wild geese flying. For the first time Crispin seemed more to her than the boy she had always known. He was a part of the wonder of it — the ineffable beauty.

When she got back to the house, the feeling lingered. She found herself watching Crispin as he had watched her earlier in the day. She found herself, too, contrasting him with the others in the room. There was supper still to be eaten, and Crispin was to stay for it. As she came back and forth from the kitchen, she was aware of him in the midst of the group of men about the dining-room stove — outranking them all in strength and good looks. Across the room she caught his quick smile for her. They had brought some leaves and berries back with them from their walk. Hildegarde was arranging a dish of fruit in the center of the table.

" I thought we might make a wreath of bittersweet and trumpet vine," she said, as he joined her.

Other people were watching. The women in the kitchen. " It would be a fine match for her," they were saying to each other as they fried the potatoes, and scrambled the eggs, and stirred the cream gravy.

The men, too, were watching over their pipes, envious of youth and beauty.

At supper Hildegarde sat beside Crispin.

" I am not hungry," she said, but she found herself eating.

Crispin buttered bits of hot biscuit and laid them on her plate. He helped her to cottage cheese and honey. As for himself, he ate the fried things with hearty appetite. He had two cups of coffee and cake and pie and preserves. And Hildegarde was glad he ate. She would have had no use for a sighing lover. His heartiness and strength appealed to her. It was as if on some wide and lonely sea she had hoisted a flag of distress, and he had come bravely to meet her.

His comforting presence kept, too, the shadows away from her. After a while she would have to go up to her room with its dreadful emptiness. The blackness would shut down on her, and she would cry out for her mother. She grew faint with the thought of it. She was glad to sit there in the light with that line of people about the table, talking, and even laughing a little. The gloom which had surrounded them for the past three days was lightening; it would not be long before everything was as it had been before.

After supper, Hildegarde and Crispin sat apart from the others, and she told him her plans. She was to go as soon as she could get ready. She was sure Aunt Olivia and Aunt Catherine would be willing. He made her promise to write him. Often.

When it was time for him to leave, she went with him to the front door. They were alone in the hall.

" Walk to the gate with me," he begged.

She took a sweater from the hatrack. It belonged
to one of the Skinners and was a bright scarlet. When
Hildegarde put it on, it wrapped her like a flame.

Crispin said, " Some day, when you are happy, you
must have a dress like that."

" I shall never be happy."

" Yes," he said, " you will. I shall make you
happy."

The night, as they went out in it, was cold and clear.
Sharp, white stars pierced the sky. Dry leaves rustled
under their feet as they walked; the wind sighed in
the bare branches.

When they came to the gate, Crispin took her hand
and said, " I shall live on the thought of your letters."

" Shan't I see you before I go? "

" I shall come as often as I can. You know that."

" And — I haven't promised anything, Crispin."

" No. I don't need any promises. I know what I
want and what I mean to have."

She was much stirred by the way he said it. For
the first time she was meeting the mastery of a masculine mind. " You mustn't expect too much."

" No." His fingers tightened on hers. " Hildegarde, let me kiss you. It won't tie you to anything.
But it will make you remember that I — care."

She stood very still, then: " Crispin, it would tie me
— I mustn't."

After everybody had gone that night, Hildegarde
and her aunts talked for a long time. They told her
many things the letter did not tell. There was some
money, they said, in the bank. Not much, but a few
hundreds. It had been her mother's share when the

lower lot was sold, and she had kept it for Hildegarde. They, too, thought she ought to go to her father. They would miss her dreadfully, but the farm was no place for a young girl. And, of course, if she found she could not stay, she could come back.

At last Aunt Olivia went upstairs and came down with a traveling bag. " It was your mother's."

Louis Carew had bought it for Elizabeth on their wedding journey. It was lined with rose-color and outfitted with ivory with the monogram in gold letters.

" Everything he gave her was like that," Catherine said. " Handsome. We had never seen such handsome things as she brought back with her. Yet she said they were nothing to what she left behind."

" If he had given her more love, she would have liked it better than anything that money could buy," was Aunt Olivia's grim response. " I couldn't ever forgive him, although she didn't want us to feel that way. He broke her heart."

Hildegarde wondered if she ought to feel as Aunt Olivia did, and Crispin. Yet, somehow, she couldn't hate her father. Her mother hadn't hated him. Whatever she had suffered, she had loved him to the end.

CHAPTER III

FINDING A FATHER

TWO weeks after her mother's funeral, Hildegarde Carew came to her father's place in Maryland. The house was set on a hill from which it took its name — Round Hill — and overlooked the Chesapeake. It was of red brick, with white-painted porches of wood, and was not imposing. It was half a mile from the station, and as there was no conveyance, Hildegarde walked, carrying her bag.

It was eleven o'clock in the morning, and Louis Carew was still in bed. It was a carved mahogany bed, with cupids and angels on the posts, and a faded canopy. From where he lay, Carew could see through a wide window the road which led from the station. And so he saw his daughter coming, not knowing that she was his daughter.

" Who's that woman? " he demanded of his secretary.

The secretary stood up. He was glad to know that any one was coming. He was bored to death. " Looks like a book-agent."

" Don't let her in."

" As you please."

The secretary was not obsequious. His social status paralleled that of his employer; they had been to-

gether since the War — and had fought together politi-
cal battles and financial ones. It had been stimulating
— exciting. Almost as thrilling, young Meriweather
thought, as the Marne and some moments in the Ar-
gonne.

He picked up his pencil. Louis Carew was dictating
an important paper. They had worked on it for several mornings. While he dictated, Carew would drink
cup after cup of strong coffee, with toast and bacon.
The secretary breakfasted early, with a ride before
his work began. Today he would have another ride
after lunch, and then type the matter which Carew had
dictated. He and Carew would dine with the Hulburts
— a mile or two away — and would come back and
work until long after midnight.

The girl was ascending the hill. The sun shone full
upon her. She walked lightly, with her head well up.
Once she stopped to take off her heavy cape. Then
she came on, all in black with her black bag.

" I can't see," Carew said with irritation, " why any
one would come as far as this on the chance of selling
books."

" They know you are big game if they can get
you."

" Not so big as some of them think, if they knew my
debts."

" But they don't. And they won't if I can help it.
We've got to pull you out."

" I'd get in again."

Meriweather laughed. " I'm not so pessimistic."

Downstairs the bell rang. " There she is," Carew
ejaculated.

A negro servant came up presently. " A young lady to see Mr. Carew."

" Did she say what she wanted? " Carew demanded.

She had not, it seemed, except that it was important.

" She's probably selling books. You go down, Merry."

Meriweather went and returned. " She says that she must see you; that she's a relative. Her name is Hildegarde Carew."

" Never heard of her."

" She insists it is important."

" But, great guns — I never get up at this time in the morning."

" I told her that, and she said she would wait."

" Let her wait then. Put her in the library and have Sampson take in something to eat. I'll finish this and dress — "

Meriweather, delivering the message, put it pleasantly. The girl was a lady and not to be treated with incivility. Mr. Carew was much occupied with an important matter until noon. Could she wait?

She could. Meriweather led the way to the library and gave orders to Sampson for refreshment.

The girl protested, " I really don't want anything."

" You must have had an early breakfast. It is a long ride from Baltimore."

" I didn't have any breakfast. I came through last night from the West and went straight up to Mr. Carew's office. They told me he was out here and that he had retired from active business."

"He has." Meriweather did not explain that Carew had failed in a crash and was out of the office altogether.

"Will you make yourself comfortable?" he said. "Sampson will bring you some tea and a sandwich or two. I am sure you need it — "

She smiled up at him, and he found something wistful and appealing in her manner. He wondered what she wanted of Carew and hoped that, whatever she wanted, she might get it.

He drew a chair for her to the fire. "There are plenty of books — and the magazines — "

"Thank you so much. I shall be all right, and glad to rest."

She took off her hat and thus proclaimed to him her lack of sophistication. The women he knew lived in their hats — ate in them, played cards in them. He sometimes wondered if they slept in them.

Without her hat, he was puzzled by a resemblance. Then, suddenly, he had it!

"You have the Carew top-knot," he told her. "Every one of them has that waved lock on the forehead."

She flushed a little. "I didn't know," she said. "I — I live in the West."

He pointed to a portrait over the mantel. "There's one of them," he said.

It was a dashing picture of a young man in the red coat of an English officer. Red cheeks, thin lips, cool gray eyes, and that sweep of black hair.

"Carew's great-grandfather — good-looking chap."

The girl's heart leaped. Her own great-great-grand-

father! This charming gentleman! It gave her a new
sense of values. Relatives had hitherto meant to her
Aunt Olivia and Aunt Catherine. There was a photograph of her mother's father, the country doctor, a
substantial old codger, but nothing like this, dashing,
gay, distinguished.

When Meriweather left her presently, she looked
around the room. The library was high-ceiled, hung
with faded yellow brocade. The walls were lined with
mahogany bookcases, and there was a drop-leaf table
with a bronze lamp. Bronze book-ends held together
a varied assortment of new books. The fireplace in
which great logs glowed was set massively in Italian
marble — and above it was the dashing portrait.

Altogether it was a satisfying room for one who
loved beauty. Hildegarde wondered how her mother
could have left it. "I would have forgiven anything
rather than go back to the farm."

When Sampson came in with the tray, he drew a
small, low table to where Hildegarde sat by the fire.
He had a fine, bronze face which seemed to match the
room. He served her deftly and left her to eat alone.
There were thin, delicious sandwiches and delicate
sugar cakes; the tea was in a slender, silver pot.
Hildegarde, as she ate, contrasted the food and service
with that she had known at home. Again she wondered at her mother's strength.

It seemed a long time before a step in the hall set
her heart to beating wildly. She had rehearsed a thousand things to say to her father, but not one of them
seemed now appropriate. Amid all this elegance she
felt an upstart. Why had she thought that she might

come back and fit herself in? Might she not find herself like her mother, crude and looked down upon?

As he entered, her father said, " I am sorry to have kept you waiting."

She rose and stood there with her soul shaken. She had not thought he would be like this. She had had in mind, perhaps, the miniature that had been in the lacquered box, or the portrait of the dashing gentleman in the red coat, the sweep of black hair, the cool, clear eyes.

But the hair of this man was gray, and his eyes were tired. His tall figure had a sag at the shoulders. He wore out-of-door clothes, a Norfolk coat and knickerbockers. He had a cap in his hand.

He came forward. " Meriweather says you are a relative. And that you are from the West. I did not know there were any Western Carews of our branch."

Her throat was dry. " I am your daughter."

A quick lift of his head, startled. " My daughter? "

" Yes. My mother was Elizabeth Musgrove."

Dead silence, then he came closer. So close that he almost touched her. " You don't look like her."

" No."

" How old are you? "

" Eighteen."

Another silence. Then, " Why have you come now? "

" My mother is dead. She died two weeks ago."

His face did not change. He put out his hand and caught at the back of one of the big chairs. Turned it so that it faced her, at the other side of the fireplace. Sat down.

Another long silence. And out of it, "What do you want me to do?"

"My mother told me to come. I have a letter that she left for me. I did not know until I read it that you were alive."

He leaned forward. "She kept it away from you?"

"From everybody except her sisters. People thought she was a widow."

He considered that for a moment. "Yet in the end she sent you to me?"

"Yes."

He did not pursue the subject. He sat there, weighing, apparently, the unusual situation which confronted him; measuring this girl, who called herself his daughter, with a keen glance.

"You're a Carew all right," he said at last abruptly. "You look like me and like all the rest of us. You've got our hair and eyes."

She felt embarrassed by his scrutiny, wished that he would talk of her mother.

"You ought to have more color in your cheeks," he went on. "Do you ride?"

"A little."

"Dance?"

"A little."

"Any accomplishments? French?"

"*Ma mère m'a enseignée ce qu'elle savait.*"

"*Vous êtes une très bonne élève.*" He surveyed her with speculating eyes, then seemed to come to a quick decision. "Is there any reason why you can't stay on for a while? We might as well settle that now. I've

a horse that you can ride, and you can dance with
Meriweather and talk French with me."

Far back in his eyes was a spark of laughter. But
she did not see it. The world was whirling about her.
She was hot with resentment. She had come on a
sacred errand, and he was talking about the color in
her cheeks and what horse she should ride!

" Oh," she gasped, " do you think I'd stay? "

" Why not? "

" I don't know whether I can make it clear. But my
mother loved you — to the very end. And because
she loved you and because she loved me — she wanted
to bring us together. Yet, when I come and tell you
she is dead, you act as if I were giving you news from
the morning paper — "

He interrupted her. " My dear child, I can't stand
any more tragedy. Life at this moment for me isn't
cakes and ale. I've been stabbed in the back by my
friends and hooted at by my enemies. I'm not in a
mood to be hurt by raked-up memories."

He was standing now with his foot on the low fender,
his arm on the mantel-shelf. " I've lost everything I
had. I'm head over heels in debt. This old house is
my final refuge. And my back's to the wall."

It seemed to her incredible that he should talk like
that. Poverty, in her mind, was associated with crush-
ing physical effort and sordid surroundings. It had to
do with scrubbing, and sweeping, and cooking three
meals a day, and washing dishes, and bending one's
back over the weeds in the garden.

And here was this elegant gentleman with a servant
to bring delicious and delectable things on a silver tray,

and with a secretary to jump at his call. A man who could stay in bed until noon!

She spoke out of her thoughts. " If I had a house like this," she said, " I would think it was all I wanted in the world. Do you know that my mother worked in the fields before she died? "

" Elizabeth? "

"Yes. The people out there say that hard work killed her."

" Hard work? "

" Yes. She didn't have any servants. She got up before daylight on winter mornings, and built the fire, and on cold nights she'd take a lantern and go out t.: the barn and feed the stock."

" And she did this rather than stay with me? "

" She wouldn't stay where she wasn't wanted."

" I did want her."

With breath almost suspended, she looked up at him. " You mean — ? "

" Yes — letting her go was — horrible — "

" But you loved somebody else."

" She told you that? Well, I did. I'm afraid I can't make you understand. I shan't try. I don't want to think about it." Again that high note of irritation.

She stood up, reached for her little hat, pulled it down over her smoky curls, and picked up her bag. " I'm sorry I came," she said. " I didn't know you didn't want to think about her. I think about her all the time."

He put out his hand. " You're not going."

He lifted the hat from her head and set it beyond her reach on the mantel.

"I like you best without it," he said. "You've got the family top-knot and the family temper — And you'll have to learn that when I am cross my heart — hurts — "

He took both of her hands in his, lifted one of them, and kissed it. "Having you here," he said gently, "will be like having my own youth back again. You're like me, and I love you for it. I've got you, and you're going to stay."

Chapter IV

ENTER SALLY

HILDEGARDE was shown to her room by Sampson's wife, a bronze negress who, like her husband, was descended from a long line of dependents who had served several generations of Carews.

Yet Sampson and Delia were modern in everything except their dialect and their grammar. They read the papers and took their airings in a rackety runabout. Louis Carew often complained that they had more unmortgaged property than he possessed.

To Delia, going upstairs with Hildegarde, the thing took on the aspect of adventure. When she entered the library Carew had made the simple announcement:

" This is my daughter, Miss Hildegarde Carew. You remember Miss Elizabeth, Delia? This is her child — and mine. She has come to me now that her mother is dead."

Delia had few sensations in her day's work. This was one, therefore, beyond her dreaming.

" You'll want a nice bath, honey," she said, as they came into the room. " You jes' set and rest while I gits it ready."

Hildegarde had never been waited on. She saw Delia take her bag and thought of the sparseness of her wardrobe. Yet she was not ashamed. Her mother had taught her that poverty was not disgraceful if one bore it with dignity. She tried to remember that. Yet she wished Delia would go down — leave her to open her own bag, hide her few simple garments in the great clothes-press.

Everything in the room was massive and old-fashioned, with the massiveness redeemed a bit by the roses on the faded chintz that covered the chairs and couch, and by the clean, frilled swiss covers on dresser and table. Two long windows gave a wide view of the Bay with gulls flashing white against the deep blue sky.

Her eyes came back to Delia, who was opening the bag. "My *chile*," she said, as the rose-colored lining and ivory fittings were revealed, "my *chile* — I 'members dis bag."

Hildegarde's voice was eager. "You knew my mother?"

"Yes, miss." Delia, kneeling on the floor, was aware of the dramatic quality of her own revelation. "Many's the time she's cried in these arms."

Their eyes met. "She was unhappy?" Hildegarde said.

"I packed her bag for the las' time, honey." Delia was in the full swing of her recital. "An' she set right where you's a-settin' now, and she look like she were ca'ved fum stone."

"In this chair — ?"

"Yes, miss, this were her room. And she set there, and downstai's Mr. Louis was rompin' and ragin'. You see, he wanted her to stay, and he wanted her to go.

Seems like he were to'n thisaway and thataway. An'
I were hopin' and prayin' she wouldn't leave him."

" You wanted her to stay? "

" Yes, honey. She loved him, and she was made
for Mr. Louis. But he's allus havin' things and losin'
'em, and then wishin' he had 'em back. Seems like
the only ones he's evah kep' on is Sampson and me."

Hildegarde wanted to ask about his second wife.
Hadn't he kept her on? She felt, however, that this
was not a thing to discuss with Delia.

" But you love him, don't you? " she said at last.
" You've stayed with him so long."

" Lord, yes, honey. Me and Sampson belongs right
heah, like the house and the trees and the garden gate.
An' we knows Mistah Louis and his ways." She hesitated a moment, then gave a warning. " Don't evah
let him see you loves him too much. 'T'aint good for
him."

A breath of cold wind seemed to blow against the
warm hope in Hildegarde's heart. Her interview with
her father had shed a ray of light in the darkness in
which she had moved since her mother's death. His
gentleness, his need of her, the things he had said to
her in those first moments of meeting — on these she
had built a structure of dreams.

The water was booming in the bath. Delia went in
to turn it off. When she came back, she said, " I'll
sen' down to the station fo' yo' trunk honey."

" I just brought my bag," Hildegarde told her. " I
didn't know whether I was going to stay or not. I can
send home if I need more."

Weighing, mentally, the clothes she had taken out of

the bag, Delia said: " I wouldn' send. Just git yo'
Daddy to buy you some."

Hildegarde flushed. " Oh, I couldn't ask him for
money."

" Effen yo' don't ask, you nevah gits," the maid
warned her. " Plums don't drop 'thout you shakes
the tree."

Leaving Hildegarde, presently, to bathe and rest,
Delia went downstairs to the front porch where Carew
and young Meriweather were smoking in the soft autumn sunlight.

" Mistah Louis," Delia remarked, " that po' chile
needs some clothes, but she say she won't ask
you."

" Why not? "

" I reckon she doan feel that you's her real Daddy.
An' I tole her she ain't gwine git no plums effen she
don't shake the tree — "

The men shouted at that.

" So I'm the plum-tree, Delia? "

The eyes of the negress were inscrutable. " I ain't
sayin' it, is I? "

" I'm not made of money, Delia."

" No, suh. But you knows the kin' of clo'es Miss
Sally wears."

With sudden decision Carew's hands came down on
the arm of his chair. " I'll run up to Baltimore with
her tomorrow and have Anne take her to the shops.
I'm not going to have my daughter put in the shade by
Sally Hulburt."

When Delia had gone, Carew said to Meriweather,
" I might as well be killed for a sheep as a lamb."

"It is all right if your credit stays good."

"What do you mean?" sharply.

"Well, there's an insistence about their demands, in this month's bills."

"I'll pay them some day. But in the meantime, if I introduce my daughter to my friends, she's got to make a decent appearance."

Meriweather, with his hand on the head of the nearest hound, weighed the matter thoughtfully. It was the dickens of a time for a daughter to appear. His employer didn't half appreciate the gravity of the financial situation. A little more, and Round Hill would go with the rest. And Carew and the girl would be high and dry.

"You'll have to have somebody here, won't you?" he said at last, "if you are going to keep her with you. Some woman."

"Anne can come down. I telephoned her. She was shocked to flinders, of course. Everybody will be." An amused light flamed in his eyes. "I'm going to take her over with us tonight to the Hulburts'."

"*What?*" Meriweather's tone was incredulous.

"Why not? I want to see Ethel's face, and Sally's. I am going to call them up and ask them to put an extra plate on the dinner table for — my daughter."

He was, Meriweather could see, delighting in the sensation he would create. He would forget his money worries in this new interest.

Carew rose. "I'll telephone, and then I'll get at those affidavits. Are you going to ride?"

"I'll take a run with the dogs, and come back and type the stuff you gave me this morning."

From the window Hildegarde saw young Meri-weather ride away, a half-dozen dogs streaming ahead of him. She liked the picture it made — the erect figure on the brown horse sweeping down the white oyster-shell road that led to the Bay.

Delia came up with a message from Carew. Miss Hildegarde would dine with her father at the Hulburts'. She must not worry about what she would wear. The Hulburts were most informal. Delia, enlarging the theme, revealed that the Hulburts had been neighbors for more than one generation. There was now only Mrs. Hulburt, a widow, and her daughter, Sally. They were not rich, but their social position was unassailable. Delia's vocabulary was somewhat limited, but she made this clear.

Hildegarde, curled up luxuriously in the puffy bed, listened. It sounded, she thought, rather like a story-book. Life, as she had known it, wasn't made up of balls and parties and hunt breakfasts.

Delia left her at last, and Hildegarde lay, very tired and very comfortable, looking out at the Bay. She had never before been near the sea. Her imagination carried her beyond the limits of the Chesapeake to the ocean that stretched to Spain. Perhaps some day she would sail it. She drifted off into sleep, waking at last to find that it was nearly five o'clock and was time to dress for dinner.

When at last she went down, she found her father by the library fire.

" I did the best I could with myself," she told him, as he rose to meet her. " I'm afraid I'm not very fashionable."

" You are very pretty, which is much better," he assured her.

Meriweather came in just then, and sat and talked with them until it was time to go. The young secretary was glad the girl had come. Carew was often overtaken by moods which made him poor company. Yet when he was in these moods Meriweather did not want to leave him, even for a game of bridge.

It was Sally Hulburt who asked a little later about Hildegarde.

" For Heaven's sake, Merry, I didn't know there was a daughter."

" There is. Long-lost, and all that sort of thing. First wife."

" The one he divorced? "

" Yes. She made him do it. She gave him his liberty to let him marry Corinne, and now here's the daughter."

" But why did she come? After all these years? "

" Her mother is dead. And made her promise to look up Carew. She stuck it out herself on an awful old farm in Missouri, but she wanted more than that for Hildegarde."

" She's a pretty thing," Sally said, " but she is not quite comfortable with us."

Hildegarde was not comfortable. Dinner had been difficult. She had known the right forks and spoons, but she had not known what to talk about. With the best intentions in the world, they had sailed right over her head with their light chatter of things which belonged to their lives, but which had never belonged to hers. She had tried not to be self-conscious. But she knew she was as different from these people as her mother had been from the old aunts — she was as different, she told herself passionately, as Mrs. Hulburt's thin, lovely china was from her aunts' thick blue dishes. There was something about the way Sally wore her clothes — she had not even dressed for dinner, but had kept on a sleeveless little coat of pale yellow over a straight dress of white silk. Hildegarde, in her long black serge, with her mother's pearls about her neck, felt awkward and over-dressed against the elegance of Sally's simplicity.

She wondered if Meriweather were in love with Sally. She thought he ought to be. If she were a man she would, she was sure, fall in love with Sally.

She was aware, as they sat by the fire, that Sally was trying to set her at her ease.

" You are all to come here on election night for dinner. Neale Winslow, a friend of Louis', will be down, and there'll be just the six of us. I wanted some younger men. But Merry won't let me have them. He's a dog in the manger. He's not in love with me, and he won't let anybody else be."

Meriweather defended himself. " Sally's a perfect queen bee, Miss Carew; she always has a swarm of adorers. I'm trying to keep away from the honey-pot — self-preservation — "

Hildegarde spoke out of her honest conviction. " I'd be in love with her if I were a man."

Sally liked that. But she laughed with the rest of them. " Why would you love me? Tell me that. The men say it's because of my hair or my eyes. Please don't say you'd like me because of my eyes or hair — "

"No," said Hildegarde, "I wouldn't. I'd love you because you are funny and sweet."

She was so very much in earnest that she was bewildered by their laughter.

"You *peach!*" Sally said. "Merry, did you hear her?"

He had heard, and something fine in him had responded to her earnestness. And her honesty. Even Sally with all her sincerity could not have said a thing like that.

During the evening his eyes were often upon her. And when they reached home, he kept her for a moment with him before they went into the house.

"I want you to see the moon over the Bay. It's rather splendid on a night like this."

The moon hung high above the water, making a wide, golden track, and in that track the molten waves moved restlessly. The wind blew softly with a little whistling sound. Except for that, all the world was still. Then suddenly across the golden radiance of the moon drifted a thin, black shadow, another followed, and another. Steadily, beating strong wings, went the wild geese — so far away that no sound of them reached the watchers on the porch.

"By jinks," Meriweather said, "that's fine. One doesn't often see it."

Hildegarde did not answer. Indeed, she hardly heard him. All that belonged to this new life had dropped away. Again she stood beside Crispin, his strong arm about her; again she was lifted up with him by the exaltation of their high mood; again his voice came to her, "*When I see them, I want to follow!*"

Her heart cried out for him, " Crispin, Crispin."
She longed to bridge the distance, fly to him with
steady-beating wings as the wild geese were flying.
What had she to do with this place and these people?
Long ago her mother had left them never to return.

CHAPTER V

NEW CLOTHES FOR OLD

BEFORE she slept that night, Hildegarde wrote to Crispin — a homesick letter. She felt he would understand her longing, her loneliness in her new surroundings. Since, for the moment, her longing included Crispin, she let him see it.

"It is wonderful here, and in a way I like it. But there is no one to whom I can talk as I used to talk to you. I feel as if all the people around me are on a stage, and that I am watching them."

When she had finished the letter, she went to bed, and lay awake for a long time in the moonlight. Writing to Crispin had given her a renewed sense of nearness to her mother, and she felt, too, secure in the thought of her lover's strength and love. Whatever happened, she had that. Instinctively she knew that she could not lean too heavily for love upon her father.

The next morning, when she went down, she found that she was to go to Baltimore to be outfitted by Miss Anne Carew, the remaining sister of the two who had been kind to young Elizabeth. Miss Nancy was dead, and Miss Anne still lived in the old house near the cathedral.

"The house belongs to her," Louis Carew told his daughter. "She wanted to give it up to help me out,

44

but I wouldn't let her. I'll run down to Baltimore with you and leave you with her for a few days."

It was in their first moment alone that Miss Anne told Hildegarde:

" You are like your mother. I was very fond of her, and Louis made a great mistake. But that is all in the past, isn't it? And you and I must begin right here without any post-mortems."

Miss Anne seemed to Hildegarde very young for her years. She was slender and dark and wore charming clothes. She had a modern mind, was ardent at sports, took a keen interest in politics, and was equally at home in the latest dances or in making speeches on World Peace. She had shaken off the shackles of conservatism which had bound the women of her family, and had emerged free in all things except in her relation to her brother. Louis was, she asserted, a Turk and a tyrant, but she loved him. And loving him, she let him bully her.

" It is the reason we live apart," she told Hildegarde. " When I am with him, I want to do the things he demands, and when I am away from him, I rage at my weakness."

There was laughter in her eyes. " Louis insists that I shall spend the winter at Round Hill with you," she told Hildegarde, " if I do, you'll have to act as a buffer. I usually stand him for a month or two, and then I pack my trunk and come back to Baltimore. He always calls me up and tells me what he thinks of me for deserting him. And I tell him it is the only way I can own my soul. I can defy him at long distance, and he knows it."

They were in Miss Anne's bedroom, where there was a riot of lovely color — burnt orange and dull old blues, and Miss Anne in a dressing-gown that was like a tangerine. Hildegarde, wrapped in a Chinese robe of silver-embroidered satin, which her hostess had lent her, felt impressively elegant as she sat curled up on the couch, one of the burnt-orange cushions behind her.

Miss Anne, looking at her meditatively, remarked, " Of course, we'll have to bob your hair."

" Oh, *no!* "

Hildegarde's shining braids hung heavily over her shoulders and down the length of the silver-satin gown. They were curled at the ends and were a lovely, living part of her. She shivered a little.

" It would be like cutting off an arm, or a leg."

" My dear, you mustn't let yourself have emotions. They aren't fashionable. Nobody suffers any more, or has rapturous moments. We are all at a dead level of insensibility."

" But — to cut these off — " Hildegarde had an end of a braid in each hand, holding them out as if they offered mute evidence of her argument. " Why, they are *me* — myself — as much as my eyes or nose — "

" But, my dear child, we won't be able to get any hats that fit, and there's nothing to be done in these days with a lot of hair like that. You'll look as if you came out of the Ark."

" Shall I? " Hildegarde's tone was anxious. She got down from the couch and surveyed herself in a long mirror. " I could twist it around my head — flat."

She tried it, turned and faced Miss Anne. "Does that look as if I came out of the Ark? Does it?"

"It looks adorable."

Miss Anne had a little leap of the heart as she saw that silver-shining figure in the mirror — the youth of it — the likeness to her own happy self so many years ago!

"I shall dress you to suit your type," she said presently. "In that mauve and silver you are like a lilac in the spring."

Again Hildegarde's face was anxious. "Do you mean that you want me to wear colors?"

"Of course. You're too young for black."

"No, I'm not. And I won't take it off. It would be like forgetting mother."

The scene at the farm swept back to Hildegarde — all the women talking together, and herself sitting on the high hard sofa. She felt that what she had not conceded to her mother's sisters she must not concede to this sister of her father.

"I had it out with father on the train this morning," she told her aunt breathlessly. "I am afraid he was terribly upset, and I'm sorry. But I told him that if he made me take off my black dresses, I'd go back to my aunts."

Miss Anne stared at her. "You *did*. My dear, he'll adore you. Opposition whets his appetite."

"Well, I didn't do it for that. I loved mother, and I told him so. And — and I told him that if he couldn't mourn, I'd have to do it for both of us."

Miss Anne surveyed her with satisfaction. "I'll dress you in black now if the heavens fall. Louis has me under his thumb. But he'll take from you what he wouldn't take from me. Hildegarde, I can see in you my buckler and shield against the assaults of tyranny."

The next morning was spent in getting the delicate feminine belongings which were to form the basis of Hildegarde's wardrobe.

" This afternoon we'll have a try at hats and shoes and dresses," Miss Anne promised. " You won't mind some white things for house and evenings, will you? I shall telephone Louise to have them ready."

The two of them were having lunch in a tea-room on Charles Street. Miss Anne seemed to know everybody, but she did not introduce Hildegarde to the people who came up to the table.

" I simply haven't the courage," she confessed frankly, " to spring Louis' daughter on them here. When I get you out to Round Hill, I'll write little notes to everybody, and they will gradually dribble out to look you over. But here — *c'est impossible.*"

The people that Miss Anne knew seemed to Hildegarde to have a sort of sharpness about them. She couldn't think of any other word. They were all so clear-cut in speech and looks. The clothes of the women were so expensively simple, and their sentences so brief. And the men all had such stiff, straight backs, like Meriweather, and moved among the tables with a grace which seemed incredible when she thought of the masculine awkwardness of her provincial friends. All except Crispin. He was not awkward. Yet, for the first time, she began to wonder how Crispin would look against this background, instead of the background of hills and sky. But then she didn't care *how* Crispin looked. Crispin was Crispin.

Miss Anne was saying, " When I get the right clothes on you, some of these boys are going to be crazy about you, Hildegarde."

Hildegarde laughed a little. " Will the clothes do it? "

" Not the clothes alone, of course. But with you in them. And if you will keep your hair long, I'm going to play up to it. Braids wound flat around your head as you did them last night — white dresses — pearls — lovely innocence. I'll make people look at you."

" I'm not sure I want to be looked at."

" Every girl does. Be honest with yourself, Hildegarde. It's a great help. Modesty is not modern. We blow our own trumpets even in our own minds."

There was no question but that Miss Anne's point of view was stimulating. Yet Hildegarde knew it would be hard to blow her own trumpet. Even in her own mind. There were so many times when she wasn't sure.

" The thing to do," Miss Anne was elucidating, " is to avoid an inferiority complex. If your mother hadn't had it, she would be here."

Hildegarde's startled eyes questioned.

" She felt that she wasn't as good as Louis — socially. Yet she had a grace of mind and body far beyond anything we Carews could hope for. Far beyond anything Corinne possessed."

" Corinne? "

" Didn't you know —? Louis' second wife? "

" No."

Miss Anne gave a brief and frank history. "You might as well have me tell it as to get it from any one else. Corinne had always had her own way. And when Louis married your mother, she was frantic. It was killing to her pride to have another woman chosen. And she made up her mind to get him back. I have always thought she staged the scene which separated them."

"Scene?"

"Yes. Your mother came upon them one night in the garden at Round Hill. Louis was holding Corinne's hand and swearing eternal devotion. I've always felt that he didn't mean a word of it. He was simply carried away by the moment and the moonlight. But when Corinne saw your mother, she jumped up and said, ' We might as well tell her the truth now, Louis.' And she told it — her version. Louis tried to stop her, but when she said, ' He has just said that he — still cares — ' what could he say? He *had* said it. And whether or not he meant it, he had to stick to it. Yet I am sure that even at that moment he loved Elizabeth."

"Love like that," Hildegarde flung out, " isn't worth the name." Her cheeks were blazing.

Miss Anne, hunting in her pocket-book for a tip to the waitress, said: " Perhaps I shouldn't have told you, but I'd rather you'd see things straight. Love Louis for what he is, and not for what you want him to be. And if you love him enough, you can sway him. Elizabeth could have done anything with him if she had only known it. But she ran away — "

With her heart beating, Hildegarde asked a question. " Was he happy with Corinne? "

Miss Anne threw up her hands. "Happy? In a way, perhaps. But she brought out the worst in Louis. She played life as a game, and he played with her. And he couldn't afford to play, and so he lost his law practice — lost everything — And toward the end they had a quarrel, and she left him. I think he was glad — She died in Italy."

So that was it! As Delia had said, he was " always losin' 'em." Would the day come when he would also lose his daughter?

Miss Anne, having paid her bill at the desk, came back.

"What will my father do, now that he has lost everything? " Hildegarde asked.

" If the election goes our way, he'll ask for a diplomatic position, and we could live more cheaply abroad. You'd like it there, Hildegarde."

As they got into Miss Anne's little car, Hildegarde wondered what else would happen. A few weeks ago there had been only the farm and its dull routine, and now there stretched ahead a vista of endless excitement.

Buying more clothes was the immediate excitement — five new frocks — three hats — two coats.

Hildegarde protested. " Do you think we ought to afford them? "

" We haven't been extravagant," Miss Anne informed her. " Louis is not so poor that he can't dress you suitably."

Hildegarde reflected that he was surely as poor as her aunts on the farm, who did not spend on clothes in a decade as much as he had already spent on her new wardrobe. Yet they owned the house in which they

lived, hadn't a debt in the world, and were guarded
against future want by a bunch of bonds in the safety
vault of the bank.

Miss Anne went out the next morning with Hildegarde to Round Hill. The Hulburts were to come to
dinner, and Hildegarde dressed early and went down.
A big fire was blazing in the library, and she stood
before it. She had on a simple little frock of white
chiffon, and her arms were bare. She had never before
had an evening gown without sleeves. She felt very
elegant and different in her high-heeled satin slippers
and sheer stockings.

When Meriweather came in, he said, " Congratulations."

" Why? "

" On the frock."

" Do you like it? "   Her flush was charming.

" More than that. I was half dreading to see you.
I was afraid they'd make you look like all the rest of
the modern young women."

" But shouldn't one in Rome want to look like the
Romans? "

" Heaven forbid!"   He drew a chair up to the fire
for her, and she sat down.

" You see, I've always lived in the country," she
said, with her eyes on the lovely satin slippers touched
with pink by the firelight.

He smiled down at her. " So did the goddesses."

" But I'm not a goddess."

" Perhaps you are and don't know it. They weren't
all heavy and blonde like the Wagnerian prima donnas.
The Germans are responsible for more than the war."

Hildegarde felt that she liked him very much. With all his sophistication, the things that he said seemed sincere, and she was perfectly at her ease with him. More at ease with him than with her father or Miss Anne, or Sally Hulburt — more at ease than with any one else in the whole wide world, except Crispin.

Yet he was not in the least like Crispin. Crispin was not a man of the world — he belonged to the sky and the woods and the sunsets. He was like nobody else in that. And he was so strong and young and beautiful.

Meriweather was not beautiful, nor was he young. He was thin, dark, tall, with a thin, dark face, small mustache, a sweep of dark brows. But it was his eyes which seemed to Hildegarde the most prepossessing thing about him. They were brown with gold flecks in them, and when Meriweather laughed they lighted his face, so that the thinness and darkness disappeared, and one seemed to see only a flashing merriment which matched his name. And even when he did not laugh, his eyes held you — deep pools of light, attentive, understanding.

He was saying now, with all the gold lighted up, " Do you know you are a life-line? "

Her eyes came up from her slipper toes. " A life-line? "

" Yes. If you hadn't come when you did, I am afraid I should have had to chuck it — Round Hill, I mean. The monotony was getting on my nerves."

Her eyelashes flickered. " You had Sally."

" But Sally isn't an angel in the house. She's great fun on the golf course, or with a horse under her. But

you can never put your finger on Sally. I like 'em to
sit by the fire and talk." His laughter was infectious.
" I always did. When I was a youngster, I wanted the
women of the household to toast their toes and be
there when I came in — "

He flung it at her lightly, and she surprised herself
by flinging back.

" And you want me to be here — when you come
in? "

" Yes — I adore a warm hearth — and a woman
waiting — "

Voices were in the hall. Meriweather stood up.
" When are you going to ride with me? "

" I don't ride very well."

" That's no answer. When? "

" Well, I have new riding clothes — lovely — " Her
voice showed her pride in them.

" Good. Shall we christen them tomorrow morning?
I have a lot of things I want to show you. The bay,
and the old burying ground, and the bronze turtle.
Have you seen the turtle? "

" No, but my mother used to tell me about him."

" He's in the pond at the foot of the hill. There was
once a garden there — your mother's garden."

" Next summer," her face was uplifted, " it shall be
my garden."

He nodded. " That's why I told you."

But he did not tell her that next to women on hearth-
stones, he liked women in gardens.

Sally came in, up to the ears in a white fur cloak.
" Are you making love to her? " she demanded of
Meriweather.

" I haven't dared — yet."

" You'd dare anything except — to marry me — "
Sally poked an accusing finger at him. " Hildegarde,
you look good enough to eat. Miss Anne has a way
with her when it comes to clothes. She hasn't spoiled
your individuality."

Until Hildegarde came to Round Hill, she had never
known she had individuality. Yet to be told it was
rather stimulating, as if she had had an unaccustomed
glass of wine.

Dinner was a dream-like affair during which Hildegarde sat at the foot of the table, opposite her father,
in what she felt should have been Miss Anne's place.

But Miss Anne would have none of it. " The place
of honor belongs to Hildegarde," she told her guests
with her hand on the shoulder of her niece. " May
I present to you the new mistress of the house? And
please don't turn her head with the nice things you are
going to say to her."

They said the nice things, coining flattering phrases
which seemed to flow over Hildegarde in soft waves
of sound. There were twelve people at the table, some
of them from Baltimore, some of them from the country, two men from Washington.

One of the men from Washington sat at Hildegarde's
right. He had a great mane of white hair which, in
spite of his short stature, gave him an air of distinction.
He had charming manners, but Hildegarde was not
quite sure that she liked him. She wondered how he
would look if he cut his hair in the prevailing fashion.
She imagined he would at once lose his air of splendor,
like a shorn sheep, or a plucked goose. He had light-

blue, keen eyes and small hands. He ate daintily, but with an appetite. The stories he told were pointed with wit, and cosmopolitan in character. He had traveled a great deal and said that Hildegarde ought to travel.

" Your father must take you to Paris."

She wanted to tell him that they couldn't afford it. But she wasn't sure that she had a right to say such things to her father's friends. And would they believe it if she said it? A man who could afford a dinner like this might find a way to go to Paris. The dinner was perfect. It was the season for game, and there were ducks — oysters had formed the first course, there were avocados for the salad, and the ices were from Baltimore.

Whose money had paid for it? Or had it been paid for? The thought troubled her. To her straight-thinking honesty, the honesty of her mother and of her aunts, there was something sinister in the fact that her father, hounded for money, could buy such dresses for his daughter, and such dinners for his friends.

Yet she was proud of him. Indeed, it seemed amazing to know that he was her father — at his ease, almost youthful in his enjoyment of the hospitality which he dispensed, he seemed utterly divorced from anything that had belonged to her before — he shone with an effulgence that startled her and seemed to separate her from him by the difference which environment had made in them.

After dinner everybody but Hildegarde danced or played cards. Miss Anne, arranging a table, said, " Will you join us, my dear, or dance? "

"Would you mind if I just looked on?"

"But why?"

"It seems so soon — to be gay — "

"Of course. I should have thought of it." She touched her niece's cheek with the tip of her finger. "They are all quite mad about you, Hildegarde."

Hildegarde would not have been human if such flattery had not thrilled her. But she managed to say, "It's my gown, and your good taste."

"Nonsense. You're different — and Elizabeth's daughter.

"Did any of them know her?"

"Yes. Neale Winslow — the one with the white hair. He admired your mother immensely. But she did not like him."

"And I don't." Hildegarde was emphatic.

Miss Anne was tolerant. "He's not so bad. He is very rich, and he has been a great help to Louis. It is his egotism that antagonizes women — I feel it. But in spite of it we are friends."

She left her niece then, and a little later Hildegarde went upstairs. She felt she would not be missed if she slipped away quietly and did not say "good-night."

Sally, dancing with Meriweather, saw Hildegarde go. "Well, the Madonna has fled," she said with her cheek against his shoulder.

"The Madonna?"

"The new daughter. Merry, I hope I'm a good sport, and I shan't be a cat and say things about her. But I'm sorry she came."

"I thought you liked her."

"I do. She's precious. But that's it. You think so, too."

Meriweather laughed. " What if I do? "

" Well, I'm always dreading the moment when you'll find the One Woman, and I won't have any one to ride with, or play golf with, or make love to — "

They were laughing together now. Sally was never, Meriweather reflected, serious for more than a minute. And the things she said to him were as light as a feather.

Yet it was not a feather-light Sally who presently slipped away and ran to Hildegarde's room. She tapped.

" May I come in? "

Hildegarde opened the door. She had taken off the pretty dress and was in the sober little robe she had brought with her. She was not yet used to wearing the fragile negligées Miss Anne had bought, and then, too, her mother had made this.

" My dear," Sally said, " I have a feeling that you are up here breaking your heart. And I hate it. I wish you would come down and let us make you happy."

Hildegarde reached out an impulsive hand. " How dear of you to say that!"

For a moment the two girls clung together. Then Sally drew away.

" Now we are friends for always, aren't we? I am really rather good at friendships."

" You are very understanding. I was feeling lost and lonely."

" Well," Sally was somewhat cryptic, " I may not know what it is to lose a mother, but I know what it is to do without somebody — I want — very much —

I am not the crying kind — but there are moments when I could weep — floods."

With that she shelved the subject, but before she went down she said: " I've got a dance with Merry, and I can't stay. Not that he would champ at the bit if I wasn't there, but I'd hate to miss it." She hesitated and went on, " He thinks you are charming."

" Oh — does he? " The red came up into Hildegarde's cheeks.

" I'll say he does, and he shows his good taste."

Sally's tone had a touch of wistfulness. Then, having proved her sportsmanship to herself, she went away — a little ministering angel in red chiffon, with gold roses on her shoulders instead of wings; and not a word did she say to Meriweather of where she had been, although she danced a dozen times with him before the night was over.

CHAPTER VI

THE BRONZE TURTLE

THE bronze turtle had seen many things in his time. There had been a century or two in old Japan, where the cherry blossoms had drifted over him, and the fogs from the sea, and where at all hours he had heard the bells of the temple.

Then one day he had found himself here in the pool with the sunshine hot upon him, and a stream of water rising up and splashing down again, so that he seemed to swim in it, and all about him were lily pads, and on the bank was a blaze of flowers, and a girl in white standing among them.

And the girl was saying, " Don't you love my old turtle, Louis? "

" I love you — "

They had come often together, these two. They had come one day when the pink lotus lilies starred the water, and the girl had said:

" All my life I have wanted a garden like this. To me it seems wonderful that this is my garden."

" It is wonderful that you are my wife, Elizabeth."

They had come at night sometimes, this Louis and Elizabeth, when the moon was reflected in the pool, and once the bronze turtle had heard the girl say:

" How old he is — my turtle! He must have seen many lovers."

" But none so happy, dearest."

Then one night, when the leaves were falling, and a chill wind wrinkled the pool, had come another woman with the man called Louis, and she had said:

" How can you bear to have that turtle in the pool? I hate old things!"

She had drawn her cloak about her as if she were cold, and her voice had sighed above the sound of the wind, " The winter is coming, Louis, and my heart is empty."

After that, the first woman had come no more. And the fountain had ceased to play. But there were springs under the pool which fed it, so the lilies still bloomed in the summer time, and the flowers still blazed bravely on the bank, and the butterflies came, and the bees, and the goldfish multiplied until they sparkled like flames beneath the surface, and there were frogs who sat sociably on the old turtle's back and kept him company.

So he was, as turtles go, content. Even in winter it was not so bad — for the birds rested on the way south, and rested again when they flew north, and in between there was the snow, soft as a blanket.

And now winter was on the way again, and a thin film of ice was on the edge of the pool, and a girl was standing where the other girl had stood so long ago, and she was saying:

" How lonely he looks!"

But the bronze turtle was not lonely, for there were

the fishes far down in the pool, and the frogs, and only
that morning a red-bird had lighted on his head to
drink.

"How strange," the girl was saying, "to have a
garden here!"

"It was because of the pool," Meriweather told her.
"The springs feed it — and so your mother had the
walk made of flagstones to lead down the hill."

"She had a garden at home," Hildegarde said.
"Things always bloomed for her. The day of her
funeral there was a white rose on a bush, and Crispin
picked it for me as we passed through."

It was the first time she had spoken his name to any
of them. She was scarcely conscious that she had
spoken it now.

"Crispin?" Meriweather asked.

"Crispin Harlowe. A friend of mine at home."

"But this is your home."

"Is it? Or is it just a stopping place?"

"What makes you say that?"

"I haven't any roots — not far-down ones like those
that hold me to the farm."

"But you don't belong to the farm. You belong
here."

"Do I? I doubted it last night. Mother couldn't
fit herself in — perhaps I can't."

"But if you should not stay, where would you go?"

She was silent, seeing Crispin as he had talked to
her under the sunset sky — "My heart is waiting."

Meriweather, watching her, was aware of something
he had not seen before, a sort of inner radiance. He
wondered what had lighted her like that.

"We are not going to let you go," he said with determination. "We shall keep you to tend our garden, and sit by our hearth, and ride with us on mornings like this." Lightly said, but with meaning back of it.

Hildegarde, missing the meaning, saw only the lightness. "It has been a wonderful ride," she told him.

"We'll have more of them. There's an old inn on the Point. Some morning we'll have breakfast there — just you and I. It's great fun — fish and cornbread and a rasher of bacon."

As he told more about the famous old hostelry, Hildegarde's thoughts were swept away from Crispin. Here was adventure close at hand. And it was pleasantly stimulating to see the admiration in Meriweather's eyes. There had been, too, her mirror before that to show a charming reflection in the new riding clothes — rough, gray homespun, smart waistcoat, shining boots, and stiff little hat.

They mounted their horses.

"Good-by," Hildegarde called back to the old bronze turtle. "We shall come again tomorrow."

She came tomorrow, and for many morrows, and always beside her was the tall figure of the thin, dark man. She called him "Merry" now, and they were great friends.

"I am riding every morning with Mr. Meriweather," she wrote to Crispin. "We had breakfast yesterday at a place on the Point which is famous all through the state. It was snowing a little, just a feather or two drifting down, and everything so still and cold — and then the roaring fire as we came in, and the gay

chintzes on the chairs. There are old hunting scenes
on the wall. Not copies of English things, but sketches
done in color by the man who owns the place. And,
Crispin, there was one of father and mother among the
guests at a hunt breakfast. Merry said that was why
he took me there. He wanted me to see it. He said
that father had tried to buy the picture, but that old
Christopher wouldn't sell. He won't sell any of them,
and there are so many famous people that his collection
is extremely valuable.

"We are to have dinner at Sally's on election night.
It seems so strange to be in the midst of things as we
are. Father's friends are men we've always read about,
and he calls them by their first names. Politics are
still a gentlemanly tradition in this old county, and a
lot of my ancestors held public office. Father will be
dreadfully disappointed if his candidate loses this election, not only because he has some personal matters
involved, but because he will feel keenly the defeat of
his party.

"Oh, I wish you were here, Crispin, to talk about
the new things that are coming into my life. Sometimes you seem so far away, and the old life seems so
far — and mother seems the farthest of all. And I
have no one to lean on, or ask things. Yet father and
I are, really, the best of friends. Sometimes he talks
to me about mother, and I really think he cares a lot.
He gave me a lacquer cabinet that was hers — the little
red box that she left me belongs to it. The cabinet
stands in a dark corner of the library, and is very old,
and on top of it is a cat of rock crystal made into a
lamp. The light flows down over the red and gold of

the cabinet and brings out all the beauty, and the cat sleeps the sleep of a thousand years. When I was a child mother told me about the crystal cat, but I never thought I should see it.

" It is queer how these inanimate things bring me nearer to mother than any of the people. She told me, too, about the bronze turtle. But she never told me about father, or his family and friends. And I always thought it was strange. But now I know the reason. She couldn't talk about them — she cared too much.

" It is queer, too, the way I feel sometimes about Daddy, as if he were an unhappy little boy and I had to feel sorry for him. Perhaps, if mother could have felt that way, she might have stayed and let things work themselves out. Marriage is ' until death parts,' isn't it, Crispin? Oh, I am not blaming Mother, but I am sure that Daddy wanted her to stay."

Hildegarde had been sure when her father gave her the lacquer cabinet. They were alone in the library, and he said:

" There are some things in the drawers that were your mother's. I have always carried the key on my ring, but I have never had the courage to open it. You may, if you wish."

He gave her the key, and she knelt before the lovely cabinet and opened it, pulling out the little drawers. And the things she found were a bunch of faded violets, little packages of letters, some old photographs.

And her father, standing beside her, said: " I remember when your mother knelt there, so pleased with it all — and her hair lighted this dark room with gold

— I am glad you are not like her, Hildegarde. I couldn't stand it."

And Hildegarde, looking up at him, said, " Oh, I wish she had stayed with you."

" And I! You have brought it all back to me — her kneeling there — and the love she gave me."

If Carew had been always like that — revealing his gentler self, Hildegarde would soon have bestowed upon him an unquestioning devotion. But there were other moments when he was cynical, hard, irritable. Moments when Meriweather warned her:

" In a mood like this it is better to let him alone."

In the days preceding the election, Carew had many moods.

" If it goes against him," Miss Anne said, " there won't be any living with him."

There were to be six of them on election night at the dinner at the Hulburts'. Neale Winslow made up the quota of men, with Mrs. Hulburt, Sally, and Hildegarde as the only women.

Miss Anne had gone to Baltimore to help there with the women's vote. Delia and Sampson were whirling around the county in their little car, excitedly, in opposition to the white families for whom they and their kind had always worked. Only in this one thing did they differ, and for them election day was the one echo of emancipation.

It was on the ride over to the Hulburts' that Carew discovered his daughter's politics were not his own.

" Do you mean that if you were old enough, you'd vote the other way? "

" Yes."

" Then it's a good thing you haven't a vote. Do you think I'd let you neutralize mine? "

Warned by his tone, Hildegarde was silent.

" Oh, this thing of women voting!" he raged. " Why should my daughter set her mind against my convictions? Why should any daughter? Why should any wife set herself against her husband? It's all wrong, I tell you. A woman like you, Hildegarde, why, a woman like you should be content to be adored. Shouldn't she, Merry, shouldn't she? "

Meriweather was driving, with Hildegarde in the seat beside him. Carew, back of them, leaned forward while he argued in his ragged, irascible voice.

" Shouldn't she, Merry? "

" Well, she is adorable, isn't she, Louis? And we will keep her from voting as long as we can."

Carew growled and settled back in his seat. They rode on in silence for a while, then Hildegarde said, very low, and only for Meriweather's ears:

" Oh, you men! With your heels on our necks!"

He gave her his amused glance. " So you feel like that about it? "

" With you and Daddy. But not with Crispin."

" Crispin again? "

" Yes. He's glad I can vote."

" Perhaps your politics agree."

" What has that to do with it? "

" He would naturally be complacent to add a vote to his." He was still smiling.

" He isn't like that. He would take me to the polls himself, no matter how I voted."

" A *perfect* young man," Meriweather emphasized.

" Oh!" she blazed. Then subsided. " You and Daddy are cave-men."

She refused, after that, to talk to him. So with Carew sulking on the back seat, they reached the end of their journey without further conversation.

After dinner, they got the news by radio — from New York and Texas, from Seattle to Florida. East and west, north and south, everybody was listening in.

" Some contrast," Winslow said, " to the days when we stood in front of newspaper offices to read the slow telegrams."

It was when things began to go against him that Carew said to his daughter, " I suppose you're happy."

Hildegarde flushed. " I couldn't be happy to have you disappointed, Daddy."

Winslow looked at her. " You're not on our side? "

Her head went up. " If I could have voted, I should have had to vote the other way."

" Why? "

She tried to treat it lightly, " Because — "

" *Because* and *because* and *because* is no reason." A dark fire burned in Louis' eyes. " If I had my way, women shouldn't vote. It's not their business."

Unexpectedly Mrs. Hulburt agreed. " Life's too short to bother with politics. I'm glad to leave it to the men."

" Good for you, Ethel," was Carew's emphatic commendation. " I hope you'll convert Hildegarde to your doctrine."

Hildegarde was assailed by an unreasonable sense of jealousy. She liked Mrs. Hulburt, but she didn't like her father's praise of her. Mrs. Hulburt was good-natured, good-looking, tactful. But, as Sally said of her:

" Mother is as comfortable as a feather-pillow, because she always agrees with everybody."

" But how can she agree with everybody," Hildegarde had demanded, " and be sincere? "

" The girls of mother's generation were not trained to be sincere," Sally explained. " They were trained to be attractive, and you can't be attractive to men if you have too many opinions."

Hildegarde thought of her own mother. Her mother's sincerity had been the stable and splendid thing about her. Yet it had never been irritating. In argument she had always been fair, laughing often at her own inconsistencies, agreeing with her opponent when she could, but waving the truth as she saw it like an oriflamme in the faces of her enemies.

Yet here was Mrs. Hulburt, soothing in pale lavender, her fair hair banded with silver, capturing Carew's fancy with her sophistries, her insincerities.

The evening was spoiled for Hildegarde. And when the returns began to show that defeat for her father's candidate was imminent, she had a feeling that she might be held personally responsible.

When the thing was certain, however, Carew rose sportingly to the occasion. "We who are about to die, salute you," he said to his daughter. Then, to Mrs. Hulburt: " Ethel, let's relieve our drooping spirits by going over to the Country Club. There's a dance — "

Hildegarde was in no mood for the Country Club.

And when, on the way over, she found that they were
to pass Round Hill, she asked if she might stop. " I'm
too tired to do any more, Daddy."

It was Meriweather who went up the steps with her
and let her in with his key. " I don't like to think of
you here alone," he said. " The chances are that the
servants are off celebrating somewhere."

" I'm not afraid."

The dogs were in the hall, eager. " You'll
have them," Meriweather said, " and you can telephone if you need me. I'd much rather stay with
you — "

" It wouldn't do. You must go on with Sally."

He hesitated. " You mustn't be too upset by your
father's manner."

He saw that her lips were quivering. " But I want
him to love me."

" He does. But he can be hard at times with those
he loves. And tonight, you know, he stands amid the
wreck of his fortunes."

She stared at him. " Does it mean that? "

" I am afraid it does."

Her hand went up to her throat. " Oh, I should
have known!"

" You couldn't, of course. But now that you do
know, it will be easier for you to understand."

" Oh, yes. And I'll write a note for him to find
when he comes in."

How dear she was in her quick repentance! Meriweather went back presently to Sally — Sally with her
sparkles, her feather-lightness, Sally in silver tissue
dancing with him to the despair of all the other men.

But through it all, the vision was with him of that child in white with the smoky sweep of hair, the tender eyes.

Hildegarde wrote her note, tucked it under her father's door, and descended the stairway. As she reached the first landing, she stopped, spellbound by the beauty which confronted her. A great window filled the high-ceiled wall space, and through it streamed the golden radiance of the moon. Everything it touched was turned, Midas-like, to gold — the cushions on the window-seat, the marble bust of a dead and gone Carew, the two dogs stealing up the steps to meet their young mistress, Hildegarde herself — a golden statue.

The window on the landing was called " the Blue Window," because by day it framed the azure of the Bay and by night the rich indigo of the sky. It seemed to overlook immeasurable distance. Hildegarde unlatched the French shutters and leaned out. As far as she could see was a wide expanse of moonlight. The wind blew in her face. She had a sense of forward movement, as if she stood on the prow of some swift-sailing vessel.

She was soothed by the beauty which surrounded her — serenity seemed to enter into her soul. She had been much shaken by her father's unsympathetic attitude, but now she felt she would be able to meet it. She would learn to understand him, and then — he would love her.

To the right of the moon and a little above it was a pale and quiet star. She spoke to it voicelessly: " You loved him, mother, didn't you? And you were sorry you left him? Oh, I want to love him with all my heart . . . and to have him love . . . me."

Meriweather, flying back from the club, found Hilde-garde still leaning forth in that golden light.

" You'll be frozen," he said. " I saw you as I drove up the road. You looked like a princess in a tower — "

" It isn't a tower;" she told him, " it's — sanctuary in this restless house."

" What makes you call it restless? "

" Isn't it? Isn't Daddy? "

" I see what you mean. Louis isn't happy."

" Do you think I can make him happy? I've been wondering about it. Sometimes he is like a wild thing that has been caged — his spirit, I mean. Will it tie him down to have a daughter? Will it? "

" Not to have a daughter like you. He is better since you've been here. Less moody."

" Yet — tonight —? "

" I know. But he has probably forgotten all about it by this time. I left him playing bridge with Ethel Hulburt and her crowd. I told him that as the servants were out, I'd better get back here to you. He'll drive the Hulburts home and bring Winslow on with him."

The wind was blowing cold through the open window. " You'll be frozen," Meriweather said again. " You'd better sit by the fire — there's one in the library."

She was chilled to the bone and found the warmth comforting. Meriweather, intent on hospitality, said:

" What you need is a cup of tea."

He brewed it for her himself. He did it easily, with an effect of delicate ceremony.

Hildegarde, watching him, remarked, " I didn't know a man could."

" Could what? "

" Make tea."

" I lived in the East too long not to have learned a few arts that the average American doesn't know."

He talked to her, after that, of his experiences in the Orient. He had the gift of picturesque expression, and he broke off suddenly to say: " You're a flattering little Desdemona. You really make me feel like a personage — a traveler of parts."

" Well, you are, in my eyes. I've been a country mouse."

It was some time later that he came to the thing that was much on his mind. " I'm afraid I am not going to be able to stay with your father."

" Do you mean that you are going away? "

" Oh, not at once. But after the first of the year, I don't see how he will be able to keep me on. He told me the other day that if the election went the wrong way, he'd take you abroad."

" But how can he afford to take me abroad, Merry? "

" Miss Anne would go, too. And a villa in Italy would be cheaper for the three of you than separate establishments here."

A villa in Italy! Magic! Her mother had told her of Sorrento, Asolo, Capri —

" I have always dreamed of it," she told Meriweather. " I am perfectly sure it will never come true."

" You'd like it then? "

" Oh, yes."

" You wouldn't mind leaving your friends behind? "

" My friends? "

" Me, for example? "

" Oh, but couldn't you go? "

" I might get a diplomatic position over there. I've some friends in high places. I wish I might show you Rome — the ruins by moonlight, the old roads, the churches."

He had opened a vista.

She spoke breathlessly, " It would be wonderful — "

More wonderful than she knew!

He was about to tell her more, when there came to them through the still, clear air the sound of a purring motor.

" It's your father," Meriweather said.

" Oh, what will he think? " Hildegarde's tone was agitated. " I told him I was tired and would go to bed."

" Then, if you're wise, you'll run along while the going's good. The chances are that things will be all right with him in the morning. But I wouldn't risk having him find you at this hour."

They scurried through the hall together, and Meriweather followed her upstairs. At her door he said, " Good-night and the best of dreams!"

She held out her hand to him. " You've made me dream — "

There was a charming flush in her cheeks. Meriweather wished that he might keep her there — prolong the moment. But her father was coming. So he let her go.

CHAPTER VII

THE WAY TO WIN A WOMAN

IT was on Thanksgiving afternoon that Crispin had a letter from Hildegarde. He was home for the holidays, had been to church that morning, had shared the thankful feast with his parents, and all the time there had been the thought that lying there in the post-office might be a letter from his love. He had not gone for it earlier in the day, because he had wanted to taste the full savor of it when he was alone. He wanted to read it in some quiet spot where he and Hildegarde had been together, and have her again with him in spirit.

So he turned from the post-office and followed a path which led along the way he had walked with Hildegarde on the day of her mother's funeral. He faced the west, and the trees of the grove as he passed through were black against the flaming clouds which swept the heavens like a conflagration. Crispin felt a sense of great exaltation as he walked in the glory of that flaming light with Hildegarde's letter in his pocket.

He ascended at last the hill where he had stood with her to watch the flying geese. He looked off again toward the south. She was there, far beyond his gaze, but tied to him still by the past which they had shared with each other and with Hildegarde's mother.

She spoke now of that past in her letter. " Do you remember last Thanksgiving Day? Mother and I went to church, and you were there, and you walked home with us."

Yes, he remembered. How proud he had been of Hildegarde's girlish beauty, of her mother's light carriage and free step! The weather had been almost spring-like, and they had loitered, stopping at last at the cemetery where Elizabeth was so soon to sleep.

Thinking of it now, it seemed to Crispin incredible that all that was left of that quick and burning spirit which had been Elizabeth Musgrove should lie sleeping in that quiet place. She had seemed to him always such an amazing and splendid person. Whether he had found her digging in the garden or tending her stock, there had been an air of detachment from toil, as if the thing she did was not a task, but an achievement.

That had been the charm of Elizabeth for him. She had set her own standards. She had wrested from what would have seemed to some women intolerable conditions a measure of contentment. If there had been a cry in her heart for what she had lost, there had been a song on her lips for what she had found — a brave woman and a royal one.

Early that morning Crispin had gone to the cemetery to lay a wreath for Hildegarde on her mother's grave. He had added for himself a little chaplet of laurel tied with gold. He had felt that the woman who lay there deserved a crown.

And she had passed her courage on to her daughter.

Hildegarde had not told Crispin all that had happened on election night, but she had told him a part of it and had ended with this:

" Father doesn't want me to have a mind of my own, but I must have it, mustn't I? Mother's love didn't demand that I should be her echo. Sometimes father doesn't seem to mind opposition. He laughs at me and says I am like him. But when he is in one of his moods I have to be careful — I wouldn't tell this to any one else in the world, Crispin, but you always understand."

Crispin's heart leaped at that. Yet, as he read on, he became aware of a sense of disquiet, almost of foreboding. For Hildegarde was talking of Meriweather.

" We are going to church together on Thanksgiving morning. No one else here goes to church — not even Miss Anne. She says she is emancipated, and father is indifferent. But I went last week with Merry to a century-old chapel at the cross-roads. There's a high church priest, so that there were candles on the altar, and there's a war memorial window, with a young soldier in golden armor and his face turned toward a great Light. Mr. Meriweather says that's the way it ought to be. That artists who make memorials of tired and stricken men don't know the Something that illumines men's souls at the very end. He says that war is beastly, but that the souls of men are not beastly. And that's why he likes the soldier in golden armor, with his eyes fixed on the Light — "

Crispin felt that it was a thing to disturb him, this growing intimacy with Meriweather. His name was sprinkled through the pages. She had called him once or twice, " Merry." She rode with him, danced with him.

" I am not doing many gay things — but we take up the rugs in the living-room and put on the records, and I am not nearly as awkward as I thought I'd be."

So, almost in spite of herself, she was being swept on to new adventures, and it was not he who shared them, but Meriweather. It was Meriweather who might in time come to share her confidences.

Then young Crispin, looking off toward the south, said in his heart:

" She is mine. No one else shall have her."

If Hildegarde had loved him, he would have felt no fears. Perhaps she did love him, but she had made no promises. And letters were a slender bond with which to hold a woman.

A little moon was hanging over the hills when at last he turned toward home. The valley lay all purple shadows below him. But it was to the sky that he lifted his face as he went along. " God give her to me," he said, and found that his eyes were wet.

That night he talked to his father and mother. " I want to go to Baltimore for the Christmas holidays, to see Hildegarde."

" Is it an invitation? " his mother asked.

" No. But no one ever gets a thing unless he goes after it."

They smiled at him. " So that's it," was what their smiles meant.

" Hildegarde's mine," Crispin told them. " I'm not going to let anybody else have her, and the way to win a woman is to win her."

" Why should she want anybody else? " his mother demanded.

" Why should she want me? But I can't see my future without her. And she's all linked up with my past. I love her childhood and her little-girlhood. No other man will ever see her as I have seen her."

He was in dead earnest. And they met his earnestness with their own.

" We'll miss you for the holidays," his mother said. " But you'd better go."

So it was settled. None of them was very practical. Crispin couldn't be married for a year or two at the best. But a woman who loved him would wait. Hildegarde was his, and he was going to tell her so. It all sounded simple.

But it really wasn't so simple as it sounded.

Crispin's letter came to Round Hill on a snowy morning. Sampson put it on Hildegarde's tray, and it lay there while he made her toast and boiled her egg.

Delia, upstairs, was drawing water for Hildegarde's bath and singing in a voice of poignant sweetness.

> *Nobody knows the troubles I has.*
> *Nobody knows — but Jesus —*

Hildegarde, listening, felt that it was delicious and delightful to lie in bed and have Delia wait on her. Delia had taken on her duties of lady's maid voluntarily. When Hildegarde had protested, she had said,

" I ain't doin' it, Honey-chile, because you likes it, but because I does."

Which was the truth. Hildegarde's coming had
given a fillip, as it were, to Delia's existence. She
enjoyed vicariously the things that her young mistress
did, and the things she wore. The new gowns which
she laid out shone and shimmered for her as well as
for Hildegarde. And Hildegarde's experiences, retailed
each morning, took on the aspect of a Thousand-and-
One-Nights enchantment to the enraptured maid.

This morning they had talked about the Christmas
party. Round Hill was to be very gay, with a half-
dozen house guests and two servants added to help
Delia and Sampson. One of these servants was Mary
Jackson — Delia's own cousin.

" I'm havin' her do the cookin'," Delia had stated.
" Ma'y kin roas' a tukkey twel hit tase like pa'tridge.
I told Mr. Louis effen he'd have Ma'y Jackson an' ol'
Edward, we could lay the res' of our troubles at the
feet of Jesus."

" *Delia!* " To Hildegarde, Delia's frankness of expression seemed nothing short of blasphemous.

Delia gave her an oblique glance. " Well, Mr. Louis
knows Ma'y, and he knows Edward. Ma'y *can* cook,
and Edward *can* wait, and that leaves me and Sampson
free to circulate."

" Circulating " was, in Delia's vocabulary, the cream
of all that was desirable. With the things of the
kitchen and dining-room off her mind, she could flit
from the room of one feminine guest to another, giving
help where it was needed, and getting in return the
gossip.

While Hildegarde had her bath, Delia went down
for the breakfast tray. The letters lay in a neat pile

beside the silver covers of the hot dishes. On the top
of the pile of letters was Crispin's!

Hildegarde read it before she ate a mouthful. The
news it contained seemed too good to be true. Crispin
was coming! He wrote that he would be in Baltimore
during the holidays, and hoped she would let him come
to Round Hill to say " A Merry Christmas."

" The darling, the darling," she found herself saying.
She had never called Crispin that even in her thoughts,
but she said it again, " The darling!"

Delia's voice came from the bathroom, where she
was scrubbing the tub, " *Nobody knows the troubles
I has —* "

Hildegarde felt there weren't any troubles in the
world — *Crispin was coming —!*

" Delia," she called.

" Yes, Honey? "

" Is there an extra room? A friend of mine has
written that he is to be in Baltimore, and I want him
here for the week-end."

Delia, standing in the bathroom door, surveyed her
mistress speculatively. " He mus' be made of gold to
make yo' eyes shine like that."

" I've known him all my life, Delia."

" They's some folks I've known all my life," said
wise Delia, " that don' make *my* eyes shine."

Hildegarde passed that over. " Do you think we'll
have a room for him? "

" They ain' one left, Honey-chile. Some of them
might double up — two beds. But you'll have to ask
yo' Daddy."

Hildegarde finished her breakfast, got up, dressed, and wrote a note to her father.

"Daddy, darling, do have lunch with me in the library. Aunt Anne isn't coming down, and I've something most important to say to you."

She was flinging her "darlings," you see, wherever they might fall. She even called the two dogs "darlings" when she found them on the hearth, waiting for her, with their tails tapping.

Her father came at last, kissed her, and put a finger under her chin. "Well, what's the important matter?"

"Daddy, Crispin is coming."

"Crispin?"

"Yes. He's a boy I've known all my life. He's to be in Baltimore, and I want to ask him here for the week-end."

Her father drew out a chair for her, sat down. "Why should you ask him here?" His tone was sharp.

Hildegarde's heart began to beat wildly. "He's my friend."

"But not one of my invited guests."

The color was drained from Hildegarde's cheeks. "But — can't I invite him?"

"As a house guest? I see no reason. The sooner you cut your ties with the farm, Hildegarde, the better."

"But he isn't on the farm. His father is a judge, and Crispin — why, there isn't any one finer than Crispin."

Her father looked at her — flushed cheeks, tear-wet eyes. " Are you in love with him? "

The flush deepened. " I haven't promised — anything — "

" But he's in love with you."

" Yes. But — "

Her father beat his fist on the arm of his chair, " I'm not going to have you in love with anybody. Do you think I am going to let any one take you away from me? "

Hildegarde's breath was quick. " But we don't have to think of that, do we? Crispin isn't coming to marry ne. Why, Daddy, he isn't out of college."

" I don't care whether he is in college or out of it. I don't want him coming here. I am not going to ask him as a house guest. You can have him down for an afternoon. That's the best I can do. There isn't a bed for him."

Sampson came in just then with a tray. Hildegarde, helping herself, hardly knew what she was doing. It seemed to her that her father, peppering a poached egg composedly, was a monster of inhospitality. Why, Crispin was her friend, her mother's friend. The one who loved them both.

Sampson left them, and suddenly, almost without her volition, Hildegarde found herself saying, " If Crispin can't come to see me here, I shall go back to the farm."

Through a blinding whirl of emotions she heard her father's violent voice:

" You'll do nothing of the kind."

" But I shall. Do you think I'd stay? "

" That's nonsense, Hildegarde. Simply because the beds are full."

" Oh, if it were only a matter of *beds*," she flung at him, " I'd give up mine. I'd sleep on the *floor*." She began to sob. " Why, Crispin — Crispin — was mother's friend — she loved him."

Dead silence. Her father staring at her.

Then, in the midst of that pause, the curtains parted, and Meriweather in riding clothes came in.

" How cozy you look! " he said.

Hildegarde could not speak. Carew laughed harshly.

" Come on in," he said. " We are not cozy. We are quarreling. Hildegarde has just told me that she is going back to the farm."

Chapter VIII

MERIWEATHER AS PEACEMAKER

MERIWEATHER never forgot the picture which they presented, father and daughter, so much alike, facing each other across the little table — Hildegarde's cheeks blazing, Carew's eyes hard. The young secretary knew what it meant when Carew's eyes were like that. In such a mood he would say bitter things, sarcastic things, cruel things sometimes, things he would regret.

Hildegarde, slim as a young birch in her white wool frock, stood up. " I'm sorry it has all ended like this."

" Ended! " The word seemed to ring through the room.

The three of them were standing now, and Carew was saying, " I am sorry you care more for this boy than for me."

" Daddy, it isn't that."

" But why should you want so much to have him here? "

" Because he was my friend and mother's."

" You've said that before. Yet your mother sent you to me, to share my life, to cut away from old associations."

" Mother would never have had me ungrateful."

" But don't I deserve something? "

Hildegarde regarded him with troubled eyes. " Yes. You do. You've given me a lovely home and a lot of pretty things. But if you haven't given me love, it doesn't amount to anything."

" Why should you say that I don't love you? "

" Because if you did, you wouldn't let me go."

" I won't let you go, if you'll give up this Crispin."

Meriweather was conscious of a surge of blood in his body. So that was the cause of it all — the boy of whom she had spoken on their ride together. Did he mean, then, so much to her? So much that she would leave her father? Well, the thing must not happen. He did not want to face the days ahead without Hildegarde.

" Oh, look here," he broke out boyishly, " I suppose it isn't any of my business, but what has happened? "

" Daddy won't let me invite Crispin here."

" Are you engaged to him, Hildegarde? "

" No."

" Good. I almost had heart failure at the thought of it. As Sally would say, ' Who would ride with me 'n everything,' if you found the One Man? "

" It is not a matter to be joked about," Hildegarde reminded him coldly. " You'd find plenty of people to ride with. And Crispin isn't the One Man. He's my friend. I've known him all my life."

" But he's in love with you," Carew interposed.

" Daddy, *please!* It isn't quite fair, is it? Merry isn't interested in what Crispin thinks of me."

" Oh, but I *am*. We both are, your father and I — we're jealous."

Carew whirled around on him. "Do you think I could be jealous of a country clod?"

"Oh," Hildegarde's voice was low and deep with anger, "Crispin's not a clod. He's — beautiful. He's like a young god out there under the wide skies."

She was so much in earnest that her poetic exaggeration took on an effect of dignity. There was dignity, too, in the way she left them, her head up, without a word.

When the two men were alone, Meriweather said, leaning forward and looking into the fire, "If she were mine, I would never let her go."

"It's not your affair, Merry. If she doesn't care any more for me that that — "

"She does care for you. But she won't be dictated to. It's your own blood, Louis."

Carew was held by that. "Yes, she's like me. That's why she means so much to me. She's bone of my bone and flesh of my flesh."

" Yet you are letting her go? "

" But what can I do? "

" Let her have him here. It is much simpler. She will see him then away from the wide skies which make him — beautiful." A faint smile curled on Meriweather's lip. "Distance lends enchantment. When she compares him with your friends, there may be disillusionment."

" You mean that he won't fit in, and she'll know it? "

" Yes."

" If I thought that, I'd let her have her way."

" Let her have it, Louis. Go up and tell her now.

You may have to eat humble pie. But it will do you good, and the game is worth it."

Upstairs Hildegarde was flying from the closet to the bed, from the bed to her trunk, with armfuls of dresses and hats and lingerie. She was packing violently, the tears streaming down her face.

She was acting as she had never acted in her life, impulsively, heatedly. But then no one had ever hurt her in quite the way that her father's words had hurt. She felt that she must get away at once, before she thought of how happy she had been that morning when Delia was singing in the bathroom; before she thought of her mood when she had said " darling," and " darling," and " darling." Would she ever again call her father " darling " ? Would her heart ever stop aching?

She threw herself across the bed sobbing. She had locked the door. No one must come in, not even Delia, until this storm within herself subsided.

There was a knock on the door. " Hildegarde."

It was her father's voice. She sat up.

" Yes? "

" Let me in."

She looked about her at the wild confusion. The mirror showed her tear-stained face, her disordered hair. How could she let him in? Yet how could she shut him out? So she opened the door.

And when he saw her, something within him broke — the hardness. Downstairs, with Meriweather, he had thought himself a diplomat, gaining his own ends while seeming to yield. But he knew now that he must yield even if he did not gain his end. The child was so young and sweet and unhappy. And in this room years ago had been another child-woman, sweet and young and despairing. And he had let *her* go.

Well, Hildegarde should not leave him. He gathered her into his arms.

" I've been a brute — "

" Daddy — "

" I want you here, Hildegarde. At any price. You're mine."

Meriweather, downstairs by the library fire, felt that he had used Machiavellian tactics. It was not fair, perhaps, to Hildegarde, but it had seemed the only way. He had had to reach back to Carew's egotism. Make him see the advantages.

As for himself, he wondered how he felt about this young god of Hildegarde's. Was she in love with him? And if she was, what had happened to him, Meriweather, that the thought stabbed him like a sword?

Miss Anne, trailing down presently in a tea-gown of bronze satin, demanded: " What in the world is the matter? Louis is in Hildegarde's room, and I heard her crying."

Meriweather told her.

" Oh, the idiot! " was Miss Anne's comment. " Doesn't he know that opposition simply fans the flame in an affair like this? "

" He wanted his own way."

" He always wants it."

" He listened to reason finally, when I insisted that he let the boy come. Hildegarde may find him less attractive in a more sophisticated atmosphere."

Miss Anne, tapping a restless foot on the fender,

asked, " Why should any one want to be sophisticated? "

" Whether we want to be or not, this boy's crudeness
may show up against it."

" That doesn't sound in the least like you, Merry."

He flushed. " I'm being perfectly frank with you.
I don't want her to love him."

She surveyed him with open eyes. " So that's it.
You've fallen in love with her yourself."

" Perhaps I have not gone quite that far. But I
know this, that I don't want any one else to have her."

Miss Anne threw up her hands in a little gesture of
despair. " Life is like the House that Jack Built —
Sally is in love with you, you are in love with Hildegarde, Hildegarde is in love with Crispin — "

He smiled at her. " I fancy that none of us has
gone as far as you think."

" But you have gone far enough." Miss Anne sat
staring into the fire. Years ago, family pride had separated her from the man she wanted to marry. Because
of that, her life was incomplete. " I'll have nothing to
do with Hildegarde's love-affairs," she declared. " Let
her choose for herself."

" By all means," Meriweather agreed. " And now,
shall we talk about Louis? You said this morning that
you wanted a minute with me to discuss him."

" I am worried about his finances. This Christmas
party seems to me a mad extravagance. He can't
afford it, Merry."

" He says he might as well be killed for a sheep
as a lamb."

" But what does he expect to get out of it? "

"Winslow wanted it. He can meet the people here who will help him — socially and politically."

"But can Louis stand the expense?"

"Yes, Winslow gave him a check for the whole thing."

Miss Anne blazed. "Do you mean that Louis is being paid for his hospitality?"

"It really isn't so bad as it sounds. Winslow wanted what Louis couldn't afford, so he put up the money."

"Oh, why didn't he come to me? I'd gladly pay his bills."

"He may have to come to you yet. He's talking about that villa in Italy for the three of you."

"I wish he'd go. Get away from Winslow, get rid of this house, look his poverty straight in the face, and find some way to rise on the wreck of his fortunes."

Meriweather nodded. "I know how you feel about it. But I know how he feels, too. Life has taken a lot out of him. The war did that for me. It was such a cataclysm that after it nothing seemed worth while. I was glad of a safe harbor here with Louis. And so I have stayed and let the world go by. But lately I have felt the stirrings of ambition. I want something for myself — a future and a name."

"Knowing Hildegarde has made you feel that way?" Miss Anne demanded.

"Yes."

Miss Anne's response was indirect. "Poor Sally, I am afraid her goose is cooked."

He laughed. "Sally isn't in earnest. You know that. If she cared, she'd never tell it."

" Yes, she would. The modern girl flings out her emotions like a banner to the breeze. She shouts them from the housetop, and sometimes her vociferousness wins."

" Sally is the moon, Hildegarde is the sun," he stated simply. " I might as well tell you. This thing has got me. My lance is against Crispin, and I shall beat him if I can. I am in the fight in earnest, and I shall stay in it until the best man wins."

CHAPTER IX

COCK–O'–THE–WALK

THE Hulburts were to spend the holidays at Round Hill, and it was on the day before Christmas — the day on which Crispin was to arrive — that Sally and Meriweather went for a ride. There had been an ice-storm the night before, and the world was of a white and glittering gorgeousness which seemed artificial in its stiffness, like the setting of a pantomime.

Sally, with her red coat and copper hair, was as vivid as a cardinal against the frozen background. Her spirits were at top-notch. There was a week ahead of her in the same house with Merry. Why quarrel with the gods?

Their horses went carefully over the slippery roads. Sally welcomed the slowness. They could talk as they rode, and there were so many things to talk about.

" Aren't you glad you are living, Merry? " she said out of a full heart.

He was glad. He might have been happier if Hildegarde were beside him. But he had had her yesterday, and it was because of yesterday that he was not un-happy, even though Hildegarde was at this moment meeting Crispin at the station, having with him the first hour of reunion.

Meriweather had offered to take her to the train, but she had said: "No, you wouldn't be interested in the things we'd have to talk about. I shall have a thousand questions for Crispin."

In spite of her refusal, however, he found himself upheld by the hope of what would happen when she saw Harlowe among her new friends. The house was full of people, the pick of Carew's acquaintances. Was it likely that side by side with these the young god would still shine?

Meriweather was not a snob, but he knew the world, and he knew women. Hildegarde had adapted herself amazingly to her new surroundings. People were saying charming things to her. As Miss Anne had prophesied, there had been great curiosity about Louis Carew's daughter. Everybody wanted to see the child of Elizabeth Musgrove who had left her husband and had gone out into a silence which had never been broken. And here was the girl, with her mother's slim grace, plus the Carew eyes and the crown of smoky curls. They made much of her.

"But they can't spoil her," Miss Anne had said to Meriweather: "she's true to the Carew tradition."

And there you had it. Back of her was the blood! But this Harlowe chap? No background apparently. Son of a country lawyer. Educated in a country college. Those things were all right, of course. But here, in the home of her forefathers, Hildegarde must see the difference.

Sally was saying: "Let's go to the Point and have tea. I haven't been there for ages, and no one will care if we don't get back."

Meriweather had been to the Point the day before with Hildegarde. They had had hot chocolate — with muffins. Not the English kind of muffin, but the crisp, golden cones of Maryland fame. And Hildegarde like a child, buttering hers, had said:

" I love it like this, Merry — with the storm outside, and all this warmth and deliciousness within."

For the storm had caught them, but Meriweather had wrapped Hildegarde in the army cape which he had carried across his saddle, and had ridden home with his hand on her horse's bridle.

He wished now that Sally had not suggested going to the Point. It was fine to ride with Sally, but to sit across from her at a tea-table was another story. Sally had no little outpourings of confidence, no wistful petitions for advice. The charm of Hildegarde lay for Meriweather in a sort of quaint childishness, in her hot little tempers, her quick repentances. She was so utterly herself, without affectation.

Sally, too, seemed utterly herself. Yet her individuality was that of premeditation. She knew the effects she wanted to make, and made them. All the girls of her set were like that. They created a rôle and played it. Just now the rôle was one of perfect frankness and ingenuousness. Tomorrow the rôle might be different.

It was yesterday at tea that Hildegarde had told him breathlessly of her reconciliation with her father.

" If he hadn't come upstairs, my heart would have been broken. I was crying my eyes out."

" Yet you would have left him? "

" I could not have stayed, could I? "

Meriweather had been daring. "Do you care so much for Harlowe?"

She had looked up at him, startled, and their eyes had held. And after a long pause, Hildegarde had said, with that startled air still upon her:

"I am not in love with him."

"Are you sure?"

She had nodded. "I have told him so over and over again. But he won't take 'no' for an answer. He says I am his. That I have belonged to him from the beginning of the world."

"Of course, you don't believe that?"

"Sometimes I do. And when I think of marriage it always seems as if it would be Crispin."

She had caught herself up. "I don't know why I am telling you all this. It doesn't seem quite right to tell it."

Yet she *had* told him. And there had been that moment when his eyes had held hers.

When they reached the Point, Sally agreed contentedly to tea and cinnamon toast. Meriweather was glad she did not demand muffins. His lip curled with laughter that the fact of eating or not eating muffins with Sally should matter. But it did. To such depths of sentimentality had he descended. Muffins and chocolate were the nectar and ambrosia of his romance!

When they came finally to the Inn, and he held the door open for Sally, there was the vision of Hildegarde, wrapped in his cape against the storm, his hand keeping her horse steady!

But this was Sally — ! He went in with her, sat

across from her, laughed and talked and ate, even flirted a little. Yet all the time he saw Hildegarde, telling him her troubles, talking of Harlowe — the look in her eyes in that startled moment!

"We've had a whale of a time," Sally said, as they left the Point behind them.

Sally loved the slang of the day. And it contrasted with her exquisiteness somewhat picturesquely, so that it seemed a whimsical adornment to her conversation rather than a defect.

The sky darkened as they rode home, spreading its deep sapphire from horizon to horizon, and under that spreading sky the countryside was flooded with the silver light of a frigid sunset. And in that light everything seemed touched by magic into an almost supernatural stillness. In the garden, when they came to it, the branches of the trees swept down like frozen, silver fountains; the bushes were a tangle of silver wires; the bronze turtle, caught in solid ice, might have been the remnant of some glacial age.

Then Sally said suddenly: "Look, Merry! Who's that?"

In the midst of the frozen garden, beside the pool, stood a young man. His face was turned to the bay, so that they saw only his profile. He had on gray knickerbockers, and a thick white sweater with the collar rolled up to his ears. He wore no hat, and above the collar of the sweater his hair was a flame of gold. There was a fine red in his cheeks, his face showed beauty and strength, and as at the sound of their voices, he turned, Meriweather received an impression of poise.

" Gee," Sally said, " he's got a peach of a head.
Who is he? "

" Harlowe."

" Hildegarde's friend? Merry, he is positively too
good-looking to be true."

He was good-looking. He was more than that.
Meriweather had to admit to himself that Hildegarde
had been right — the boy there in the frozen garden
belonged to the beauty of this silver scene as Lohengrin
belongs to his swan and his silver star.

He rode up to the fence. " Harlowe? "

Crispin came forward. " Yes. You are Meriweather, aren't you? Hildegarde told me to look out
for you. Some more people have come in, and she's
giving them tea. And I wanted to see the turtle."

Meriweather presented him to Sally. " I should
think you'd want to look at something warmer than
turtles," she told him, " on a day like this."

" Red coats, for example? "

He was at his ease. Utterly without self-conscious-
ness. That was, Meriweather was to find later, the
secret of his poise. He didn't know that he was good-
looking. He didn't in the least care. He didn't know
that living in a small town was a handicap. He didn't
know that there was any essential difference between
himself and the smart and sophisticated crowd in
which he found himself. And he didn't know because,
as has been said, he didn't care. He was interested
in life, eager. He swept everything else away. At this
very moment he was telling Sally:

" I'm middle-western, and there's no large body of

water near us. Did you ever see anything like the blue of that bay? It's like a Madonna's cloak."

Think of saying a thing like that! Where did he get that " Madonna's cloak " ? But Crispin wasn't thinking of what he was saying. He was thinking of the Bay and of its beauty, and of how glad he was to be near Hildegarde, and he was saying it all to Sally — all except the nearness to Hildegarde — in his fresh young voice. Meriweather felt suddenly old.

When they came to the house, they found Hildegarde in the library alone.

" We had tea at the Point," Sally told her, " so we won't have any. But you can talk to Merry while I get acquainted with Mr. Harlowe."

" Crispin! " Hildegarde said. " You musn't call him ' Mr. Harlowe.' Nobody does."

" Oh, don't they? Well, then, I want to get acquainted with — Crispin."

She flashed a challenging glance at the newcomer. " Merry will feel that we are public benefactors if we leave Hildegarde to him. Just for the moment he's at her feet."

Meriweather protested, " Do you mean that at other moments I am at other feet? "

Sally shrugged. " I said it, didn't I? "

" ' Just for the moment ' sounds too temporary to be true to fact," Meriweather stated. " I am under the heel of Hildegarde's slippers ' pummanently and f'ever' as Sampson would say."

Crispin, going upstairs to shed his sweater and get into a coat, reflected that at least Meriweather made no secret of his infatuation. And he was no mean rival, with his dark good looks, his pleasant and perfect manner.

When he came down, he stood for a moment outside the library door looking in. The gay group around the fire had the effect of a painting. Hildegarde, with her hair done in that new and beautiful fashion of braids, sat in a high-backed chair of stamped green velvet. Her white tea-gown was edged with soft feather trimming, and she wore silver slippers.

Crispin remembered her as she had walked beside him in her mother's black cape. He had thought her lovely then, but this was a different loveliness — the loveliness of Cinderella after the wand was waved, the loveliness which money makes possible, the loveliness which belonged to the portrait above the fireplace, to the pomegranate bloom of the lacquered cabinet, to the crystal cat and her sleep of a thousand years. It was the loveliness of enchantment. This Hildegarde was a dream-woman. Tomorrow he would wake and find her walking beside him in her stout little shoes and red sweater.

When he went in, Sally claimed him. She had taken off her hat, and her hair was gold. She was extremely pretty, Crispin decided. But not with Hildegarde's loveliness.

He was quite content to talk to Sally because he could feast his eyes on Hildegarde, and willing to let Meriweather talk to Hildegarde because when he was near his love, he felt that nothing could ever come between them.

He had a few moments alone with her before she

went up to dress for dinner. Meriweather had had a
message from Carew calling him away. Sally stated
with great regret that she must leave at once. Her
dress for the dance that night had come from Baltimore.

"There may be something to be done to it, you
know. And I must look my best for — Crispin."

She was off with a wave of her hand.

The dance was to be at the country club, after dinner
and the tree at Round Hill.

"The country club is adorable," Hildegarde told
him. "They have used an old manor house, and have
made as few changes as possible. This part of the
country used to be famous for its hunts, and that's
the keynote of the decorations. It's wonderful,
Crispin, to read in some of the old records that
my grandfather, up there, was among the best of
them."

Crispin had no hunting grandfathers. Or, rather, if
they had hunted, it had not been with hounds and
horses. They had conquered the virgin forests with
axes and guns, but there had been no red coats, no
banquets, no balls, in their social scheme. There had
been judges among them, a clergyman or two; and
there had been sporting blood and to spare. It had
taken strength of fiber and a high spirit of adventure
to pioneer in that western wilderness.

Yet Crispin's imagination was held by the thought
of the history of this different country — a land where
ships had come up from the sea by way of the blue
bay, and where men of rank and title had arrived,
bringing their luxurious habits with them, and had

found on the Chesapeake good living and gay, and had gone no farther.

He spoke of this now. " It's all so different. And you're like an enchanted princess."

" Do you like enchanted princesses? "

" Love them," he smiled at her.

She smiled back. " Sometimes I have to pinch myself to be sure it's true."

He agreed. " I know how you feel. That you'll wake up some morning and find yourself on the farm."

She asked wistfully, " Do Aunt Catherine and Aunt Olivia miss me? "

" They have your letters. You've been good about writing, Hildegarde."

" Oh, *no;* they did so much for me. Sometimes I feel like a deserter."

" But you're happy here? "

" Crispin, I want my mother. There's never a moment — " She stopped and could not go on.

" I often think of her," the boy said, " and of how different she was from all the others. She was a wonderful woman."

" None of the women here is like her," Hildegarde confided. " Somehow they all seem to live on the surface. And Miss Anne says emotions aren't fashionable."

" That's all bunk," explosively. " Living at top-notch means *feeling* at top-notch. I'd rather love and hate like an untutored savage than be so desiccated that I couldn't enjoy everything from a sunset to a good dinner."

Hildegarde was lighted up and laughing. " Crispin, how utterly like you! "

" Well, why not? "

" It's so *good* to have you here."

" That's why I came."

He was standing on the hearthrug, his hands in his pockets. She was aware of that touch of masterfulness in him which she had felt on the night of her mother's funeral. No other man had ever given her that impression of strength, of mental and physical poise. She had a sense almost of panic.

" Cock-o'-the-walk," she said suddenly, " the conceit of you! "

" It isn't conceit. It's sense. I came to let you know that you belong to me. I was afraid you might forget."

" I haven't promised."

" I don't need any promises. When I am ready, I am going to pick you up and carry you off."

" You say it as if you believe it."

" I do believe it. You'll see."

She had a feeling that he might do it at this very moment. She rose.

" I must go up and dress."

" Are you sure you must? "

" Yes."

He walked with her into the hall, stood at the foot of the stairs, and said, "Where's your balcony, Juliet? "

" My what? "

" Your room."

" Second floor, front."

" Sunrise side? "

" Yes — "

" Good. If you hear a pebble on the pane early
tomorrow morning, will you look out? "

" Yes. Why? "

" I am going to take you to church." The laughter
died out of his eyes as he stood looking up at her.
" Hildegarde, I want to say my prayers with you —
on Christmas morning."

She had nothing in answer to that but quick-drawn
breath, tear-wet eyes.   " I'll go," she whispered
after a moment, and he watched her as she went upstairs.

Delia, waiting for Hildegarde, was arrayed smartly
in a maid's dress of gray, a swiss apron with ruffles, and
a matching cap with a lavender bow. Miss Anne had
given them to her, and Delia was ecstatic.

" Honey-chile," she said, as Hildegarde compli-
mented her, " I has dreamed of lookin' like this in
Heaven, but nevah on dis yearth."

" What does Sampson think of you? "

" He say I'll be gittin' a *de*vorce and marryin' a hand-
somer man. Sampson's got rheumatism in his feet,
Honey-chile, an' he say he's got no eye fo' fumdiddles."

But whatever Sampson lacked in appreciation of
sartorial attractions was made up by his wife's absorp-
tion in them.

" Mis' Sally's got on silver lace," she said, "an' 'er
head's tied up in a silver ribbon. An' if she doan tek
her death of col' 'thout anything on her back and arms,
I'll miss my guess."

She said this over again when Sally came into Hildegarde's room.

"You'll tek you' death, honey."

"I'm used to it," Sally said, "and anyhow I'm not ready to die until I know whether I am going to marry Merry."

She flung this at them airily, surveying herself meanwhile in Hildegarde's mirror. Delia, doing Hildegarde's hair, remarked:

"You know right now you ain' gwine marry Mr. Merry. You wouldn't have him, not ef he axed you on his bended knees."

"Oh, but I would, Delia."

"You thinks you would," said Delia sententiously, "but I ain' known you all yo' life fo' nothin', Miss Sally."

When the two girls went down together, Crispin was waiting for them, and there were a lot of other people. The drawing-room was full of color, rose and jade and sapphire in kaleidoscope combinations as the women moved about. Miss Anne was in amethyst velvet, Mrs. Hulburt in gold brocade. Crispin had never been a part of a group like this. At college there had been dances and dinners, but the students had been a heterogeneous mass, and the dresses of the women not gorgeous. Here was perfection of line, opulence of hue, elegance balanced by exquisite and artful simplicity.

Characteristically, Crispin was not in the least embarrassed by the opulence and exquisiteness. He was much too interested. It was all like a lovely play, with the actors and actresses at close range. He stood alone by the fire and looked on, enjoying himself, waiting for Hildegarde.

And when she came in simple white with a knot of violets on her shoulder, he liked the fact that she took the center of the stage — took it not because of super-elegance and opulence, but because she was, in effect, the heroine of the drama, the leading lady. As she went from one guest to the other, greeting them, she was for him no dearer, than she had been when, in the old farmhouse, she had greeted the Skinners.

She went out to dinner on the arm of a distinguished diplomat. Crispin took Sally. Hildegarde had managed that and had put Meriweather on the other side of Sally, who was in her liveliest mood.

" Hildegarde is wearing Merry's violets, did you know it? " she demanded of Crispin.

He had not known it. And anyhow what did it matter? She was his! So he said to Sally easily:

" There are flowers that she likes better than violets."

" What are they? "

" I shan't tell you. Meriweather might hear."

Meriweather, turning at the sound of his name, asked, " What might I hear? "

" Hildegarde's favorite flower. Crispin knows it, and it isn't violets. And it serves you right, Merry, for sending them to her instead of to me. She didn't tell me where they came from, but I was up in her room and saw the card with your name."

Meriweather flushed. Sally's frankness had ceased to be amusing.

She was aware she had gone too far, and saved the situation. " Somebody lend me a pencil," she begged.

Crispin had one. Sally decorated a placecard with a bit of green from her plate and wrote:

> Here's parsley, that's for that.
> I would give you violets,
> But they withered all,
> When my dear rival wore them —

She laid it before Meriweather, and in spite of himself he laughed.

" She wears them well."

" She does. But next Christmas I shall be wearing your flowers, Merry."

" Is that a prophecy or a threat? "

" Both."

" There's a present for you on the tree," he digressed.

" Tell me about it." She clapped her hands like a child. " I can't wait. I can't wait."

" I ought to make you wait for your — impertinence." His tone was light, but she knew he meant it.

" I'm sorry," she said softly.

Her eyes, as they came up to his, had tears far back in them. How could he know that the card she had read in Hildegarde's room had stricken all the brightness from her day. For the card had said:

" Wear them, won't you, Hildegarde? They'll be awfully proud to be worn by you."

And now here she was saying, " I'm sorry," and her heart was heavy. And she looked so like a repentant child that Meriweather laid his hand for a second over hers.

" I'll forgive you. And — it's a doll."

" Not really? "

"Yes. The one we saw in Baltimore."

"Merry, you're precious! "

"I thought you'd like it."

"Oh, I do. And I'm going to call her 'Sarah.'"
She turned to Crispin, 'That's my real name, but nobody ever gives it to me. This doll is dressed like Queen
Victoria. She's fat and short and wears a little cap.
I fell in love with her at first sight. She's just what I'd
like to be when I grow old. But I shan't be like that
at all. I shall be thin and all strung up with beads and
things, and my cheeks will be red, and my hair touched
up." She stopped from sheer failure of invention.

"But you won't have to look like that, will you? "

"Yes, I shall. You watch the old women of our set.
They've got a youth-complex. Can you see mother
wearing a cap when her hair gets thin? Or having
flat-heeled slippers? But I'll bet that deep down in
her heart she envies my Sarah-doll."

Crispin laughed a little, and then, as she talked to
Meriweather, turned his attention to the people around
him. This was, for him, the second act of the play.
And the setting! He had never in his life seen such
silver and glass and china. The strip of Italian embroidery down the center of the table might have belonged in a palace — the flower-holder was a silver
pheasant, and smaller silver pheasants, placed at inter-
vals down the table, held the salt. The grandfather
in the red coat had had the pheasants made by an
English silversmith, and they were brought out only on
grand occasions.

Like Hildegarde, Crispin wondered at the effect of
extravagance. Carew had, he knew, lost his money.

How could he afford a feast which would have paid the bills of the Harlowe family for days to come?

He found himself weighing Louis Carew against his own father. Weighing the tired eyes, the restless hands, the stooping elegance of the tall figure against the middle-aged serenity of the country judge. Clear-eyed, quick of step, not rich, but with not a money worry in the world, the judge went back and forth to the county court, a wise and just man, with a sense of humor and a love of living which saved him from a provincial point of view.

Yet there was a charm about Carew. Crispin had to admit that, and to admit, too, that he was like Hilde-garde — like her as a shadow is like the bright figure by which it is cast. Crispin found himself resenting the likeness. It was as if he saw in the father some prophecy of what the daughter might be. Would he ever see her with that burnt-out look? With fingers tap-tap-tapping on the arm of her chair? Would he ever see her fighting a losing fight against the world?

Well, not if he could help it. He could give her more than her father gave. If he had no silver pheas-ants, he had at least no debts. His head went up a little. He caught Hildegarde's glance and smiled at her. He was eager to slay the dragons which lay in the path of his beloved — a young St. George in even-ing dress.

From the other end of the table Louis Carew saw Harlowe smile at Hildegarde. Saw the look she gave him in return, and was infuriated. Things had not turned out as Meriweather had prophesied. The boy was not a clodhopper. He was a gentleman. He had manners and ease. And while he was not so good-look-ing in his evening clothes as he had been in his white sweater, he was good-looking enough to cause much comment, and to have people ask about him.

" A friend of Hildegarde," Carew had told them, and had resented the fact that Hildegarde should have such a friend.

He had had only a moment's conversation with Cris-pin, and he had recognized in that moment a force stronger than his own, and he had feared it.

And fearing it, he had only one recourse. To run away. He would take Hildegarde to Europe. He and Merry had talked it over — a villa in Capri or an apartment in Venice. A new world for Hildegarde! A world in which young country lovers would have no part. A world in which Carew would have his daughter to himself.

And Winslow had said that this would all be possible — if Carew would say a good word for him here and there to the other men who were dining tonight at his table. It was not a thing that he liked to do, to use his guests for his own advantage. But he was up against a blank wall, and he would sponsor no cause that he did not believe in. Thus it became for him a matter of taste, rather than of conscience. He would do no act of dishonesty, no matter what happened. But why should he question, if he knew that by obliging a friend he could help himself? Once upon a time he had been squeamish in such matters, but Corinne had laughed at his " knightliness " and had called it out of date. Elizabeth had never laughed. She had loved it.

But he did not want to think of Elizabeth and of the

love he had thrown away. He had never let himself
brood over it. He did not intend to begin now. He
turned to Mrs. Hulburt.

"What about Europe in the spring, Ethel?"

"Do you mean that you are going?"

"Yes. I'll take Anne and Hildegarde. And with
you and Sally over there the thing would be perfect."

"I'd like it. I don't need to tell you that, Louis.
But I don't know what Sally will say."

"Are you going to let Sally manage your life for
you?"

"Well — why not? There isn't any one else to do
it."

It was an opening of a kind. But he did not take it.
He liked Ethel Hulburt, but he was not in love with
her.

"If we let our daughters get the upper hand," he
said, "we might as well be slaves."

Mrs. Hulburt knew the thing he liked, and gave it.

"Hildegarde will never rule you. You've always
been king of your own domain, Louis. You will always
be."

Chapter X

THE CLODHOPPER

THE great tree in the hall was hung with gold and silver balls which caught the light, and festooned with shimmering tinsel. On the topmost branch was a gay little Santa Claus, red as a flame and powdered with snow. Under the tree, and on the low tables which flanked it, were tissue-wrapped parcels — hundreds, it seemed to Crispin — mountains of treasure.

Carew, thin and dark, excitement in his gray eyes, read the names on the parcels, and Sampson and Delia, in fluttering ecstasy, distributed them.

For Hildegarde there was, from her father, a sapphire hung on a fragile platinum chain. It had belonged to her grandmother and had been reset. Miss Anne gave her crystal bottles for her dressing-table; Winslow, a gorgeous fan of sapphire feathers.

"Your father and I have decided," Winslow told Hildegarde, "that this deep blue is your color. Women with your smoky hair and white skin can always wear blue, but some of them don't know it."

Crispin, standing by, hated Winslow's manner of close intimacy. He did not like the man. There was something frigid about him, brittle, insincere. His own gift to Hildegarde had been book-ends which he had carved for her. They had ships on them, ships with wind-filled sails.

When Hildegarde thanked him, Crispin said: " They are our ships. We shall reach harbor together. No storms can stop us."

And Hildegarde, thrilling to the romance of the thought, flushed and sparkled. " What a voyage that would be, Crispin! "

After the presents had been distributed, everybody motored to the country club. Hildegarde danced several dances and went home at midnight with her father and Mrs. Hulburt and Crispin. Sally begged to be left with Meriweather to finish the night out.

" There are plenty of mothers staying," she told her own. " I'll be more than chaperoned."

" I suppose I shouldn't have left her," Mrs. Hulburt apologized on the way home. " But I must have my beauty sleep, Louis."

And so it happened that Sally and Meriweather danced until morning, and had bacon and scrambled eggs at dawn, in the club grill, with other revelers. And Sally set the doll, Sarah, in the center of the table.

" She is really my subconscious self," she informed her friends. " You see only the surface — the Sally Hulburt that I let you see. But underneath I want to wear caps and part my hair and warm my toes at the fire."

They roared at that — Sally, with her impertinences, and revealing franknesses. Sally, with her copper-colored bob, and her lip-stick.

"The only kind of cap you'll ever wear," Meri-weather told her, "is a liberty cap."

She shrugged. "That shows how little you know me, Merry," and was presently laughing and roaring with the rest of them.

And outside in the Christmas sky a star shone, and in the throbbing darkness under young Juliet's window, her lover waited.

Except for the dim light in Hildegarde's room, there was only the lamp in the hall left to guide the returning revelers. As she came out of the door, the two dogs followed her — not making a sound. They seemed to grasp the secrecy of the adventure and the need for silence.

As she and Crispin walked along, Hildegarde said, "I suppose I should have told Daddy."

"Why tell anybody?" Crispin demanded. "This is our hour, isn't it?" He took her hand and tucked it within his arm. "I wish I were running away with you."

She laughed. "But where could we go?"

"To a little house deep in a wood, with a big fire blazing on the hearth, and angels spreading their wings over the roof."

"But there isn't such a house — anywhere."

"There is. I am sure. For every pair of lovers. But not all of them find it. Most of them crowd their romances between stone walls in efficiency apartments."

She loved to hear him talk like that. To Crispin's imagination a primrose by the river's brim was not merely a yellow primrose. He believed it, rather, a golden star, and had a way of making others believe.

When they came at last to the church, they were both sorry. It had been glorious to walk along arm in arm, and to talk of the dream-house in the deep wood.

Within the church there were candles on the altar. The figure of the young warrior on the window showed pale in the dim light. Crispin and Hildegarde knelt side by side in one of the back pews, and suddenly through the church surged the music, echoes of the song the angels sang one sacred, shining night. And rising above all the other voices, clear, triumphant, Hildegarde seemed to hear her mother singing.

Through all the years she and Crispin and her mother had gone to early Christmas service. They had always walked, and Crispin had met them at the edge of town. Those had been glorious pilgrimages. Things to remember. Perhaps, some day, this would be a thing to remember — this dim, little church with its illumined warrior, and its candles shining, and Crispin beside her — a warrior, too, of a kind, fighting as youth must always fight to hold its bright ideals.

When, after the service, they came out of the church, they found the pale gray of the dawn. The waters of the Bay were opalescent, and as they walked along, the trees and bushes, and the hills behind them, had a spectral look like a mirage, or a reflection in a mirror. The dogs ran ahead of them, loping along in a sort of rapturous joy of movement, running back now and then as if to double the delights of the distance.

" How happy they are! " Hildegarde said.

He looked down at her. " Hildegarde, I want to make you happy."

" I wish you might, but we are both so young to

settle such things.   And — and Daddy wouldn't be willing."

He turned to her his startled face.   " Do you mean he has said so? "

" Yes.   I didn't intend to tell you.   But I think I ought.   He didn't want you to come — "

" Why not? "

" Well — " it was a rather difficult confession, " he asked if you were in love with me.   And I said — that you were — but that there wasn't any . . . promise."

" You mean that he played the heavy father? "

" In a way, yes.   You see, he doesn't want me to marry."

" The cheek of him! " Crispin commented.   " He married twice."

" Crispin! "

" Well, he did, didn't he? "

" Yes.   But he says he wants to keep me for himself."

" He can't have you.   Of course, you know that. You're *mine*."

It was thrilling, the way he said it!   " Cock-o'-the-walk! "   Hildegarde teased, but her heart was beating.

And who knows what might have happened, in that moment, if Meriweather's big car had not come whirling down the road, with Sally on the back seat with the doll, Sarah?

When he saw Crispin and Hildegarde, Meriweather stopped.

" By all the gods! " he ejaculated.   " Where are the two of you going? "

" We've been," Hildegarde told him.

" Where? "

" To church."

Meriweather's eyes weighed the pair of them.
Happy? More than that. Radiant! And he had
been dancing with Sally! Sally, dead for sleep and a
little dazed, the doll, Sarah, cradled in her arms. And
here was Hildegarde with the radiance of Crispin's
love-making upon her. Meriweather knew it must be
that.

His voice held a touch of irritation. " Oh, well, get
in. I'll take you home."

" We don't want to be taken. We'd rather walk,
Merry."

He was insistent. " Don't be selfish. Sally is too
tired to be companionable." At last Hildegarde got in
and sat beside Meriweather, Crispin on the back seat
with Sally and the doll.

" Sarah is thoroughly ashamed of me," Sally said.
" I suppose I ought to be ashamed of myself. Stay-
ing out until morning. But everybody does it. And
I'm dead for sleep."

She was silent after that, and Crispin was glad not
to have her talk. He was content to sit there silent,
with Hildegarde in front of him — to see the soft wave
of her hair against her cheek, to catch the murmur of
her voice as she talked with Meriweather.

When they came to the house, Sally went at once to
her room. Meriweather had taken the car round to
the garage, so for the moment Crispin was alone with
Hildegarde.

He took up the conversation where they had left
off when the big car whirled up. " You called me

cock-o'-the-walk, Hildegarde. And I rather liked it. I am Chanticleer this morning. And it isn't because I am conceited. It is because you are here, and I am here, and nothing else matters."

She was standing a little way up the stairs, and he was below her. "Hildegarde, do you feel that way about me?"

Before she could answer, the library door opened. Her father stood on the threshold.

"I thought I heard voices," he said. "Where have you been, Hildegarde?"

"To church with Crispin."

"You might have told me you were going."

"Oh, perhaps I should have, Daddy."

"Why didn't you?"

She was honest. "It was such fun not to."

"I don't understand."

"You might not have let me do it, if I had told you. And I wanted to do it."

"I should certainly not have let you run around alone in the dark with a young man if I had known —"

"But *Crispin*, Daddy. I've known Crispin all my life."

His face darkened. "I haven't known him twenty-four hours. And I mean what I say. I don't want you running around with him."

She stood very still, looking at him. She had a puzzled air of not understanding what he was saying. She was like a child, bewildered by reproof. Carew found his rage leaving him. He had said more than he had intended to say. But to find her there on the stairway with her lover —

Then, quite suddenly, Hildegarde came toward him, took hold of the lapel of his coat. "*Daddy,* do you know you haven't said? — 'A Merry Christmas!'"

A moment's suspense. Then all the darkness went out of his face. "Haven't I? Well, why should I? I'm not merry. Life is just one darned thing after another."

"Are things darned-er this morning than usual?"

"Yes. I've been up all night. And if I go to bed, I can't sleep. And then to find you — keeping things from me — "

She was patting the lapel of his coat, smoothing it, playing little tunes with her fingers on it. "You see, I've never been bound much by rules. I wanted to go — and I went."

He was apologetic. "I don't want to bind you, Hildegarde."

Her cheek was against his shoulder. "Say it."

"Say what?"

"'A Merry Christmas.'"

It seemed to Crispin that he had never seen anything so charming as her coaxing way with her father. Ignoring the blackness of his mood, bringing him out of the darkness.

Suddenly Carew caught up his daughter's hand and kissed it.

"A thousand Merry Christmases, Hildegarde! Is that the way you want it?"

"Oh, yes."

His arm went around her, and over her head he looked at Crispin. "You are not to make love to her, do you understand? She's too young, and you're too young. I am not going to have her getting married."

Surging up through Crispin came that almost overwhelming impulse to shout, "She's *mine*," but he restrained himself. "Of course, I'm in love with her," he said, "but I'm not going to run away with her — yet."

"Perhaps she doesn't want to run away with you. Do you, Hildegarde?"

She hedged. "I don't want anything, just now, but to have you get some rest. If you'll lie down in the library, I'll read to you."

"Have you had your breakfast?"

"No."

"Run along and eat it. I'll wait for you by the fire. Don't keep her too long, Harlowe."

Sampson, in the dining-room, welcomed the two young people with a Christmas salutation. Then he voiced a complaint.

"Nobody comin' down to brek'fus. 'Taint much like the ol'-time Christmas. In dem days eve'body was up an' shouting w'en the day break. But now they dances all night and fergits that the good Lord was bo'n in Bethelum."

He set their grape-fruit before them and went out for the sausages and waffles, and Hildegarde, with a little flame in her cheeks, said to Crispin:

"You didn't mind what father said, did you?"

"I minded it when he scolded you."

"He didn't mean it. He is so unhappy."

"And because he is unhappy you'll forgive him.

You'll give and give and give, and he'll take and take and take."

Hildegarde nodded. "I know what you mean. It isn't easy to help giving when he asks. Sometimes I think it must have been hard for mother. She had a free spirit."

"Some day," Crispin prophesied, "you'll leave him as she did."

"Oh, *no*," Hildegarde protested. "Don't say such things, Crispin."

The waffles arriving, with Sampson in devoted attendance, made further confidences impossible. And when breakfast was over, Hildegarde went back to her father, and Crispin, feeling like a castaway stranded on an island in a lonely sea, made his way to the deserted drawing-room, where the great tree stood, its lights out, its shine and radiance dulled. The shimmer of its gold and silver balls was deadened by the daylight. Its tinsel chains seemed tawdry; the little red Santa Claus on the topmost bough was tilted and had a slightly drunken look.

To Crispin the tree was symbolic. Last night in its shine and glow it had been the expression of the things that Christmas means. Two thousand years ago, wise men had brought gifts. So here was the tree — "These are your gifts," it had proclaimed, "for remembrance."

But who in all that throng had remembered? Upstairs they were all sleeping the morning away. They would drift down at noon, bored by the thought of the mid-day dinner. Night would come with a big supper

party at a neighbor's some miles away. Everybody
would wake up, dance some more, and go to bed again,
to wake late again in the morning.

Hildegarde had come to her father's house, and this
was what she had found. And everybody was com-
menting on her good fortune. But was it good fortune? In the home of her aunts there had been a
standard of simple and severe living. But there had
been that last Christmas morning when he had come
back from church with Hildegarde and her mother.
There had been the warmth and brightness of the big
kitchen. Miss Olivia and Miss Catherine about the
table, and Elizabeth Musgrove saying grace:

" O Thou, who wast once a Babe in Bethlehem,
make us love good things and peaceful things and keep
our hearts strong."

Well, her heart had been strong, dear lady! And
her child had leaned on her strength. And now that
same child was shut in with a selfish man, subject to
his whims and tempers. Was this life any better than
the other? He found himself chafing at the thought of
it, restless, and after a while he got a horse from the
stable and went at a good pace down to the Bay,
where there was a low pier that extended well into the
water.

The ice was thick near the shore, but grew thinner
farther out, until at last the water was free from it.
And in that free water a few ducks were swimming.
They rose as they saw him, and were off in a low
flight above the rushes. He reflected that if he had
had a gun he might have brought down one or two of
them. He wondered if the game laws prohibited shoot-

ing at this season. It was a thing Hildegarde did not like about him. She hated to see things killed.

Yet — after all — a quick death was not the worst thing that could happen to these flying things. Death was indeed not the worst thing that could happen to anybody; a chaplain who had come back from France had told him that.

" I did not pray to save my life. I prayed only to be kept from cowardice, and that if death came it might come quickly."

Strange thoughts for a boy on a morning like this. But youth dwells easily on these things. It is only when we are afraid of death that we dare not think of it.

He rode on, too, to the Point, and went in and sat down at one of the tables, wishing that Hildegarde were there. He spoke to the old man, Christopher, who pointed out Elizabeth and Louis Carew in the picture on the wall. Crispin stood for a long time looking at the picture. It was hard to believe that that young and gallant figure in hunting pink was the same Louis Carew he had seen that morning standing in the library door.

When he got back to the house he found no one was down. The drawing-room had been set in order, and a fire was blazing on the hearth, but it was still deserted; so, ascending the steps to the first landing, he sat by the Blue Window. Today it justified its name. The sky was swept clear of clouds, and there was little wind to ruffle the Bay. The blue sweep of water rose to meet the blue above it. It was like a sapphire curtain hanging down from the heavens.

Hildegarde had written him of the window —
"Sanctuary" she had called it. "Whenever things
get too much for me, I go and look out. And my
thoughts fly straight to you and to my mother. It's
a wonderful feeling!"

What a child she was! Needing a heart on which
to rest. And she would never rest with her father.
Instinctively he felt it. Louis Carew would always be
flung from one thing to another. It was his tempera-
ment, a part of his selfishness, that he sought eternally
new sensations.

He heard a step in the hall below, and, turning, saw
Hildegarde climbing the stairs. He spoke her name,
and she looked up at him. There was something so
unutterably forlorn in her look that his heart was
wrung by it. As she reached the landing, he went toward her and took her in his arms. She made no protest. She simply hid her eyes against his coat and
sobbed as if she would never stop.

He did not ask questions, and after a while she said:

"Daddy's asleep. . . . I read to him until he was
. . . quiet. But before that. . . . I tried to tell him
. . . how I felt . . . about you . . . that we had always been . . . friends. . . . And he wouldn't . . .
listen. . . . He said . . . we wouldn't talk about it
. . . and made me go on . . . reading. . . ."

She lifted her head; tears were streaming down her
cheeks. "Crispin, I want my mother. I want my
mother."

"I know." His arm was still about her shoulders.

Oh, why shouldn't she want her mother? That sure
affection, serene and steadfast. This father-love was
a will-o'-the-wisp, unsatisfactory, uncertain.

They sat down presently on the window-seat, and he told her of the things he had thought as he rode that morning — of her mother and of the contrast between their Christmas day last year and this.

And Hildegarde said, when he had finished, " It's because you knew mother that — that you mean so much to me, Crispin."

It was not all he had hoped for, but it was at least something. He said quietly: " I want to help if I can. You must always remember that. Whenever you are in trouble, I wish you might come here and look out of this window and wave a thought to me. I'll try to answer. No matter where I am, I think I shall know."

She looked up at him. " Do you think you would, really? "

" Know that you were unhappy? I think I should. Such things are not impossible."

To their youth it did not seem impossible that heart could speak to heart across the miles. They were very much in earnest, and things of the spirit were as real to them as things of the body.

And now there was a stir in the house, servants passing to and fro in the lower hall, voices in the hall above them.

" I don't want to see anybody just now," Hildegarde said, " so I'll run along." She laid her hand on her lover's arm. " You've been such a help, Crispin."

After she left him, Crispin unlatched the window and leaned on the sill. Far below against the sapphire background was the silver sweep of the snow. Everything glittered. And the wind sang, " *You've been such a help, Crispin . . . you mean so much to me.*"

CHAPTER XI

HILDEGARDE OVERHEARS A CONVER-
SATION

THE doll, Sarah, serene and trim on top of the bookcase in Sally's room, looked down upon a devastating disorder.

Sally, flung among her pillows, showed a wild mop of copper-colored curls. The silver dress which she had discarded hung precariously on the back of a chair, and small, silk garments lay like pink snow everywhere.

From among her pillows Sally was saying: " I've got to get up, Sarah. I've got to get up."

Sarah's eyes seemed to hold a calm rebuke. " I know," Sally agreed, " you don't approve of me. Well, I don't approve of myself. But what do you expect? I'm like the rest. They all stayed up, didn't they? Until morning? "

Sarah did not open her lips, yet Sally had an impression of speech, " *All except Hildegarde.*"

" Hildegarde? Well, give her time, Sarah. And anyhow she's a prig. Oh, yes, she is. She's the kind that used to be in the old novels — *the queen can do no wrong*, and all that. And men still fall for it — Crispin and — Merry."

Her voice held on that. She dropped back on her pillows, turned her face to the wall, pulled the rose-colored cover over the mop of curls, and lay still. But she was not asleep. Her mind was on Hildegarde walking home with Crispin in the dawn, and the look that had been in Meriweather's eyes at the sight of her.

No man had ever looked at Sally like that. She had had admirers a-plenty, and many proposals. But that touch of worship! She had not known until this morning how much she wanted it! And so she had flung herself among her pillows.

When Mrs. Hulburt came in later, Sally was having her breakfast on a tray.

" Louis wants us to go abroad next summer," she told her daughter. " What do you think? "

Sally set down her cup of chocolate. " Who is going with him? "

" Hildegarde and Anne."

" And Merry? "

" Probably."

" Then I won't go."

" Sally! Why not? "

" Well, if you think I am going over to watch Merry make love to Hildegarde — "

" My dear child, if you could know how glad I am that he isn't making love to you."

" What makes you say that, mother? "

" You couldn't marry him, if he loved you. He hasn't a cent in the world."

" Do you think I care for that? "

" You ought to care. It is just as easy to love a rich man as a poor one."

" Not if the poor one is Merry."

" Sally, I wish you'd have some reticences. In my

day girls didn't admit they loved a man until he asked it."

" In your day girls lied about it, mother."

" *Sally.*"

" Oh, well, I mean that they let concealment prey on their damask cheeks and that sort of thing. We moderns know that suppression of emotion is fatal. That's why I talk about my feelings. I haven't proposed to Merry yet, but I may if I don't say things first to you and Sarah."

Mrs. Hulburt's eyes went to the doll. " I don't see why you like her."

" Don't you? "

Sally had a fleeting wish that her mother wore caps and had a mid-Victorian mind. She felt this morning as if she needed the stimulus of sternness and rigidity. Her mother would scold a bit, but in the end would be that smoothing, feather-bed softness of heart which got nobody anywhere, and meant nothing. Yet at the moment Mrs. Hulburt was trying to do her best.

" I want you to be happy, Sally."

" I know," Sally said, and flung a hand up across her eyes. She sobbed in a dry, gasping fashion.

Mrs. Hulburt bent over her. " My dear, do you really care like that? "

" Oh, mother, I care like the — dickens — " And the thing was not funny, but tragic.

Yet, two hours later, when Sally went down for dinner, she was clothed and in her right mind, and as saucy as ever. After dinner all the young people went for a walk in the snow, and came back to have tea in the drawing-room, rosy with its lights.

Sally flung off her hat and sat down at the piano. She was in knickerbockers and a muffin-colored sweater, and looked like a slender boy. She played a chord or two and then sang softly, a bit here and a bit there from popular musical plays. Crispin, leaning over the piano, looked over a pile of songs and found a group of Chinese lyrics. He chose one.

" Do you know this? " he asked.

Sally nodded, and he set it before her. Her fingers rippled an accompaniment, and as her voice was lifted in the haunting melody, one after another of the people in the room stopped talking, and listened.

Among the others Winslow listened, weighing Sally's charms of sprightliness and sophistication against Hildegarde's youth and innocence.

How oft against the sunset sky or moon,
I watched that moving zigzag of spread wings —
In unforgotten autumns, gone too soon,
    In unforgotten springs —

Hildegarde, behind her tea-table, failed to fill the cups. The great room with its gay groups, its gay lights, its great fire, fell away. She and Crispin were once more out under a wide sky — and the wild geese were overhead —

Creatures of desolation far they fly,
Above all lands bound by the curling foam.
In misty fens, wild moors and trackless sky,
    These wild things have their home.

Across the room her eyes met Crispin's. He lifted his hand in recognition of her glance. He, too, remembered! Somebody brought a cup for more tea, and she poured it, put in lemon, two lumps of sugar, smiled, was to all outward appearances a hostess intent on her duty. Yet her pulses were pounding.

They know the tundra of Siberian coasts,
And tropic marshes by the Indian seas.
They know the clouds and night and starry hosts,
    From Crux to Pleiades.

Dark flying rune against the Western glow,
It tells the sweep and loneliness of things,
Symbols of autumns vanished long ago,
    Symbols of coming spring. . . .

Sally, having finished her song, turned and spoke to Crispin.

" Did you know that Hildegarde is going abroad? "

" No."

" Mother told me this morning. They want us to go with them. And Merry."

He had nothing to say to that, and presently Sally went on.

" If I were you, I wouldn't let her go."

" How can I keep her? "

" Do you think, if I cared for a girl, that I'd let the ocean yawn between us. Not if I had to use caveman tactics. I'd carry her off — Oh, why aren't men like that! I wish somebody would pick me up and run away with me."

" Heaven help him, if it wasn't the right man! " His eyes twinkled.

Sally was wistful. " It is never the right man, is it?

It is nearly always the wrong man who does the masterful stunt, and they live unhappily ever after."

Crispin, only half-hearing, was eager to get to Hildegarde. " It's because people don't pray for good wives and husbands."

Sally stared. " Does any woman ever pray for a good husband? "

" Well, is there anything better that she can do? " asked this astounding young masculine.

Then, seeing an empty chair beside Hildegarde, he went to her, while Sally, left behind, wondered if she dared ask the Lord to give her Merry!

She had a half-feeling that it wasn't the sporting thing to do. What had she ever given the Lord that He should grant her this great favor?

When Crispin came up to Hildegarde, he said:

" Can't I get you away from these people? I want to talk to you."

" I mustn't now. But I could dress early and come down."

" Good. I'll wait for you in the library."

After that Crispin moved about in a dream, saying pleasant things in his gay young voice. One woman described him afterward:

" That young Harlowe is as vivid as a torch. He positively lights the room."

Moving, too, among the guests, was Winslow. He was not vivid, nor did he light the room like a torch. Yet he shed around him a sort of artificial brightness, like steel or the surface of a shallow pool. And as he and Carew stood in the big window talking together, there was about him a baleful glitter.

" We must settle the thing before we go to Stabler's tonight, Louis. Suppose you meet me in the library after you are dressed for dinner."

" I hate to use Stabler — "

" You are not using him. You are simply bringing two friends together for their mutual benefit."

" For your benefit, Neale."

" Stabler will get something out of it. And anyhow why should you worry? "

" Because I am in your power."

" Nonsense!" Winslow's hand came down on his shoulder. " What have I done that you should think that, Louis? "

" If it wasn't for Hildegarde, I'd cut the whole thing. She couldn't have come to me at a more inopportune moment. But now that she is here, I shall keep her, and if I keep her I've got to have more money."

Thus did Carew quiet his conscience. He was, he argued, asking all this for his daughter. He did not face the fact that if his daughter had not been there, he might have asked it for himself.

It was Hildegarde who came into the library before the others. When she entered, there was no light in the room but that which shone from the crystal cat. It seemed an eerie thing to see the cat in her cold, white beauty, curled up in her eternal sleep. The fire on the hearth had died down to pale ashes.

Hildegarde went to the window to draw the curtain. A little moon sailed in a sky that was clear after the snows. She sat on the window-seat and looked out at the moon, and because it was cold she drew the velvet curtain about her.

And so it happened that when the library door opened, her light dress was hidden. She was, indeed, completely screened as, when she saw who had entered, she drew back behind the hangings.

It was Winslow. He crossed to the hearth and stood rubbing his hands by the fire, making a dry sound. It seemed to Hildegarde that in the dim room, lighted only by the pale glow from the white cat and from the ashes, he was more than ever sinister.

She hoped he would go out. It would be most embarrassing if he should find her. She drew closer within the shelter of the curtain and waited.

When her father arrived, she felt that all hope was gone. They would sit and talk, and Crispin would come. And, oh, what was she going to do about it?

The best way seemed to do nothing. . . .

Carew sat down. "I very nearly stayed upstairs, Winslow. I hate the whole thing."

"Don't be a fool, Louis. This is the best way out for you. You know that, and I know it."

"But Stabler is my friend. And to go to him to-night. Accept his hospitality!"

"You've said all that before. It isn't going to hurt him, I tell you, Louis."

"Perhaps not. But it's the idea of the thing. If I can pull it off with him, you'll pay me for it. That's putting it straight, Neale. I'll be selling my influence for money."

Winslow would not argue. He simply asked a question. "What's the alternative?"

Louis' voice raged. "Oh, I know. I know. You've got me."

After that they made their plans, and Hildegarde,

curled up in the window-seat, had to listen. She had to see her father, trapped like a hunted thing, yield bit by bit. She had to know him weak. She had to learn that he was if not actively dishonest, at least acquiescent in the dishonesty of another.

And in the back of her mind was always the thought that if Crispin came, she might be discovered. And that if discovered, her father would have to know she had heard!

Yet when Crispin came, she was not discovered. He stood in the door. " Have you seen Hildegarde? " he asked the men.

" No." Carew's voice had a touch of impatience. " She's not down."

Crispin lingered for a moment, then went away. And when, after a few minutes, Winslow was called to the telephone, Carew sat alone.

He was, as he stared into the fire, a tragic figure. Above the mantel his bright-eyed ancestor met the world with a straight glance. Hereafter Carew would look at no man like that. He had broken the code of those who had preceded him. However he might excuse it, he was not one of them.

Hildegarde had a sense of revolt. She didn't want a weak father. She wanted him strong, brave, his head up, fighting. Her mother had been like that. She wondered what her mother would have thought of the man she loved, if she had seen him now.

Would she still love him? And why should he expect to be loved? One loved people for the fine things that were in them — Yet . . . oh, she was sorry for that tired, tragic father by the fire. She wanted to go up to him, to put her arms about his neck, to ask him to let her help to free him from the coils that Winslow had wound about him.

She forced herself sternly to stop being sorry. One should not forgive weakness or love a weakling. . . . She was swept by a sense of desolation. She had hoped for so much and had found so little. It was dreadful to remember all that she had hoped. She felt as if the world had fallen about her, and that she walked alone amid the wreck of it.

When at last Carew left the room, and she came out from her hiding place, she felt her knees weak under her. She sank down in a chair. . . .

And after what seemed a long time, she heard Crispin's voice saying:

" Hildegarde, what's the matter? What has happened? "

" I thought you were never coming."

" I came, and you weren't here."

" I was here. Hidden in the window-seat."

" Hidden? "

" I was sitting in the window when Mr. Winslow came, and I didn't want to see him. So I covered myself with the curtains. And then father came, and — they talked."

Her voice dropped away into silence. " I can't tell you," she told him finally, " what they said. But it changes — everything. Crispin, I want to go back."

He did not understand. " Go back? "

" To Aunt Catherine and Aunt Olivia. I can't stay here any longer. I've got to — get away — "

Chapter XII

THE BLUE WINDOW

THE Blue Window framed tonight a gold-powdered sky. Hildegarde, ascending the stairway after the talk with Crispin which had followed her dramatic announcement of departure, knelt on the window-seat and looked out. Here was sanctuary — but it was some time before the serene beauty of the night stilled the tumult within her.

She held a far-flung argument with the quiet star which burned bright against the darkness.

"Mother, I am going back."

Then, as if in answer to some protest from the quiet star: "You went, Mother. And if I stayed, I should be sharing things that are dishonest."

Again, after a long pause: "Oh, of course I love him. Who wouldn't? But I can't stay."

Crispin had gone to his room to write a letter. She had talked over her plans with him. He had begged her to marry him. But she had been firm.

"I won't promise anything. I can live with Aunt Olivia and Aunt Catherine. It won't be so bad, with you coming on for week-ends."

It would be heaven, he told her, to see her so often, to know that she was close at hand. Yet he hated to have her at the farm with its hardships. If she would

only marry him, his father would see them through
until he finished college.

" I mustn't think of it. Not yet, Crispin. I don't
even know that I — love you — "

While she would not promise, she had been glad of
his sympathy and strength, and had found herself
leaning on them.

So it had been settled. In the morning she would
tell her father that she was going. No more than that.
It would not be easy to tell him, but it must be done.

She was startled to hear Carew's voice on the stairs.
" All alone in the dark, Hildegarde? "

He came up and stood beside her. " Your mother
always waited for me on this landing when I came up
to dress for dinner. It is because of her that there are
never any lights. She said it spoiled the view of the
sky. After she left, the window seemed blank."

She wondered if he expected her to sympathize. His
hand was on her shoulder, but she drew away a little.

" If you had never let her go, I should have looked
out of this window when I was a child. And I should
have met you when you came to dress for dinner."

His voice had a note of surprise. " You say that as
if you blamed me."

" It is something to think of, isn't it? " There was
a touch of hardness in her tone.

He turned and looked at her, trying to pierce the
shadows. " Why talk of that now? We've had it all
out. Do you suppose I don't think of it? Of what
I've missed. If you could know how often I've longed
for a child to go up and down these stairs!"

She had a wild feeling that she was going to be sorry

for him, and she wouldn't. *She wouldn't.* If she was sorry she would weaken. And she had made up her mind.

If she left him, it would be his own fault. He didn't deserve better. He had had her mother, and he had had Corinne. He couldn't have his cake and eat it, too.

So all she said was: " Isn't it late? Sampson was to have supper at seven."

" Nobody is down." He hesitated. " Is anything the matter, Hildegarde? "

She was honest. " Something I want to talk over in the morning, Daddy."

" I never talk things over in the morning. Is it about young Lohengrin? I fancy I haven't been as polite as I might be. But I can't help it. He's too young and too good-looking to make me comfortable. I feel my age and my infirmities when he's around, Hildegarde."

She found herself wanting to pat him on the cheek and say, " You're not old, Daddy." But she wouldn't. That was the worst of it; disapproving of him, she still loved him.

She was glad, therefore, to hear people coming down the stairs — gay ladies in their ball gowns, the men at their ease, distinguished. Would she ever again see their like if she went back to the farm?

The thought recurred to her at supper. Winslow asked her, " When is young Harlowe going? "

" Tomorrow. He had expected to stay longer, but things are calling him back."

There was a secret excitement in the thought that the things which called him back had to do with her own departure. He would prepare the way for her, talk with her aunts. And it was best that he should not be at Round Hill when she broke the news to her father. They could not, of course, travel together.

Winslow said, " You mustn't let yourself fall in love with him."

" Why not? "

" There's too much ahead of you here. Paris in the spring! Scotland in summer! The Nile, perhaps, next winter!"

Paris! Scotland! The Nile! And set against all that, the farm. She had a sense of panic. Everything in the lovely room seemed to mock her — the silver birds trailing their shining tails on the satin-smooth cloth, the glow of the tall candles, the red of the Christmas roses in the Sheffield bowl, the glimmer of pearls on the white necks of the women.

Aunt Olivia and Aunt Catherine wore gingham gowns, and there was an oil lamp in the center of the table! All the food was put on at once! And they were such silent women! There would be nobody to talk to, now that her mother was gone.

At the end of the meal Sally rose to propose a toast to Crispin.

" He goes tomorrow. Can't somebody do it in verse? ' When Crispin goes ' — it rhymes with ' rose,' and ' watch and ward ' with ' Hildegarde.' "

Sally's hair was a blaze of gold. Her slender figure in flame chiffon was like the calyx of a bright flower. Winslow, leaning back, watched her with narrowed eyes. He had a decision to make. He was indeed an ice-cold Paris with an apple to award. As things looked at the moment, Sally would win.

Crispin was on his feet. " I'll write my own valedictory," he announced, " if you'll let me rhyme ' Sally ' with ' ally '." He paused, then gave the four lines:

> When Crispin goes,
> He leaves an ally.
> Her cheeks are red,
> Her name is — Sally.

They shouted at that. Hildegarde was blushing, her father frowning. Meriweather, self-controlled, tapped the table with the tips of his nails. He did not like the trend things were taking. As if Hildegarde belonged to Harlowe. He wished Sally had let the thing alone.

After dinner he wandered away from the rest of them, coming finally to the first landing and the seat under the Blue Window. There in the half-dark he smoked one cigarette after another. He was restless, moody. His life seemed spanned at the moment by futility. If Hildegarde loved Harlowe, the thing was over. . . .

Sally's voice: " I saw your cigarette. May I have one? "

" They aren't good for you — and I hate to see a woman smoke."

" Archaic!" She curled herself up on the other end of the window-seat. " Well, I won't if you don't like it. Anything to please you."

He did not answer.

" What's happened? " she demanded.

" Nothing."

"Then cheer up. We all have our troubles. I have mine. One of them is Neale Winslow. He's trying to make love to me, Merry."

Meriweather lifted his head. "*Winslow?*"

"Yes. And I wish you'd see the way he goes about it — as if I were Red Ridinghood and he wanted to eat me up."

"He can't eat you if you don't want to be eaten."

"Oh, yes, he can. Some day, when I am walking alone in the wood, he'll come along, and he'll say, 'Little Red Ridinghood, why should you be walking through the wood alone, when you can ride in a coach-and-four, and have two men on the box and two behind, and have plumes in your bonnet, and pearls as big as roc's eggs in your ears?' And I'll listen, and let him go along with me, and then — he'll eat me up."

Meriweather gave a short laugh. "If you let him do it, I hope you won't expect any sympathy from me."

"I don't expect — anything — from you. But why shouldn't I take the plumes and pearls and the coach-and-four if he asks me?"

"Let's drop the fairy tales," he said with irritation. "If you marry Winslow, you'll simply be having him for his money."

"That's not what I should call an original remark, Merry."

"Oh, if you are going to look at it that way!"

"What other way can I? Mother wants me to do it. She says she has seen it coming on for a long time. And she doesn't believe in romantic love as a basis for marriage. She says the things to go for when you marry are the things that will make life easy."

"She's wrong." Meriweather was tense. "If I could have the woman I want, I'd tramp the roads with her."

A pain stabbed Sally's heart. She knew the woman he wanted, and the woman was not herself. Yet how gladly she would have tramped with him — muddy roads, dusty roads, in any weather!

"I wish I were back again in the diplomatic service," he was saying. "I've half a notion to get back."

"But you mustn't go away. We can't spare you."

"I'm not so important as that. If I dropped out, the world would go on just the same."

"Not my world, Merry."

She said it lightly, and he took it lightly. He could not know, of course, how he was hurting her — shallow little Sally, who had no depths.

And now Winslow was coming up the stairs. "You two are selfish," he said. "May I help you look at the stars?"

He sat down and talked with them. He had no idea of leaving the field to Merry. He had definitely made up his mind to marry Sally. And always when he made up his mind he got what he wanted. That was his way.

Years ago there had been another wife, a plain little thing, incurably domestic. She had not kept step with her husband's growing prosperity and had died just in time to escape acute unhappiness. What Winslow needed now was some one to crown his possessions. He had felt that he must not hurry in his choice — that the golden apple he held in his hand was a treasure not to be lightly bestowed.

He had considered, in turn, three women — Mrs. Hulburt, Sally, Hildegarde. Early in the race Mrs.

Hulburt had been eliminated. The assets of her social experience and mature charms were offset by the ease with which she could be won. He could, he knew, pick her like ripe fruit from the tree. And he preferred some effect of resistance. He knew instinctively that Sally would offer it, and Hildegarde.

And he wanted, too, youth. His own years would soon be heavy upon him. He must have gaiety about him, and laughter. It was, perhaps, because of this need of laughter that the balance had dipped in Sally's favor. She would dance through life to a rollicking measure. He liked to think of her dancing while he piped the tune.

Hildegarde, finer than Sally, might prove to be too fine. She was burdened with that uncomfortable thing called conscience. Her mother had had it. Winslow remembered her mother. A beautiful creature. He had once tried to make love to her. Her scorn had withered him.

And so it was Sally — Sally who at this moment, curled up on the window-seat, was like an enchanting child.

She liked Meriweather, of course. Anybody could see that. But Merry could be disposed of. There was that diplomatic post he talked of now and then. A little influence would do the trick, and Merry would be on the other side of the world.

Winslow smiled in the dark at the ease with which it could be done. Then, as the chimes of the hall clock came up to them: " I am taking you and your mother over to Stabler's, Sally. She said she would be ready at ten."

" Who else will be in your car? "

"Hildegarde and Harlowe and Anne Carew."

"And Merry?"

"Sorry. But there'll be a full house without him."

Sally rose with some reluctance and ran back up the stairway to say to Merry, "I told you he would eat me up."

"Don't let him, Sally. Promise you won't. You're too fine for such a future." He laid his hand on her arm.

Thrilled by his touch, Sally wanted to turn and fling herself into his arms — to cry out, "Save me." But she couldn't, of course. Life wasn't like that.

"I'm not fine at all," she told him, "and I am as mercenary as they make 'em."

For just one fleeting moment she let her cheek rest against his coat. Then she ran down to the waiting Wolf.

After a few moments Merry also went down, and rode in the car with Carew and a lot of chattering house guests, talked with them, and laughed as if his mood matched his name, while all the time his mind was on Hildegarde riding with Harlowe in Winslow's car.

And so midnight came, and the early morning, and the stars grew pale before Hildegarde and Crispin stood for a moment under the Blue Window to say good-by. In the hall below was a brilliant, noisy group. Looking down upon them was like viewing from a balcony a scene in a play.

"Shall I ever see anything like this, Crispin?"

"Are you sorry you are going back?"

"I hate to leave it all . . . there's a part of me

that loves it . . . that wants it . . . at any price. But there's another part that can't stay."

It was, he knew, the mother in her that gave her that sense of pride and independence. Hildegarde had told him she was leaving because she could not be a burden to her father. She had found out, she said, that he was spending more than he could afford. But not a word had she divulged of Carew's capitulation to Winslow's cupidity.

" Whether you are here or there, I shall always love you, Hildegarde. You know that? "

" Yes."

" And I can make you happy."

She gave him a flashing smile. " Cock-o'-the-walk," she whispered.

He held her hand in a tight grip. " Well? Why not? Wherever you go — wherever you are — you are mine to the end of the world!"

It was perhaps the bravery of his words, which helped Hildegarde the next day when she faced her father in the library.

" Why are you leaving me, Hildegarde? "

" Because I shouldn't have come, Daddy."

" Why shouldn't you? "

She flushed. " Daughters are expensive."

" Have I made you feel that way? "

" No. You've been wonderful. But I can't stay."

" You are not going to give me any explanation? "

" I can't."

He crossed the hearth-rug and laid a hand on her shoulder. " Look at me."

Her eyes, so like his eyes, gave him a straight glance.

" You don't love me? " he asked.

" You know I do."

" Then why? "

" I can't tell you."

His hand dropped to his side. " You won't, you mean. And you leave me to my own conclusion, that you are going back because of Harlowe."

Her head went up. " I'm not."

" You're in love with him? You want to be near him? "

" I'm not in love with him. But I'd like to be." She flung it at him gallantly. " He's worth loving."

One on each side of the fireplace, their likeness to each other was amazing — upheld heads, the touch of haughtiness.

" Oh," Louis said at last impatiently, " we can't part like this. Do you think I'll let you go? "

" I must."

" You said you had written to your aunts. What reason did you give them? "

" I didn't give any. I simply said I was coming back."

" You'll hate the farm, Hildegarde — after this."

" Daddy . . . I'm sorry."

His voice had a high note of irritation. " If you were sorry, you'd stay. Have I been so — impossible? "

" It isn't that."

He began to walk the floor. " I've never loved anything that I haven't lost it."

Silence. What could she say?

After a while he went on. " Of course, the inevitable

thing will happen. If you go back to the farm you'll marry Crispin Harlowe."

He ceased speaking, but the echo of his words seemed to persist, " *You'll marry him, marry him, marry him. . . .*" It swung like a peal of bells. " *You'll marry him, marry him, marry him.*"

And now Carew brought out with violence, " A crude countryman!"

" He's splendid."

" You'll be buried. As my daughter, there would be opportunities to see the world, to broaden your life. And you love luxury, Hildegarde. You're like me in that. Your mother could do without it. But you can't."

Argument upon argument. Blaze meeting blaze. At last Carew pushed back his chair and stood up. " All I ask is that you'll think it over. Talk about it with Anne. She's sensible. I'm afraid I'm not patient. The thing is too theatrical."

He flung himself from the room, and Hildegarde, numb with distress, sat where he had left her. Now that the thing was done, it seemed to her dreadful that she had done it.

The two dogs came in presently, dropped down beside her, waiting patiently. It was the hour for her morning ride, and she had put on her riding clothes, but inertia gripped her. She had not expected to find her father up so early. He was rarely out of his room before noon. But coming upon him in the library, she blurted out the whole thing, shaking a little from nervousness, but none the less determined to get it over.

And now it was over, and she was going away. She was going back to her little room, she was going back to her somber aunts — she was going back to Crispin.

For her father had, perhaps, been right in that. If Crispin had not been within reach of the farm, would she have gone? Was it, after all, entirely her sense of integrity which was taking her back?

She stood up. The dogs, eager, followed her through the door, led the way toward the stables. But she was not going to the stables. She turned down the hill and made her way to the pool.

There had been a day or two of warmth, and the bronze turtle was free from ice or snow. He rested placidly on the surface of the water, his head raised a little as if to catch the sound of Hildegarde's step.

She stopped at the edge of the pool. All about her the dry rushes rustled. Her mother's garden would never bloom for her. She was going away. All this, the house on the hill, the gay company within, would be as if they had never been. She would go back to her aunts and Crispin, and if some day she married Crispin, they would have a little house. . . . Were people happy in little houses? Was her father right? Was she like himself in needing luxury? Not strong enough to do without it?

Her mother had been strong enough. Her mother — up there somewhere in the infinite blue. Hildegarde lifted her face to the sky. " I want to be happy," was the cry of her heart to that unseen presence.

And was happiness here? Had her mother found it on the farm? Or had she acquired only a sort of sublime serenity which had served her until the end?

Meriweather, riding along the road, saw Hildegarde standing with uplifted face. What a little thing she was under the wide heavens! And how his heart leaped at the sight of her!

He got down from his horse and joined her. " Hello, pretty thing."

" Hello." She was not smiling. Wistful.

" What's the matter? " he demanded.

" Life's a puzzle."

" My dear child, don't talk philosophy on a morning like this. You're missing Harlowe, and I won't have it. Did you ever see such air? Like a thousand cock-tails. Let me get your horse, Hildegarde. And we'll have lunch at the inn."

She brightened. Anything to run away from her thoughts. " I'll wait here for you, Merry."

He was off with the dogs after him. Back again, two horses, two dogs, streaming down the hill. A sapphire sky. Clouds racing. Could she leave it?

Merry was in a gay mood. " Am I glad Harlowe's gone? I could shout to the skies."

In spite of her depression she laughed. " Silly."

" I'm not. A man like that hasn't any right upon the earth. He ought to be up in the clouds with the other gods. When you fall in love, Hildegarde, try something human."

" Crispin is human."

" He's too good to be true."

Their horses were off like the wind. Thoughts of the dark library and her conversation with her father receded; thoughts of the farm receded; thoughts of

Crispin! The real things were the blue Bay, the red dogs, the bright sky, the touch of warmth in the sun!

When at last they arrived at the inn, light had come back to her eyes. "I am as hungry as a bear, Merry."

Old Christopher, welcoming them on the threshold, was as ruddy and round as a host should be. At this time of the year he did the cooking and served the guests himself. A helper in the kitchen and a housekeeper to look after the beds and linen formed his retinue. He knew Meriweather well, and Hildegarde. And he had known Hildegarde's mother. He had known the tragedy which had followed her marriage to Louis Carew. Carew had come clandestinely to the inn with Corinne, the woman who was to be his second wife. At such times Christopher had envied the methods of medieval justice which would have permitted poison in the food of such a pair. He had had to see Elizabeth robbed of her radiance. He hoped that Carew would not dim the radiance of Elizabeth's daughter. A man like that was a menace to the happiness of women. He was, indeed, a menace to the happiness of anybody. He took everything and gave nothing.

"Steamed oysters," Christopher advised. "I've got some Hampton Bays fresh this morning from the boats."

While they waited, Meriweather and Hildegarde sat in chairs drawn up to the great fire. The dogs, who had come in with them, flopped on the floor at their feet.

Above the fireplace was a wide shelf, and on the

shelf lay Christopher's big cat, Columbus. He was black as the ace of spades and as plump as a feather pillow. His head hung over the edge of the shelf, and his eyes were green slits as he surveyed the dogs. His faint mew was a challenge to them and showed his pink tongue. Except for a wave of the tail and a cock of the ear, the dogs paid no attention to him. They had barked at him as puppies, and he had scratched their noses for them. Their silence under his scrutiny was therefore discreet.

" He's a beauty," Hildegarde said, and stood up to rub the old cat's head.

He settled himself against the warmth of her shoulder, his paws hanging down, his sable blackness showing up the whiteness of her skin.

" The dogs are jealous," Meriweather said, " and so am I."

The dogs were, indeed, on their feet, stiff as ramrods, their muzzles upturned.

A light flickered in Meriweather's golden eyes. " They feel about Columbus as I do about Harlowe."

They laughed together. The whole thing was light-hearted. Hildegarde had a sudden sense of relief from tension. Oh, things couldn't be so bad if she could feel like this!

Christopher, coming in, set in the center of the table some white-starred flowers in a blue bowl. And presently he brought the oysters in their deep shells on blue platters — and outside was the blue of the Bay.

Hildegarde ate with an appetite. It was delightful to be here with Merry in this wide, bright room and to have him talk to her.

He was telling her something of his life. " My uncle brought me up. I was to have his money. So I played around a lot and then finally got into the diplomatic service. There was a year in Siam. You'd love it there, Hildegarde. The white days and the white nights. And the strangeness of it all. There was a sacred elephant who sounded his trumpet when his keeper left him, an infernal racket that waked everybody, and we'd all go hunting for the keeper and bring him back before we could get any sleep. And there was a little prince, only a baby, who wanted his mother, yet was forced to play the king. And there were the temple bells and the gay bazaars."

" Why did you leave? "

" The war came. And after that, the deluge! You see, my uncle didn't want me to fight. Oh, he was conscientious enough — a pacifist. But when I told him I was going, he said if I did, I could shift for myself. But I went — and I haven't seen him since. Not long ago he wrote me a letter, making overtures. But I won't go back and eat out of his hand. Not after the things he said to me. And so I came here with your father."

A little tale of heroism. And how simply put! She was aware of a feeling of warmth about her heart for Merry. Of admiration.

" It was fine of you," she said heartily.

" Oh, I didn't tell you to show myself off. Only I had to explain that I wouldn't be playing jackal to Louis if things hadn't been just as they are. I wanted you to understand."

His hands lay quietly on the table; his golden, attentive eyes had a deeper glow.

" I do understand, Merry. . . ."

" Hildegarde — if you would go with me — hear the temple bells —!" . . .

Old Christopher, coming back and forth from the kitchen, weighed Meriweather's chances with Hildegarde against those of young Harlowe. Crispin had come often to the inn, with Elizabeth's daughter during his sojourn at Round Hill. And Christopher had liked him. But then he liked Meriweather. Would Carew let either of them have her? And would he think of her happiness or of his own?

He watched them as they went away, riding down the beach road. Well, anyhow, good luck go with her! He felt a little lonely as he turned back to his empty hearth and his green-eyed cat.

The beach road was wonderful — the waves tumbling noisily over the sands, the gulls shrieking, the horses at a gallop, the dogs in a mad race —!

What a world, what a world! Hildegarde could not withstand its gay challenge. She was young, and her blood was warm. Why worry about tomorrow? Crispin loved her, and Merry. She flung care to the four winds. She would live life for the moment, with the gulls, and the wild breeze, and the tumbling waves!

CHAPTER XIII

RED RIDINGHOOD WALKS IN THE WOOD

ALL that day Louis Carew shut himself up in his room, admitting no one, not even Meriweather. He came down for dinner, was gloomy, abstracted, and went upstairs again immediately after.

Most of the house guests had departed. There remained only the Hulburts and Winslow and two bridge-mad gentlemen who were to have a final game that night with Mrs. Hulburt and Miss Anne.

Sally was bored. " There's a peach of a picture in town," she said. " Let's go and see it."

Hildegarde was glad when Winslow and Meriweather agreed. The glamour of that wild ride with Merry on the sands had departed. The shadow of the big house once more depressed her; her mind was on her father, shut up alone in his room.

There was moonlight, and Sally sat beside Winslow.

" I shall ride back with Merry," she told him with a touch of defiance.

" As you please," Winslow said, smiling; " at least you are mine for the moment."

So they sped on through the moonlight, with Winslow the only one at ease among them. The other three were restless with the emotions which swayed them, none of them happy. But Winslow was playing a game that he loved — with great odds against him, he had no doubt of the outcome.

The moving picture theater was an ambitious affair for the small town on the edge of the Bay. It was filled with a holiday crowd, and the film showed a star of great popularity. He thrilled his audience with acts of incredible heroism. He rescued, single-handed, from a forest fire, the woman he loved, his faithful hound, his faithful horse, his faithful servants, and the villain he had foiled!

Sally, between Meriweather and Winslow, asked Merry daringly, " If there should be a fire, whom would you save, Hildegarde or me? "

" Both of you," promptly.

" You wouldn't. You'd be off with Hildegarde."

She turned away from him and began to talk to Winslow. There was an intermission, and the lights were on. Meriweather was aware of the densely packed condition of the house. He noted the exits. It was as if Sally's words had rung an alarm bell somewhere deep within him. When darkness again hid the audience, his imagination was still at work. It had always been a boyish trick of his to see himself in the center of the stage. It was that which had carried him so successfully through the war and had won for him his honors. He had dramatized himself in the midst of danger, had seen himself doing big things, and had done them. He had only been sorry there was so little chance for the spectacular. He would have liked waving plumes, flashing swords, and coal-black chargers thundering to the fray!

He smiled at himself in the dark. His sense of humor had always saved him from conceit. Yet he toyed with the idea — to play the hero for Hildegarde!

There is a school of thought which contends that catastrophe is created by anticipation of it. There are, too, the amazing facts of coincidence. However that may be, whichever it was, the thing happened! The moving picture house caught fire that night. Crossed wires were, it was learned afterward, responsible.

Hildegarde was the first to realize that something was wrong. There was a thickening of the atmosphere, a veil-like haze that blurred the screen, the thin, crisp smell of smoke!

Somebody's cigarette? That was it, of course. She settled herself back in her chair. How silly — to be afraid — she was such a coward. . . .

But it was not silly. Fire was there — a spurt of flame in a corner; the strange, loud sound of startled voices; a mass of ominous figures rising in the dark.

And then Meriweather's sharp, " We must get out of this, Hildegarde."

His hand was on her arm. But she wrenched herself away.

" Take Sally. You *must*. I'll be all right."

Winslow was speaking! " Sit still, all of you; it's the safest."

But she wouldn't sit still. She was desperately afraid. She found herself running along the open aisle. Then a wave of humanity closed about her — everybody was fighting to reach the doors ahead . . . squeezing the breath out of her. She, too, fought

. . . straining toward the moonlighted world outside
. . . the safe, moonlighted world. . . .

Some one fell down in front of her . . . some one
else was falling. . . .

She stumbled, was dragged up by a strong arm, and
heard a great voice rumbling, " It's Carew's daughter."

After that she fainted.

When she came to herself, she was out under the
wide, white sky, and old Christopher was bending over
her.

" Are you all right? I was just behind you and saw
you fall."

" Where are the others? "

" I'll look for them. But I must get you out of this."

His car was not far away, and he carried her to it.

After he left her, she watched the excited crowd
pouring down the street. Engines were coming! Men
were shouting! Women screaming. Bedlam . . . !

Christopher returned with news. The fire was out.
There had, indeed, been little fire. The panic had been
the worst. He had found Hildegarde's friends. Two
of them were hurt, Mr. Meriweather and Miss Hulburt.
Not badly, but a doctor was looking after them, and
they would come on at once to the inn in Mr. Winslow's
car.

" You can't do any good," Christopher stated, when
Hildegarde insisted she must go to them. " They'll
follow us, and I'll get there first and have things
ready."

It seemed heavenly to Hildegarde to come into the
safe haven of the firelighted inn, with Columbus purring serenely on the hearth.

Christopher put her in a big chair and bustled off to give directions. " I'll have coffee for them, and the beds made."

Hildegarde was glad of the warmth and quiet. In her mad rush she had left her coat behind her, and Christopher had wrapped her in his own. She took it off and sat in her white evening dress, with her arms bare. Her hands were held out to the blaze. She could see them tremble. She was completely unnerved. She wanted her mother. She wanted. . . .

The front door opened. She turned and faced it. Somebody was calling hoarsely, " Christopher!"

It was her father.

" Daddy!" she cried. " Daddy!" And went swiftly toward him.

He took her in his arms. " I've been mad with fear." His voice was shaken by emotion. " They telephoned that there was a fire. I got the car and went at once, but I couldn't find you. Then I came across Winslow, and he said Christopher had brought you here."

Carew wore no hat. A fur coat was thrown over his evening clothes. His face was white with anxiety. His eyes burned in their deep sockets. He put Hildegarde in the big chair and knelt beside her.

" Promise you won't leave me," he said. " All day long I've been wanting to come to you and beg you not to go. I don't know what I've done. But whatever it is, I won't lose you. You are my child. Bone of my bone and flesh of my flesh. I've always wanted you . . . you're mine."

She touched his bowed head with shaking fingers.

" Promise me you'll stay, Hildegarde."

" But, Daddy."

" Promise — " Then when he had wrung it out of her, he held her close. " I'll make up to you for everything, my darling."

She felt it was wonderful to rest there in his arms — to know that he needed her. It was almost like having her mother back. And her mother had loved them both.

When Winslow's car arrived, it was learned that Meriweather had a broken arm, and Sally a cut shoulder. The doctor ordered Merry upstairs to bed and went with him. Sally, with an emergency bandage half hiding her silver gown, sat smiling by the fire. Her shoulder ached, but her eyes were bright. What did she care for a cut on the shoulder when Merry had saved her from the fire. He had turned to her and not to Hildegarde, and he had fought his way through the crowd with Sally in his arms. If death had come they would have died together. There were shallows in Sally, but there was this to say for her, that the thought of death had held no terrors with Merry by her side.

The doctor, coming down shortly, said, " It will be best to have Mr. Meriweather stay here until I can see him tomorrow. I must put his arm in a plaster cast."

Christopher, bringing in a tray, asked, " Won't you have a sandwich, doctor? "

" If I can eat it standing. There are other cases waiting."

Sally did not eat. And when the doctor was ready to go, she followed him into the hall.

"May I run up and see Mr. Meriweather for just a moment?"

"He is in great pain. The housekeeper is looking after him. She is a very sensible woman."

The doctor felt that Sally was not sensible. She seemed to him, indeed, a silly little minx in a silver gown. He had rather rigid ideas. In his lexicon there was no such word as "play." He had his work to do, and he was tired.

"You might look in for a moment," he agreed, finally.

He went on, and Sally sped upstairs. The door of Merry's room was open. He lay with his eyes shut. The housekeeper was at the end of the hall getting out blankets. So Sally tip-toed in and dropped on her knees beside the bed. Merry's unhurt hand was on the outside of the counterpane. She laid her cheek against it.

He opened his eyes. "Sally!"

She nodded, tears near the surface. "Oh, Merry, you're such a darling!"

He was puzzled. "Why?"

"To look after me as you did — when Hildegarde was there."

He saw the mistake she had made, started to speak, stopped. Might it not be kinder to Sally if he sailed under false colors rather than tell her the unflattering truth?

So, as she still knelt beside the bed, he touched her bright locks with his finger-tips. "How's the shoulder?"

" Just a scratch."

" It's more than a scratch. You're a bit of a good sport, Sally."

" No, I'm not." Then, " How am I ever going to thank you, Merry? "

" Don't try."

" I wish there was something I could do."

" That's dear of you. But there isn't, Sally."

He reached for her hand and held it. " Don't think of me as a hero, Sally. I'm not."

" You are!"

She stood looking down at him wistfully, then, suddenly lifted his hand, planted a shy little kiss on it, and was off, leaving him startled, disturbed, half-sorry that he had not faced the situation and shattered her illusion.

But it was Winslow who shattered it. He was waiting at the foot of the stairs when Sally came down.

" The others are in my car. They thought it best to go on at once and send Sampson back to look after Meriweather for the night."

" I went up to see Merry."

" So I judged. You are making a bit of a hero of him, I fancy."

" Why shouldn't I? He saved my life, didn't he? "

" Yes. But it was Hildegarde he tried to save."

Dead silence. Then, " What makes you say that? "

" Because it is true. He started to get her out, and she wouldn't let him."

" How do you know? "

" I heard him speak to her, when I leaned over to tell him to sit still."

Her voice was tense. "If you are not telling me the truth, I'll never forgive you."

"I am telling it. You ought to know it. You are too wonderful to waste thought on a man who doesn't care for you, Sally."

She swept past him out into the moonlight. He helped her into the car, and she sat silent until they reached Round Hill. Then, as she went up the steps with him, she said, "If I find you were right, I'll say I'm sorry."

An hour later, Hildegarde, propped up on her pillows, was writing a letter, when Sally came into the room, clothed picturesquely in a Japanese robe of clear red sprinkled with small gold flowers. The red of the gown reflected the red of Sally's cheeks.

Hildegarde, surveying her, asked anxiously: "Is your arm hurting? You look feverish."

Sally, at the foot of the bed, was tense. "I came to ask you a question. Did Merry want to get you out of the fire before he got me?"

"Sally. . . ."

"Don't try to save my feelings. I've got to know."

"Well, yes. He did."

Sally's small hands clung to the bed-post. "What a little fool I've been!"

For a moment she stood like a small frozen statue. "Lend me your pen, Hildegarde."

She wrote three words on a sheet of paper, folded it, and gave the pen back to Hildegarde.

"That's that," she said.

"That's what, Sally?"

"I am going," said Sally, "to walk in the wood."

Hildegarde stared at her. " I don't know what you mean."

But Sally was gone.

A few minutes later, Winslow, in his room, heard a rustling sound and saw pushed beneath his door a folded paper. He picked it up and read the scrawled words:

> " I'm sorry,
> SALLY."

He read the note again, smiling; then put it in his pocket. The game was his! Red Ridinghood had walked in the wood, and the Wolf had caught her!

CHAPTER XIV

THE OLD KITCHEN

THE old kitchen was in winter the most attractive room in the farmhouse. Aunt Olivia had pots of flowers in the windows, shining pans were hung about the walls, and blue platters were set on the shelves. The cushions of the chairs were of a clear, bright red. Elizabeth had bought the covers for the cushions.

" They match your geraniums, Olivia."

Tonight two of the geraniums had been robbed of their blossoms to provide a centerpiece for the table. Crispin was to have supper with the aunts and to talk to them about Hildegarde. He had telephoned soon after his arrival and had set Saturday night for his visit, and now it was Saturday, and he was coming.

As the two aunts went about their work, they were thrilled by the things that were ahead of them. It seemed an amazing thing that Hildegarde was coming back. They had felt, when her letter reached them, that it was incredible she should leave luxury behind for what they could give her.

Yet they agreed they would be glad to have her. They had missed her more than they had anticipated. More than they had missed Elizabeth when she had

married. But they had been younger then and had
had more in their lives. They had felt it reasonable
that the child should not care to stay with them, but
when in a house where there had been four there were
left only two, a silence had fallen and a shadow. They
had found themselves listening for the sound of Elizabeth's rich voice or of Hildegarde's light laughter.
When they ate in the kitchen, there had been the
thought of Elizabeth's insistence upon the dining-room
as the place for their meals. "We must keep up to
more formal standards for Hildegarde's sake."

They had cared little for formalities. They had,
indeed, thought them foolish. Yet they had yielded
gradually to the charm of the atmosphere which Elizabeth had created when she came back to them — although they had set themselves in some ways against
her.

They had made up their minds not to set themselves
against Hildegarde. If the child could restore something of what they had lost, they would let her do it.
They were, indeed, hungry for the brightness she would
bring.

It was a bitter day outside — one of the ragged,
blustery twilights with slate-color and black in the
sky. The sun had set, leaving a hard gleam on the
horizon like burnished metal, crisscrossed with the
bare branches of the tree.

Within, the old kitchen had a still radiance and was
fragrant with the smell of hot food. The two aunts
had wanted the best for Crispin, and there was chicken-
pie and hot gingerbread. They were a bit shy about
entertaining him. All young people were, they thought,

terrifying. They hoped he would entertain himself by talking about Hildegarde.

Looking out of the window, they saw far down the road the lights of his little car. They had a vision of him snug within it — cheeks red, eyes bright. That was one of the things about Crispin — his youth shone with such effulgence.

But as he entered the big room they were aware of something wrong.

"I have bad news for you," he said. "Hildegarde is not coming."

They stared at him. "Why not?"

"I had a letter this morning. She says she can't leave her father."

"What made her change her mind?"

"He told her it would break his heart."

They burst forth indignantly:

"He hasn't any heart to break," from Aunt Olivia.

And Aunt Catherine, "He will squeeze her dry like an orange."

"No," Crispin told them in his sure voice, "he shan't squeeze her dry. I won't let him."

He seemed to the two women a wonderful creature, there in their old kitchen, unafraid and flinging his defiance at Louis Carew.

"I was afraid it would happen," he said, "when I left. He appeals to Hildegarde's sympathies. And she's so tender-hearted. But he can't make her happy, and I can."

Standing under the hanging oil lamp, he read them parts of Hildegarde's letter. She told of the fire and of how her father had begged her to stay with him. "So I promised."

"You see," Crispin said, "perhaps it is natural that she should want to stay. But it's a mistake."

He took off his fur coat and hung it up in the hall. When he came back in his rough tweed suit with belted coat and knickerbockers, the old women thought him beautiful. If he had worn silver armor, he could not have been for them more imposing and impressive.

He insisted on helping them serve the dinner. He carried the chicken-pie, brown and bubbling, high on its platter like a boar's head. He took the head of the table and said grace. The aunts had a fluttering sense of the strangeness of it all, yet liked it, and were flushed with pleasure at his praise of the good food.

While they ate, Crispin told them of his visit to Round Hill and of his impressions of Louis Carew. He pictured Hildegarde's life of luxury.

"You should see her in the gowns they have bought for her. She takes to it all like a duck to water. She's lovely, and Carew's friends are crazy about her. He thinks I'm crude and a country clod. But I don't care. There are things I think about him which more than match his opinion of me. It is a duel between us — I shall fight to the finish."

He spoke frankly of his feeling for Hildegarde, and as they listened, the two dark old women were aware of a sense of vicarious adventure. It was wonderful to sit there with that young voice beating against their hearts. Crispin was deeply moved, eloquent in his disappointment; they felt his tragedy, suffered with him.

"Carew thinks only of himself," he said. "He would clip her wings. He would like to have her flutter wounded about him. I want her to fly with me in the upper air — to own her soul."

Aunt Olivia's mind, trained to Scriptural phrases, found a verse that fitted, "They shall mount up on wings like eagles." She saw Hildegarde and Crispin beating their way toward the sun together.

Aunt Catherine, with less poetic fancy, said, "Most men think they leave a woman free, but after they get her they tie her down."

"I shall never tie her down," Crispin protested. "I shall want her to think and act for herself. Even now I am not begging her to change her mind. I wrote this morning and said that no matter what came, I should never give her up — that a few months more or less of separation would make little difference since she is mine."

The old aunts gloried in his strength. He had, they felt, a will like Elizabeth's. Elizabeth had never bent her head to fate. They remembered when she had said in this same kitchen, "Life shall not beat me." And it had not. And it would never beat Crispin.

When they had finished supper, they sat by the big black stove in the sitting-room. The wind howled outside, but they were safe in a circle of warmth, with the red coals back of the mica doors shining upon them.

Crispin's voice had a vibrant softness as he spoke of Hildegarde. "She's such a gentle little thing. She needs somebody to fight her battles."

Aunt Catherine did not agree with him. "When the time comes, she will fight for herself. She is not so

gentle as she looks. Elizabeth seemed yielding, too.
But in the end she showed her fortitude. If she had
been weak, she would have stayed with Louis and
tried to win him back. But her self-respect wouldn't
let her do it. She couldn't sue for something which had
once been given freely."

"I had thought," Crispin said, "of going to Round
Hill and telling her father that I intend to marry her.
What do you think?"

Aunt Olivia shook her head. "I wouldn't. He
might make it harder for Hildegarde. He is a man
of strong likes and dislikes. I remember Elizabeth
told us of a man friend of Louis', named Winslow.
Elizabeth had reasons to distrust him. More reason
than she dared tell Louis. But she knew his influence
was bad. He was comparatively poor then, but she
heard afterward he had made a lot of money. And
he used Carew to help him in his schemes. And when
Elizabeth wouldn't help him, he worked against her.
It was he who told her first about Corinne. Little
things — planting suspicions. But she could never
make Louis see that Winslow was a snake in the grass.
They are still friends, I presume. Hildegarde has
mentioned him in her letters."

"He's there all the time," Crispin told them.
"Hildegarde hates him."

"If he finds it out, he'll hate her," Miss Olivia
said.

"That's why I want to get her away from it all,"
Crispin asserted. "Oh, why should I let things drift
when it means so much to me?"

He got up and walked around the room, talking to
them. He seemed to the old aunts rather like a splen-

did lion roaring in a cage. They were fascinated, yet half afraid.

"You mustn't do anything rash," Aunt Catherine warned.

"Well, I look at it like this. I can't give her what she's got. But I can give her happiness. I've talked to father about my future, and I saw a friend of his, Mr. Rutledge, when I was in Washington. When I finish college, Mr. Rutledge will have a place for me in his office, and I'll have time for a course in law at the University. And Hildegarde and I could have a pretty little home somewhere in the suburbs. We're young — but that's nothing against us. I'm going to think about it, and plan for it, and marry her in the fall."

"But she hasn't promised anything," Miss Olivia reminded him.

"I don't need promises. I can't think of life without her. I won't think of it."

Neither of the old women had ever had a lover like this. Their lives had been barren of romance. Olivia's marriage had been a matter of propinquity rather than of choice — commonplace, unexciting. She had simply left one farm for another and had come back unchanged. She and Aunt Catherine had satisfied their suppressed emotions somewhat by reading Scott and Tennyson and the other sentimentalists. Outwardly they were dull creatures, leading drab existences; inwardly they took the center of the stage in more than one adventure.

They wondered that Hildegarde could resist this wooer. What a vivid thing he would make of life! It would be a journey packed full of events. A voyage with the sails full set.

They were eager to show him their appreciation of his friendliness. They brought out things which had belonged to Hildegarde — an album with photographs, a drawing or two she had done as a child. They took him into the seldom-used parlor that he might see a boat in a bottle which had delighted her young eyes.

He liked the photographs best. There was one taken with her mother, when Hildegarde was ten. Even then there was the sweep of smoky hair across Hildegarde's forehead, and the straight clear glance like her mother's. He asked for it, and they gave it to him.

When he reached home, he put the picture on his desk. The house was still, his father and mother in bed. They had left a light for him in the hall.

He was restless and not ready for sleep. He decided to take a walk. When he went out, the wind was blowing, and it was very cold. The night was lighted by the moon, spectral among the ragged clouds. He followed the way which led to the hill where he and Hildegarde had watched the flying geese. As he went along he thought of the old aunts and of their kindness to him. He had been amazed that he could speak to them so freely, but there had been something in their hard and homely faces which had touched him. It was as if the loneliness which had come to them in the knowledge of Hildegarde's change of plan had echoed in his heart and had brought the three of them close together.

In spite of his loneliness, however, he felt no sense

of discouragement. He was secure in his ability to bend life to suit his purposes. And Hildegarde's letter had been very sweet. There had been parts of it that he could not read to the aunts. They had seemed only for himself and were sacred.

He hoped, when he reached the hill, he would find waiting for him the slender wraith of his dreams — Hildegarde of the farm in her black cloak. It was this Hildegarde who seemed nearest to him — the daughter of Elizabeth, not the daughter of Louis Carew.

But tonight it was Louis' daughter who kept him company. A vision, fairy-like in floating tulle, against a background of Christmas roses and tall candles and silver birds on a satin-smooth cloth. How like she was to Louis! And why should she not be held by the things which held him — luxury, ease, the companionship of people like Meriweather and the Hulburts? She was not Cinderella to sit among the ashes. In her father's house she lived like a princess. Why should he want her to come back to what her aunts could give her? Why should she sit by the black stove between those dark women? Why should she stand at the sink in the oil-lighted kitchen, washing dishes, scrubbing pots and pans? She loved beauty, and beauty belonged to her.

Thinking these things, for the first time hope left him. He had nothing to offer but his love, and she had known. If she had not known it, she would have come.

As he looked out over the valley the world seemed empty. The wind had died down; there was a shadow over the moon. Then suddenly he was aware that he was not alone. A gracious Presence moved near him in the silence of the night. The empty scene was filled gloriously with life and meaning. A voice spoke to his heart — the clear, sure tones that he remembered:

" Have faith in her, Crispin. She is my child as well as her father's."

Light came back to him; the warm blood surged once more in his body. His courage returned. His love was the daughter of Elizabeth Musgrove. Why should he care for Louis Carew?

CHAPTER XV

SALLY SEES THE SUN RISE

MERIWEATHER had a distinct shock when Sally showed him her ring. Winslow had given her an enormous emerald.

"So the Wolf has caught you?" he said.

"Well, he's rather a nice wolf, and he has such a lovely den."

"Don't!" sharply. "Sally, I can't believe you are selling yourself."

"Why shouldn't I? Oh, don't preach, Merry. It is the chance of my life — mother says so — Neale's giving a costume dance for me on the eighteenth. You must get well and be there."

"I don't want to be there," his arm was aching and, perhaps, his heart. Sally was his little friend.

"My dear," he said earnestly, "I can't bear to think of it."

"Can't you?" coldly. "You might as well. The deed is done. I shall have the plumes and the coach-and-four, and — "

She stopped there. She couldn't go on. Not with Merry's eyes asking questions.

"Wish me happiness," she said wistfully.

"You know I want you to be happy." He took her hand in a tight grip. "I shall miss my pal."

" Don't — " she jerked her hand away. " Neale might come in and think you — loved me. And you don't, Merry."

He was dumb. He knew he did not love her. And he knew that if he did, she would never marry Winslow.

She went away then, leaving him with a strange sense of desolateness. He felt useless, set aside. He was good for neither work nor play, and nobody cared.

He was glad when the others came in and dinner was served. It was at dinner that Winslow announced the engagement. He smiled complacently, and the hairs of his white head sparkled like icicles in the light of the candles. The old comparison of May and December occurred to Meriweather. To see Sally's youth, April-like in a daffodil frock, was to foretell the blight of Winslow's wintriness.

Sally carried it off well, head up, light words flung here and there in answer to congratulations. After dinner she went to the piano and sang love songs with Winslow standing beside her.

" Very bad taste, I call it," said Miss Anne to her niece, " to pretend there's any romance."

Hildegarde blazed. " It's a dreadful thing for her to marry him."

" Oh, Neale's not so bad," Miss Anne defended, " but it is such a clear case of Sally's selling herself."

Mrs. Hulburt bore down on them. " I know you are criticizing me, Anne, for letting Sally do it. But I was as surprised as you when she told me."

" You ought to put her to bed on bread and water."

" My dear, she'll be much happier than to throw herself away on a poor man. I know Sally."

But Mrs. Hulburt did not know the Sally who wept all that night into her pillow, and who, in the early morning, knelt by the window to watch the sun rise.

It was a slow-rising sun, but at last there was a rift of gold through the gray, and another day had dawned for Sally, another day in which she had to know herself bound to a man for whom she cared nothing.

She stood up and cast a wild look around the room. From the top of the chiffonier the doll, Sarah, stared at her.

" Oh, you needn't look so smug," Sally blazed. " It's the way of the world. Why shouldn't I? "

The doll Sarah, voicelessly, " Have you looked into your heart? "

" I haven't any heart," Sally flung back at her, and threw herself face downward on the bed.

After a while she got up, dressed, and had a long ride alone. She came in to breakfast with her cheeks glowing.

" Am I the first? " she asked Sampson.

" Yes, Miss Sally. I done took Mistuh Louis' breakfus up to 'im."

As she sat down, Meriweather came in. He was pale from pain and a sleepless night. A wave of tenderness surged over Sally.

" Little boy, little boy," she said, " come and eat your breakfast."

He dropped into a chair. " I don't want any."

" But you do — I'm going to fix it for you, and you've got to eat it."

She unfolded his napkin, ordered orange juice for him, buttered his toast, broke his egg into its cup and sat beside him — helping when she could to relieve the awkwardness of his left-handed service, for it was his right arm which had been broken.

It was when she brought his coffee, a second cup, with Sampson out of the room, that he surprised a look in her eyes — a mother-look of brooding tenderness. It waked something in his heart for her that had never been there before. Not the feeling he gave Hildegarde, but a wistful longing for what Sally could give, gentle ministration and devoted service.

Winslow, coming in and seeing the two of them there together, was gripped by jealousy. But he did not show it.

" Going to town with me this morning? " he asked Sally.

" Anything special? "

" Decorations for the dance. I'd like to have your taste. Sorry you can't be with us on the great night, Merry."

" Oh, but he can," Sally said. " It will do him good. You didn't think we were going to leave him out of it did you, Neale? "

" I really hadn't thought about it," with a touch of insolence.

" Merry's always the life of the party."

Merry settled it by saying, " I am afraid I shan't be up to a thing like that."

Yet, he did go to the dance. Willingly. Gladly. And not because Sally wanted him, but because of Hildegarde.

Miss Anne had insisted that Hildegarde must have something exceptionally charming in a costume.

" It will really be your introduction to Baltimore society. And everybody is interested in Louis' daughter."

The two of them were in Miss Anne's room. Miss Anne, by the window, was working on a needle-point chair-back. Hildegarde was curled up on the couch, her arms about her knees.

" Aunt Anne, aren't we extravagant, Daddy and I? Aren't we spending too much money? "

" All the Carews are extravagant. I am. But I'm not in debt, if that's what you mean."

" I do mean it. I can't be comfortable. It doesn't seem quite — honest."

" It wouldn't be honest, if you weren't a Carew. But the Carews are buccaneers, doing the thing rather grandly."

Hildegarde surveyed her with puzzled eyes. " You aren't in earnest? "

" Well, there does seem to be a different code," Miss Anne admitted. " If you're a gentleman of Louis' type, the world owes you a living and all that sort of thing."

" Mother was a lady," Hildegarde said practically, " and she wasn't in debt."

" And you want to be a lady out of debt — even if Louis is a gentleman in debt? "

" I want Daddy to be out of debt, too."

" I see.   But I am planning to pay for the costume, Hildegarde."

" I'd rather have you pay for other things. You really shouldn't have to pay for anything. Daddy and I ought to live on our income."

" Or lack of it? " Miss Anne studied her embroidery thoughtfully, and threaded a needle before she went on. " There are two ways to economize, if we can get Louis to agree."

" I can make him agree," Hildegarde said. " Tell me what they are."

Miss Anne looked at her. " How can you make him agree," she said in a surprised voice.

" I'll tell him I won't stay — that I'll go back to the farm — "

" Do you think he'd believe that? "

" Why not? "

Miss Anne, shading the crewels for a fat plum from damson to deep purple, answered after a moment: " You could never go back, my dear. You couldn't endure the hardships."

" My mother endured them."

" She was different. You have a lot of Louis in you. You love luxury and lovely things."

" Mother said that. She said that I had Daddy's gaiety — his faun-like quality of enjoyment."

Miss Anne nodded. " You belong in this environment."

Hildegarde hesitated, then flung out, " But I can't be happy at the price of dishonor."

Miss Anne laid down her work. " What do you mean? "

Hildegarde told her what she had heard behind the curtain. " Aunt Anne, I felt as if Mr. Winslow was a spider and was weaving a web about Daddy."

" Louis is to blame," there was red in Miss Anne's

cheeks, " for weakly letting himself be used. Some-times I feel as if my patience is at an end." She stopped, then went on more quietly. " The thing to do is to go abroad. Louis won't live with me in Balti-more. He says all the world would think he was down and out. But if we were in France or Italy, one es-tablishment would do for all us. Neale will marry Sally in June, and she ought to keep him occupied until we get Louis' affairs straight. I've an antique or two I can sell, if necessary, and there's a bunch of bonds in the safe deposit."

" And my pearls." Hildegarde's breath came quick.

Miss Anne shook her head. " We won't be up-stage. We'll do our best for our bounding buccaneer without sacrificing our treasures. If the worst came to worst, there's the crystal cat — she's worth thousands and ought to be shut up in a glass case in a museum. But Louis would rather owe all the trades-people in the world than go into the library and find that space empty. His great-grandfather put the cat there — and there it will stay until the crack o' doom! "

Hildegarde, turning that over in her mind, said, " Things don't mean so much to me. Perhaps because I've always been poor. The most precious thing I had at the farm was a little ship in a bottle. It was made by a seafaring brother of my grandfather and was brought from the East. It always stood on the mantel in the parlor, and I used to go in and look at it. It seemed very wonderful to me. And mother used to tell me then about the crystal cat and the bronze turtle — and they were like something in a fairy tale."

It was growing dark, and Miss Anne laid her work aside. " If Elizabeth could have stayed with Louis," she said, " she would have been a great help to him. And you can be a help. I'll talk to him about Europe. And of what life over there would mean to you. It would never do to approach him on the angle of economy. It would simply make him obstinate."

They talked then about the costume dance. " This will be our last fling, Hildegarde," Miss Anne said, " our final extravagance. I won't let you go unless you can look your best. And what you said just now has given me the key to your costume. You shall go as a dryad and Louis as a faun — oak leaves and a green gown for you, and pointed ears and a goatskin for Louis. The thing will be enchanting."

So it was settled, and the order for the gown given — floating, lovely chiffon and silk oak leaves — emerald and fawn and silver — the whole thing was exquisite.

And as for the cost, who cared? It was the final extravagance. Henceforth and forevermore, the Carews of Round Hill were dedicated to economy!

Chapter XVI

THE GREEN DRYAD

ABOUT ten days before Winslow's dance a letter came to Meriweather. It was from his uncle and contained surprising matter.

" My dear Boy:

I know you've given me up as a narrow and not-to-be-considered person. We did not agree about the War, and that was enough for you. Hot blood and youth cannot always see the reasons which age advances for tolerance. However that may be, I am not well, and I want to see you. I have asked this before, and you have refused to come. I hope you won't refuse this time, for the doctors are not encouraging, and I feel a loneliness that has made me put pride in my pocket and write to you. And if you need more assurance of the change that has come over me, you may find it in this — that I am glad you fought in France. I am not so cold-blooded as you may think, and I have thrilled more than once at the thought of a hero in the family.

Is this apology enough? Well, let it go at that, and come to me. I am winding up my affairs in Baltimore and shall go up to the old house in Harford. It is as good a place as any, and there's pleasure in the thought that I shall end my days where other Buchanan Meriweathers have died. I am glad you have the name, too,

Merry, and while you are my nephew and not my son, it will be my hope that some day your son will carry on the name and the traditions of the family. All that I have will be yours, but I know you well enough to understand that your coming to me will not be affected by what I have to give you. You have demonstrated your independence.

What about this week-end? And telephone me if you will. I am rather impatient — it may be a matter of blood pressure which makes me anxious to have news of you as soon as possible, but again it may be a matter of affection. My heart will beat a bit quicker at the thought of seeing you. Perhaps, you thought I hadn't a heart. But I have, and I am, therefore,

Affectionately, your
UNCLE BUCK."

Meriweather laid the letter down with a feeling of intense emotion. So there it was. The old chap really had a heart. Who would have believed it? Was it the thought of what was ahead that had changed him? Some of the fellows had been like that on the eve of battle — revealing themselves for the first time. Had his uncle, brought face to face at last with that dark opponent, found his fighting blood?

Something he had felt as a boy for the man for whom he was named rushed back upon Merry. It would seem good to go up to the old house — to be at peace once more with this remaining member of the family. And anyhow, who could resist that poignant appeal?

Three days later the two men dined alone in the oak-beamed dining-room, with a tenant's wife to wait on them.

" I've made arrangements for Minnie and her husband to take care of me — and I'd like to have you
with me as much as possible, Merry."

" I'll come up every week-end," Meriweather offered.

He felt he should have promised more than that —
to keep the old man constant company. Yet he had
not the strength to divorce himself utterly from the life
at Round Hill — not with Hildegarde under that roof
and with the chance of winning her.

After dinner they talked of business, and Merry
heard the details of his financial future. He had not
dreamed Uncle Buck had accumulated so much. He
found himself protesting, when he was made to understand that he would inherit everything.

" It doesn't seem as if I ought to have all that."

" Why not? It is not in any sense a fortune. Only
enough to make you comfortable if you marry."

" But I may not marry, Uncle Buck."

" Why not? "

" I am in love with a girl who isn't in love with me.
If she should marry some one else — there would never
be another in my life."

Silence for a long moment, then: " Don't carry con-
stancy to the extreme, Merry. I did it. I've wanted
a home — wife and children."

Meriweather shook his head. " It's Hildegarde for
me, or nobody. Carew's daughter. I want you to see
her. Perhaps some day I can bring her up here. You'd
find her charming."

" There was a lot of talk about it at the Club," old
Meriweather said, " when people learned that Louis

had a daughter living. And there's much curiosity to see her."

" Well, society will have a chance at Winslow's ball," Merry told him. " Miss Anne is counting on the sensation she will make. She looks like Louis, but she isn't like him — finer; takes after her mother, I fancy."

" I knew her mother — a wonderful type. Utterly thrown away on Louis. Couldn't we have Hildegarde here, Merry, for a visit? Perhaps we could make her see what it would be like to be mistress of this old mansion."

Merry, going up that night with his candle, had a vision of Hildegarde ascending the steps ahead of him — high-held head, crown of smoky hair. How wonderful it would be to see her turn and smile down at him — to kiss her on the stairs!

When he went back to Round Hill, he said little of what had happened. He spoke of his uncle and of their reconciliation.

" We have let bygones be bygones," he told Hildegarde. " He needs me, and his illness has made him very different."

Of the chances of his inheritance he said nothing. Dead men's shoes! The thought was distasteful. He wanted Uncle Buck to live as long as he could. He earnestly and honestly wanted it. He saw in the old man's attitude toward the inevitable something heroic. It entitled him to respect. It entitled him, too, to love.

Yet, though he would not let himself count on it, the fact that he might some day be financially independent lay in the back of Merry's mind. Some day he would have a home to offer Hildegarde. It increased his determination to win her. Happiness would come to him in such a consummation, and it would please Uncle Buck. As for Crispin Harlowe, he could take care of himself.

It was because, therefore, of this secret and stimulating knowledge that he had a right to woo, that he went gladly and willingly to Winslow's dance.

He talked about it to Hildegarde one night as they sat on the wide seat under the Blue Window.

" What are you going to wear? "

" It's a secret, Merry."

" You might tell me."

" Well, then — I'm to be a dryad — a green one. You've never seen anything so lovely as my dress."

" I'm not sure I like it. Dryads haven't souls — and you are all fire and spirit."

" Sally says souls aren't fashionable!"

" Poor Sally!"

" I feel that way about her, too, Merry. But the queer thing is, she seems to be happy. She says Neale's house is a dream."

" Haven't you seen it? "

" No. But I shall on the night of the ball. I can hardly wait."

" It's a gorgeous place, and in good taste. Neale knows all about tapestries and pictures, and old china and old books. And since he has made money, he has indulged himself. And Sally fits in with the rest. That's why he wants her — she's the final art object to complete his decorations."

Merry felt his point was proved when, on the night of the ball, he came down early and had the place quite to himself. He was a house guest. Winslow had, of late, been friendly enough to his rival. The time for jealousy seemed past. The Wolf was, indeed, secure in the thought that he was making Red Ridinghood happy. Sally, lapping up luxury as a kitten laps cream, had not time for old love affairs. And Winslow knew enough of human nature to realize that the less emphasis he placed on his fiancée's feeling for Merry the better. If he were slighted and set aside, she might feel called upon to come to his defense.

So Merry, alone in the ballroom, studied the decorative effect and once more commended Winslow's taste. The whole scheme was French — garlands of roses tied with lover's-knots of blue, gold chairs, pale brocades, thousands of candles in crystal chandeliers. Electricity there was, of course, for additional illumination but the thing was so cunningly accomplished that the effect was of sunlight, and the shepherdesses and shepherds on the Fragonard panels seemed bathed in it.

Sally, too, as she came into the room, was a shepherdess bathed in light — her hair powdered, rose silk panniers over azure, patches on her pink cheeks, a little hat with floating ribbons, a ribbon-tied crook. She had been wise enough not to let Winslow load her with jewels, or perhaps it had been his taste to show her to society in elegant simplicity.

Merry's own costume was simple — a dark wig tied at the back with a ribbon, black satin coat and knee breeches, a lace frill, paste buckles on his shoes, a black scarf over his broken arm.

"What do you represent?" Sally asked him.

"I am, I hope, a Gentleman."

"You're stunning, if you want my opinion."

"Thank you, I could say more than that, but I won't. You'll have enough compliments without mine."

"They wouldn't be worth much without yours," Sally said with a seriousness she rarely showed. "Please be nice and friendly tonight, Merry. I need it."

"Has anything happened?"

"Only this," she waved her hand to include the great empty room. "It's going to be mine. And I am wondering what I am going to do with it."

Under the high ceiling, and in that vast desert of polished floor, the two of them seemed no bigger than china figures set on a shelf. Sally with her crisp silks, and Merry with his lace frills, might have been made of Dresden porcelain, so utterly artificial were they and so absolutely in keeping with the rose garlands and the Fragonard panels.

Then, suddenly, in the arched entrance to the ballroom appeared a figure that was not in keeping — a figure which belonged not between walls, but to the out-of-doors — to summer twilights with a thin moon gleaming — to spectral midnights with a wild wind blowing — to clear, white dawns in a birch forest — !

It was Hildegarde!

"Oh," she said, when she saw them, "everybody is

asking for you, Sally. I came to see the ballroom —
I had heard so much about it. I couldn't wait — "

She was talking with an excitement which was
not usual. She was lighted, too, by excitement. She
seemed incandescent. The effect was startling. Merry's
breath came quick at the sight of her beauty.

" Sally," she was saying, " I never dreamed of such
a house. It's wonderful."

But Sally was not interested in talk of the house.
" Hildegarde," she demanded, " who planned that costume for you? "

" Aunt Anne."

" Do you know what she's done to you? You're
utterly *perfect*. Everybody will be mad about you
won't they, Merry? "

Meriweather nodded. He had no words. He had
known her lovely, but this — a wreath of oak-leaves
binding her smoky locks, her eyes lighted by that new
look, her slender body sheathed in the bright green of
young trees washed by spring rains, with more oak
leaves bordering the hem — with the curl of a leaf on
each shoe for a buckle below her silver hose — this
was loveliness with a difference. And that new look
in her eyes? Where had he seen it?

All in a moment he had it! Carew's eyes were
like that when he entered upon some new adventure!
He had marked it a thousand times, luminous, eager,
almost uncanny.

Winslow joined them. " Our guests are waiting,
Sally," and gave her his arm.

He wore a court costume which linked him with
Sally's panniers and patches. It was all of white

brocade with many glittering stones — and it made him more than ever an icicle.

There were a dozen guests for dinner, and there were other dinner parties whose guests would come on for the dance. Hildegarde, sitting next to Meriweather, ate and drank like a person in a dream. Winslow's great house had been a revelation. It was so beautiful it made her heart beat almost to suffocation. All the things she had ever read, all the poems, seemed packed into it. Its richness, fragrance, color, gave her tonight a feeling of pure ecstasy.

When she came later into the ballroom with her father, she was aware of the attention they attracted. Yet even she could not know the full effect of the sensation their appearance made — he with his furry cap with pointed ears, his goat's skin and his Pan's pipes, his wild gaiety of manner, his lighted eyes; she, reflecting the wild charm of him, and adding to it her own naiveté and young beauty.

Everybody was talking about them. So this was Carew's daughter! She looked like Louis. Was like him. What a pair they made — faun and dryad!

Louis, elated over Hildegarde's success, told Meriweather: " It's surprising how she keeps her head. She might have done this sort of thing all her life. Nothing awkward about her. Blood will tell, Merry."

Merry was not dancing — his arm made it impossible. When he left Carew, he went up to the balcony which overhung the ballroom. Many of the older guests were there, but he found a corner where he could sit alone and gaze down upon the dancers. If he could not dance with Hildegarde, he wanted at least to look at her. And she had promised to eat supper with him, which was a pleasant thing to contemplate.

The ballroom floor was crowded, but he saw only one figure — the one that belonged to moonlit groves, to silver pools among white birches. Oh, who could have dreamed of this when he gazed from the window at Round Hill and saw her coming up the road on that warm October morning?

All at once he missed her from the floor. His eyes swept the room, but she was nowhere to be seen. He decided to search for her, and took his leisurely way down the balcony stairs.

There was another stairway, the grand one which led up from an entrance court to the galleries which surrounded it. This was remote from the ballroom and was at the moment empty, except for a figure in floating green which fled lightly up until it reached the third landing.

Hildegarde could not have told why she had left the others. She knew that at this very moment a partner was hunting for her — one of the brilliant youths who had been making much of her since her spectacular introduction to them all.

She had simply felt that she must get away, still the beating of her heart, take stock of herself, find the Hildegarde she had always known. She was half-frightened by this new Hildegarde — this wild, gay creature! Her real self was quiet, a little sad, looking back somewhat wistfully, wanting her mother, longing for Crispin, hating Winslow and all his ways. Surely that Hildegarde must be waiting somewhere on the

stairs? And this other Hildegarde would at once give
way to her.

For this couldn't last, this throbbing, triumphant
sense of her own powers. How could it? Life wasn't
like that, a game, a mad dance while Pan piped. Oh,
the enchantment of the moment when her father had
played the pipes, and he and she had danced together!

Breathing rapidly, she ascended another step and
stood facing a great mirror set into the wall opposite.
It gave back her reflection, full-length.

Poised on tip-toe, she leaned forward.

" Oh," she said in a tense whisper, " am I like that?
Am I? "

Oak leaves — flaming cheeks — emerald sheath —
and silver slippers. A vision came to her of a girl
in a red sweater who had walked with Crispin in an
October twilight. That was the old Hildegarde. Did
she want to be again like that? She saw herself in
her little black dress and her mother's black cloak.
How intent she had been on wearing black!

Oak leaves . . . flaming cheeks . . . emerald sheath
. . . and silver slippers. . . . This was the new Hildegarde! Well, why not? Why not be admired and
sought after, submerged in unthinking gaiety?

" You're a darling," she said to the girl in the mirror.

Then she turned and sped down the stairs, and as she
went, all the beauties of the big house which was to be
Sally's seemed to shout at her — the tapestries, the
shimmering rugs, the priceless paintings, the pale mar-
bles. " You belong here," they vociferated. " How
could you ever think of going back to the farm? "

It was queer how the thought of the farmhouse was

like looking through the small end of an opera glass and seeing it dim and distant, with two dwarfed, dark figures moving about. . . .

As she entered the ballroom, her searching partner rushed to meet her. Other eyes were upon her. The people in the balcony craned their heads.

Carew's daughter had come back!

CHAPTER XVII

A SMALL FAT BACCHUS LAUGHS AT LIFE

MERIWEATHER was never to forget Hildegarde as she was that night. Watching her from his balcony, he saw her as a green flame streaming meteorically among the dancers. Nobody else counted. The rest of the people in the ballroom were pale phantoms; merged into a paler background. Hildegarde drew to herself all the light, leaving the others drained of brightness.

His search for her earlier in the evening had been fruitless. Passing one of the lower rooms, he had seen Sally, a maid on her knees beside her.

"Come and talk to me while I am being mended," Sally said, "if you have nothing better to do."

"I am looking for Hildegarde."

She was petulant. "Oh, well, I won't keep you."

He smiled at her? "She's probably back in the ballroom by this time."

"She and Louis are creating a great sensation. Everybody is talking about them."

"Louis is great stuff, isn't he? He looks twenty years younger." Meriweather did not say what he thought of Hildegarde. But Sally knew.

The maid had finished mending the flounce. "Let's find a quiet corner," Sally suggested. "I want your advice, Merry."

The quiet corner was found in a gallery which adjoined the ballroom, and where Winslow's art treasures were displayed. Sally and Meriweather sat on a carved Florentine choir seat and faced an ancient mosaic of a small fat Bacchus with a wreath of purple grapes.

"Neale wants me to marry him right away," Sally said, abruptly, "And I can't. I've got to be free a little longer."

"Sally, Sally," Meriweather said, "why did you do it?"

The Florentine seat was very narrow. It had a high back, and high curved arms, so that the two of them were shut in like people in an old-fashioned hansom cab. As Sally turned towards him, Merry saw in her eyes, so close to his, a strained and wistful look. "I was mad I think, Merry. But I've got to go on with it."

He was sorry for her. Little Sally. "I suppose it would do no good to beg you not to marry him?"

Her voice was low, "What else is there for me to do?"

"Wait until some one comes along who will make you happy."

Her laugh was hard. "Happy?" she jumped to her feet and stood there — gay in her shepherdess' dress, her eyes no longer wistful. "I shall be happy enough when I am spending Neale's money."

He laid his hand on her arm, "Sally, don't."

"Don't what?"

"Talk like that."

"How shall I talk."

He was impatient. " The whole thing is monstrous. You know it, and I know it. And you are too good for this sort of thing."

He saw her face change. " Hush, Neale is looking for me."

Meriweather's glance followed hers. At the other end of the long room, in an archway from which hung a priceless silver lamp, stood Winslow in white brocade. His white wig swept down on each side of his pale face. Even at that distance, they caught the glitter of his diamonds.

He saw them and spoke across the intervening space. " Were you looking at my treasures? "

Sally told him the truth. " We were talking."

Merry commended her frankness. The thing which would help her in her dealings with her lover was her lack of fear of him.

" It is time to go down to supper," Winslow said, " I've been searching for you everywhere."

Sally tucked her arm through his. " I tore my flounce and had to have it mended. Then Merry and I came here and sat in your Florentine seat, and looked at your horrid little Bacchus."

" What makes you call him horrid? " Winslow demanded.

" Because he laughs at life," Sally told him, " and it isn't a thing to laugh at. It is a thing to cry about, and if your little Bacchus had any sense, he'd know it."

At supper, Meriweather sat beside Hildegarde, but he might have been miles away for all the chance he got to talk to her. Other men kept coming up — Bob Gresham among them — the slight, girlish-looking

young Croesus, who had won honors as an aviator
during the war, who wore his diminutiveness with an
air of distinction, and who hid his super-sophistication
under a manner youthfully ingenuous.

Bob hung over Hildegarde; asked if he could serve
her. "Please give me something to do for you —
throw a glove into the arena! Or let me cut off the
head of a dragon!"

Hildegarde laughed. She thought Gresham a nice
boy. Funny.

He wanted to fill her glass. And when she wouldn't
let him, he crowed with delight. "D'ye mean you
don't touch it? Champagne? By Jove, you don't need
it. The other girls drink it to jack 'em up —. And
I'm so tired of 'em tipsy."

Meriweather was a man of the world. He knew all
the patter of the younger crowd. But he was aware,
more than ever, while Bob Gresham talked that he
·didn't want Hildegarde to be like the rest of them.
He didn't want her to learn their ways. He wanted
her sitting by fireplaces; in gardens; or going up the
stairs of an old house with a candle in her hand.

When Gresham left them, Merry said. "Do you
know I am wondering —? Do you really like all
this?"

"Like it?" she threw her head up with a quick and
charming gesture. "I love it. All my life I've wanted
beauty, and now I have it," her glance swept the great
room with its flower-wreathed pillars, its rosy lamps.
"Its a fairy tale. Unbelievable romance!"

So that was it? She was Carew's daughter — liking
the things he liked. Wanting what he wanted. The

Hildegarde of the fireplace and of the garden had been a girl lacking only the opportunity to be luxurious.

Well, whatever she was, he loved her. Yet he saw little hope for the future. In spite of her warm friendliness, he knew that she cared nothing for him. And besides Crispin there were others now in the field — Bob Gresham's manner was unmistakable. And Bob could make any woman the fashion.

It was after supper, that Merry saw Hildegarde as a green flame among the dancers. A will-o'-the-wisp? Like Carew? Or an unquenchable torch of inspiration?

It was after supper, too, that Carew sat in a niche on the wide stairway and talked to an abbess in gray with a ripple of red beads hanging from her belt.

" How austere you look, Ethel."

" I need to be to offset your *abandon*, Louis."

" But you are not really austere."

She smiled at him. " Perhaps you don't know the real me."

It was provocative. And she was very pretty with the soft folds of white linen concealing the lines of her throat and forehead; bringing out the fine darkness of her eyes, the delicate aristocracy of nose and chin.

" What is the real ' me,' Ethel? "

She ran the beads through her fingers like a rosary. At the end, in place of a crucifix, was a ball of red roses. She detached one of the roses and inhaled its perfume, looking at him above it with those dark smiling eyes.

By Jove, she *was* pretty. " Give me the rose," he said.

She shook her head, and slipped from her high seat. Her gown had a train and slid like a gray snake on the stairs. She lifted her hand and scattered the rose leaves. " Better scatter them like that than give them to you."

" Why? "

" You'd wonder tomorrow morning which woman you danced with gave it to you."

" I would not. . . ."

" You would. . . ." The gray train slid further down the stairs. He followed it, protesting, " I am not as fickle as that. . . ."

" You are a faun. . . ."

He was at her side. " Well, you are not an abbess. I'll swear to that, Ethel. In spite of your nun's gray. And some day you are going to give me a rose."

She knew that she was going to give it to him — some day. She wanted to give it to him now. But she too knew how to play the game. One must never give Louis, easily, the thing he asked for.

So " I must look for Sally," she said, and left him.

Sally was in the ballroom with Winslow. Most of the guests were gone. Once more the great room seemed to dwarf its occupants. Sally, seeing her mother, far at the other end, said, " Thank you, Wolf, for a very happy time."

" Why do you call me ' Wolf '? " he demanded.

" Because I met you in a forest."

" I don't know what you mean," he said, impatiently.

Sally didn't explain. There was, indeed, no tactful explanation. So she said, " I shall feel very small in this big house."

"You are big enough to fill it for me," he told her gallantly.

"I don't want to be married for a long time, Neale."

"What do you mean by ' a long time.' "

"Months and months."

"Why delay?"

"Oh, one's girlhood is so short. And married life is so long."

It was a poignant note. But his egotism glanced away from it as an arrow from an iron shield.

"I shall make you happy, Sally. We'll travel everywhere. See everything. And there won't be a wish of your heart that I shall be unwilling to grant."

What did he know of the wishes of her heart? What did he know of the Sally who would have shared a crust with the man she loved?

Well, he should never know. Her head went up, and she gave him a gay little glance. "I walked in a forest, and the Wolf ate me up. But he is a nice Wolf."

Neale was smiling. "So that was what you meant."

Sally was truthful! "Well, it was part of what I meant," she told him, and went to join her mother.

Chapter XVIII

A CAT IN THE WIND

DELIA explained, perhaps, the change in Hildegarde better than any of the others. " She certn'y am *be*-witched," she told Sampson. " Effen I shut my eyes an' didn't see 'er, I'd think 'twas Miss Sally."

Sampson nodded. " She sure am diffunt," there was a hint of criticism in the way he said it.

Delia surveyed him scornfully, " Ain' she got a right to have a good time? "

" I ain't sayin' she ain't."

" You didn't expect 'er to sit aroun' wearin' moanin' weeds for her Ma forever, did you? "

" I ain't expectin' nothin'," said the goaded Sampson.

" Well, then. 'Tain't for you and me to tell 'er what she is and what she ain't."

Sampson mumbled something under his breath. Delia caught it up and flung it back at him. " Why shouldn't she be like Miss Sally? "

" You said it yo'sef, Delia. She's like Miss Sally. An' I ain't struck on Miss Sally's ways."

Neither was Delia, but she refused to admit it. " She ain't like Miss Sally *insides,* I was talkin' 'bout the *outsides.* Eve'y since that ball at Mistah Winslow's, Miss Hildegarde's been playin' aroun' like a cat in the wind."

If Delia had set herself to coin a phrase, she could not have found one more fitting to describe the Hildegarde of the moment. " Like a cat in the wind " was the excited, shining, graceful creature who had replaced the old Hildegarde. " Like a cat in the wind " described perfectly the effect of the mysterious forces which had caught her up, and which kept her spinning around until she was assailed by a sort of mental and spiritual dizziness.

" I feel," Miss Anne said with some dismay to Ethel Hulburt, " that when I planned that costume I sowed dragon's teeth."

Mrs. Hulburt stared, " What in the world are you talking about, Anne."

Miss Anne was a bit vague. " Oh, you know, there's that old story about the man who sowed dragon's teeth, and reaped a crop of warriors. That costume seemed to have an affinity with all the dead and gone Carews. Anyhow it brought out in Hildegarde everything that has made the men and women of our family fascinating since the beginning of time. I never had it. But Louis has, and now — Hildegarde."

The two women were having lunch at the tea-room on Charles Street, where Sally and Hildegarde were to join them. Miss Anne and her niece now spent most of their days in town and many of their nights. Hildegarde had so many invitations. Everybody wanted her.

" You needn't blame yourself about the costume, Anne," Mrs. Hulburt comforted, " what's in the child would have come out anyhow. Up to this time there's been the effect of her mother's influence. But it couldn't last forever. And now she's thrown it off. That's a part, too, of what attracts people to her — the mystery. Nobody knew through all these years that Louis had a daughter."

"The distressing thing," Miss Anne asserted, "is that we can't afford a popular debutante. But Louis won't listen to reason. He says he'll eat and drink and be merry — and end in the poorhouse. You know that sort of thing."

"What does Hildegarde think about it."

"She told her father flatly she wouldn't have any more new clothes. And that he mustn't entertain for her. But she loves it. You can see that. And Louis is inordinately proud of her. He says it's a shame she shouldn't have her chance."

"Well, it is," Mrs. Hulburt agreed.

"I won't ride for a fall," Miss Anne said, with decision. "I've told Louis. And he says he doesn't want my money. It seems that Neale sees a way out for him financially; but I am not very hopeful. I've counted too many chickens."

Mrs. Hulburt interrupted: "The girls are coming."

Hildegarde and Sally, passing other tables on their way to their own, were much observed. Sally's engagement and Hildegarde's success at Winslow's ball had given the two of them an almost sensational prominence. And now, slim and straight in their dark coats, Sally with a close scarlet hat and Hildegarde wearing the new broad effect with a bunch of violets flat on the brim — they gathered to themselves all the eyes in the room. And the whisper went around "Carew's daughter."

Vivid, swift in her movements, with an effect of restrained high spirits that gleamed in her eye and curled her lip, Hildegarde was transformed. *A cat in the wind! A cat in the wind!* Miss Anne had not heard Delia's phrase, but if she had she would have confirmed it. She was aware in Hildegarde — of the forces which had always swayed Louis — modified, perhaps, but to be reckoned with none the less, and to fear.

She was half-afraid now, though Hildegarde sitting opposite her was saying, mildly enough, " Did you order for us? " and receiving a negative answer had demanded of Sally, " Shall we have the table d'hôte? I'm starved."

They had, they explained, been walking for hours. "With Merry and Bobby Gresham," Sally elucidated. " Hildegarde was a whirl — with her eyes under that hat. Bobby is simply limp with love for her."

" Sally," her mother reproved.

" Well, you know what I mean. Mad about her."

Miss Anne glanced at her niece. Not a sign of embarrassment. How the child had changed. In three weeks. Taking admiration with an air as if she had always been used to it. And before that there had been no lovers, except Merry, and that country boy, Crispin.

Which reminded her: " A letter came to you, Hildegarde, just before I left. Special delivery. I intended to bring it, but forgot it. I think it was from Crispin Harlowe."

" Crispin? "

" Yes."

A fleeting shadow across the shining eyes! Then the soup came, and Hildegarde went at it with an appetite. Miss Anne like Delia was obsessed by a phrase. Who was it, in the face of great emotion, " went on cutting bread and butter? " Werther's *Charlotte*, of course. Well, Hildegarde was like that — eating chops and salad and strawberry tart with an effect of insensibility which was astonishing. A month ago she would have blushed herself to death at the mention of Crispin's name. And now, did she ever think of him?

That she was thinking more of him than was apparent on the surface was evidenced when she finished her strawberry tart. " I'm going to run up to the house, Aunt Anne, while you and the others finish your shopping. I want to get Crispin's letter."

" Is it as important as that? "

" Crispin's letters are always important," Hildegarde said coolly, " and I am wondering why he sent this one special."

Miss Anne's house was not far away from the shops. It was on an old-fashioned street near the Cathedral, and had fan-lights over the door, and a fenced-in garden at the back. It was charming, quaint, and with the other houses around it formed a little island of seclusion against the encroaching wave of commercialism which had swept down upon the residential streets and turned them from their ancient purposes. Its drawing-room was on the second floor, and what had once been a bay window had been enlarged into a sun-room which overlooked the garden.

It was to this sun-room that Hildegarde took her

letter. It was a delightful place with green parrots on its chintzes and a real green parrot on a perch. A lacquered table or two in black and gold and a mirror framed in lacquer gave a modifying touch to the brightness. There was a shallow bowl of goldfish, and another bowl held narcissus.

The real parrot said, " Hello." Her name was Dickory, and she liked company.

Hildegarde stopped for a moment by the perch. " Hello," she responded and scratched Dickory's head.

Dickory gave a little chuckling murmur. She was quite content. Life in Miss Anne's sun-room had its monotonies. But it was, in the main, safe. For a philosophic parrot it was, perhaps, more satisfying than a native jungle. No enemies lurked, there were no alarms.

Hildegarde sat down on one of the chintz sofas and took off her hat. It was a lovely hat. She put it on again, and peeped into the mirror. Then, with it still on her head, she began to read Crispin's letter.

And as she read she forgot the lovely hat. She forgot all the frivolities that had been in her mind that morning. She forgot Bob Gresham and the excitement of his pursuit, she forgot everything but the words that Crispin had written, and the spell they cast upon her.

" I had to write. I've just come in from a walk. The wind was blowing so that I had to struggle against it, and at last I stopped and got in the shelter of a big tree, and watched it streaming by — all the leaves flying and the clouds racing. And then, suddenly, just as if it were real, I saw you, Hildegarde. I wonder if you remember? The day you were coming from town and found me under the oak? It was that same tree, and you were beating your way up the road against the wind. Your hair was blown straight back from your face so that it gave you a different look, and your cheeks were red, and there was a red scarf like a banner! "

" And when you saw me, you ran and got in the shelter of the tree with me. You were out of breath and beautiful —! And in that moment I knew that you were mine forever. Am I claiming too much? Well, we'll let it go at that. I shall claim all I can get, Hildegarde, even while I'm sure that I don't deserve half of it.

" And now, when are you going to write to me? When you have read this? Why not? I shall be waiting, and watching every mail."

She laid the letter down. Crispin under the old oak? Of course she remembered. She could see him now as he had stood there — strong and young and laughing.

She had laughed a great deal in the past three weeks. Bob Gresham was very funny. He said comic things with such a solemn face and only the flick of an eye towards you to see how you were taking it.

Yet when Bob was not with her, she forgot him. He was no more interesting than a lot of other people. Indeed, she much preferred to talk to Merry. Yet she had to admit that Bob's devotion flattered her. She was, after everything was said, very human, with a feminine liking for adoration. No one but Bobby had ever sent her such flowers and candy or bought tickets for all the plays, or placed such stunning motor-cars at

her disposal. Gresham was only a part of the "unbelievable romance" as she had called it. He wasn't a
fairy prince. He was, rather, a court jester — and
she liked his cap and bells. Everyone tried to tell her
of his importance, but she felt that if he had not had
money people would have laughed at him, not with him.
He was, it were, a pole on which to hang his posessions.

And here was Crispin without any possessions and
needing none. His manhood was, as a matter of fact,
worth all of Bobby Gresham's millions. She couldn't
think of Bobby under the old oak in a streaming wind.
Bobby did not fit into such backgrounds. With a
sparkling sense of the fantastic, she saw Bobby caught
up by the blast and blown away with coat-tails flying!

She re-read Crispin's letter. And sat down at her
desk to answer it. She had plenty of time. She was to
meet Sally and the others at Winslow's for tea. There
was nothing on hand until then.

"Of course I remember that day. It was great fun.
Sometimes I think that nothing I am doing here
matches such moments. But it is a different Hildegarde who likes all this from the one you knew then,
Crispin. Everybody here calls me "Carew's daughter." Does environment make such a difference. And
if I were back would I be just as I used to be? Not
knowing anything different or wanting it? I'll admit
that I don't know. I am having a gorgeous time. And
I love it. That's the truth, and the whole of it. I
sometimes wonder what mother would think of me.
Yet she knew when she sent me to father what I would
find. I think she had faith to believe that my head

wouldn't be turned. I hope it won't be. But it is all rather wonderful! "

"When are you coming to see me? Soon, please? For a week end? Can't you? I'd love it."

When she had signed and sealed the letter she changed her dress, and walked down to Mount Vernon Square. Winslow's house was one of the huge old-fashioned mansions which gave no hint without of the magnificence within. It had for its neighbors other huge mansions, a tall spired church, the Peabody Institute, the Washington Monument, and the Barye bronzes.

It was while she was making her way across the Square that her father joined her. " Anne said you were coming. So I watched out for you."

She tucked her hand in his arm. " I like to be watched for, Daddy."

He smiled down at her. " You're wonderful in that hat."

Hats! Yet . . . there had been a time when she had run bare-headed in the wind!

Her father brought out a bit of news with the effect of a thunderclap. " How would you like to sail early next month? "

" Sail? "

" For Paris. Anne and I have been talking about it. She tells me we've got to tear ourselves away from all this or sell the family jewels! "

Startled, she said the first thing that came into her head.

" I thought we were to stay for Sally's wedding."

" Ethel says that Sally is putting Neale off again.

She insists she is going to take the trip with us. That she can buy her trousseau abroad, and come back and settle down. I am not sure that Neale will stand for it. But Sally's elusiveness may have its charm."

" I hate that type of man." Hildegarde blazed: " If he loves Sally, why should it increase his interest to have her want to run away from him? "

" The eternal masculine — my dear — "

" Crispin isn't like that — "

His face darkened. " Young Lohengrin? How do you know? You fly from him and he follows — ."

" He cared when I didn't fly."

" Oh, well . . . we won't argue. And wait until you see Paris. You'll love it, and the life we'll lead. It doesn't take much money — and there's color to it, and glow. You'll forget the Puritan in you and be pure pagan for a bit. And we'll play together."

He laughed light-heartedly: " Wait till you see — Paris," he said again.

She found herself laughing with him. She had always dreamed of Paris . . . ! was she going to let that dream be spoiled by a vision of an old oak, a streaming wind, flying leaves, and a young and laughing figure?

Chapter XIX

SALLY FACES THE TRUTH

TEA was being served in Winslow's art gallery, where a carved screen had been set to cut off a corner of the long room.

As Hildegarde and her father rounded the edge of the screen, they were hailed with enthusiasm by the group which had gathered.

Mrs. Hulburt was there and Miss Anne and Sally and Bob Gresham, and a half dozen young people who belonged to Sally's crowd.

They had made Hildegarde one of them. Yet she was not like them. She was surrounded, as it were, by little walls of reticence and aloofness, which none of their modern ideas had as yet battered down. Just as she wore her hair braided, while other heads were bobbed, so she kept the habit of her mind different. It was, perhaps, this very difference in her which drew Bob Gresham. He was satiated by modernity. " I wish the girls would go back to their grandmother's ways," he was at the moment declaiming, " I'd like 'em afraid of mice. They made a man feel like a conquering hero — . He could save her from a mouse and she fainted in his arms."

" Hildegarde's afraid of mice," Sally informed him.

" Are you? " Gresham demanded of Hildegarde.

" Well, I don't like them.   But I wouldn't faint in your arms! "

She felt quite breathless as she flung that last sentence forth.   That was the way Sally said things.   But Hildegarde was not accustomed to the easy give and take of conversation as these young people knew it.

" Just for that," said Bobby, " I am going to drink a third cup of tea with you in that corner over there with the Chinese lady.   She'll be a silent and efficient chaperone, and I can make love to you — "

Hildegarde shook her head, " I loathe the Chinese lady, and I don't want any tea."

But she let Bobby sit at her feet and drink his third cup while Winslow showed them his collection of jade.

It was a wonderful collection, and he had some white pieces for Sally — a pendant and a bracelet.   They gave the effect of snow against his glitter, and Sally had a shuddery feeling that if she put them on they would freeze her where they touched.

She wished that Neale wouldn't give her things.   She wished that she wasn't going to marry him. . . .   She wished that Merry hadn't been called back to his uncle's place in Maryland . . . so that for the next few days she wouldn't see him.

Of course, she knew that she would have to get used to not seeing Merry.   But she didn't want to think about it.   If Neale would be reasonable there would be the summer in Paris . . . with Merry in the party.   And after that?   Why think about it?   The thing to think about was whether she could again get Winslow to put off the wedding!

When the time came for departure, she lingered behind the others. " I want to talk to you, Neale," she said.

" Stay here, then, and I'll come back — " he went down the length of the room with his guests, and returned presently to say, " Louis is taking your mother to the hotel. I told them I would bring you on in a moment."

Sally having met her lover midway in the big room, sat down in the alcove in which hung the Chinese painting of which Bob Gresham had spoken. It was of a woman with a long white face. The whiteness of her face, and the blueness of some butterflies which fluttered about her were the only high lights. The background was dull and drab, but the whole effect was beautiful.

Opposite the painting was a king's chair which stood on a dais. Sally sat down in it, and her scarlet hat blazed against its purple. Winslow sat on the steps of the dais.

Sally, looking down at him, said, " Neale, I want to go to Paris with the rest of them."

" With the rest of them? What do you mean, Sally? "

" Haven't you heard? Louis and Anne and Hildegarde are planning it for the summer."

He considered it. " It isn't a bad idea. A couple of months on the other side. You could get some of your pretty things in the Paris shops."

" Yes. But Neale — I want to stay longer than a couple of months."

His face did not change. " How long? "

" Until fall."

Silence for a moment. Then, " You are asking a great deal of me, Sally."

" I know, but — if I am married in June, none of them will be here for the wedding."

" I see." And after a pause, " Just whom do you mean by ' them '? "

" I want Hildegarde for my maid of honor, and Merry for one of the ushers."

He demanded; " Is Merry going across? "

" Of course. He always goes with Louis."

" I see. Do you think you are playing quite fair, Sally? "

" Perhaps not. But Neale . . . if you feel that I must marry you in June, I'm afraid that I can't marry you at all. . . ."

As if she had struck him, a red flush flamed across his whiteness. That, sitting in his king's chair, amid all the splendors which were to be hers, she could give it up with a gesture! It was incredible. Sally had nothing. She was, in effect a beggar maid spurning a crown.

" Suppose," he said, drily, " that I should take you at your word and release you."

She had a wild glimpse of freedom. " You'll have to do as you think best, Neale? "

" You won't be married in June? "

" No."

He knew that she meant it, and that if he pressed it she would give him up. And his world and her world would laugh at him. They would say that in spite of his wealth he could not hold her. That it was youth rejecting age. He was an egotist, and the thought that he might be joked about was unbearable. And besides he loved Sally. Perhaps, as Carew had said, he loved her more intensely when she flew from him and he had to follow.

Her hand hung over the back of the king's chair. He bent his head and kissed it. " Your wish is my law, Sally."

She slid down from the chair and knelt beside him. " Neale, do you mean, I am to do as I please? "

" Yes. If you'd rather be an October than a June bride, it is for you to decide. And while you are there, I'll run over to Paris."

" Neale, you're a darling."

His smile glittered, " Am I? "

" Yes. I'm afraid I'm not always nice to you. But I mean to be."

Kneeling beside him at the foot of the king's chair, she was like a pretty child. His aesthetic taste was satisfied. He was glad he had pleased her. He must give her her head a little. But in the end she would obey the bit.

He took her presently to the hotel, where she and her mother stayed when they were in town, then he went back to his own big house and to the art gallery where he had left his jades. When he had locked them up, he sat for a long time in the king's chair which faced the Chinese lady. With his icy glitter he belonged to the chair as Sally in her scarlet hat had not belonged. His thin, pale hands hung over the arms as one sees them in the pictures of royalty. They needed only lace ruffles and heavy rings.

As he gazed at the Chinese lady with the long white

face, Winslow's own face had something in common with its sinister effect of immobility. He was thinking of Merry. And of Sally's summer in Paris. Together. The two of them. With romance rampant. Winslow knew all the witchery of old gardens and dim churches and gay little inns. And Merry sharing all that with Sally! The thing was not to be thought of. It seemed to him as he gazed at the Chinese lady as if she ought to see some way out of it. She was so inscrutably wise as she sat there among her blue butterflies.

Yet it was not the Chinese lady who found a way out for him. Fate took things into her hands, and kept Merry at home.

" I can't leave my uncle," he wrote to Carew. " At first he urged me to do it, and it seemed settled. But I have had a talk with the doctor and he gives little hopes of many months ahead for Uncle Buck. So I must stay here. It would be too unutterably selfish to go when he depends so much on me. I can't tell you how sorry I am. And I shall see as much as possible of you all before you sail."

Carew read Merry's letter at the luncheon table at Round Hill. Sally and her mother were there for the week-end, and when she heard what Merry had written, Sally's heart stopped beating.

It seemed to her a long time before she got her breath, and nobody, apparently was aware that anything was the matter. She heard her mother say; " Well, one man more or less won't make much difference."

Sally knew that her mother was glad that Merry wasn't going. Mrs. Hulburt had been much upset by the postponement of the wedding. " The first thing you know you'll let Neale slip through your fingers," she had said, and Sally had flung back, " I wish he would slip. When I am in his big house, I feel as if it would crush me."

And Mrs. Hulburt afraid that she had gone too far, had said soothingly, " It's your nerves, Sally. The trip over will do you good."

Sally managed to get through luncheon without showing what she felt. Then she had a horse saddled and galloped down to the Bay. Furiously. And as she rode, she faced the truth. She had wanted to go to France because Merry was going. And now she wanted to stay at home because he was staying. And she couldn't stay. All of her plans were made, . . . she had burned her bridges. . . . The only light in the darkness was the fact that she would not have to be married in June.

The clouds were low, and as she started home it began to rain — a chilling downpour. She turned her horse's nose towards the Inn. Christopher would give her a cup of chocolate.

Christopher was glad to give it. " I haven't anybody but Columbus for company."

Sally picked up the big cat. " Cats are sometimes better than people " she said, briefly.

The big man took a look at her white little face, and said, " You put your feet up here by the fire, and I'll get your chocolate."

So Sally sat hugging Columbus up to her breast as if, with his friendly song, he was a buckler and shield against the arrows of outrageous fortune.

Christopher having served her, stood by the window. "It's a bad storm."

"I like it."

"Well, so do I," said Christopher, "if there's somebody I like to sit by my fire."

Sally looked up at him, "Suppose you knew that for years and years somebody was going to sit by your fire that you didn't like? What would you do? "

Christopher stood with his hands on his hips, considering it seriously, "I'd ask the good Lord to deliver me — "

Sally, out of a long silence, said, in a little voice, "Do you think the good Lord would — listen? "

"Sure thing. . . ."

"Oh," said Sally, and that was all. She finished her chocolate, gave Columbus a farewell hug, and was off in the rain, unheeding Christopher's advice that she'd better wait until the downpour lessened.

Galloping back, her head down against the beating storm, Christopher's words seemed to beat an echo to the horse's hoofs:

"I'd ask . . . the good Lord . . . to deliver me. . . ."

Did people really pray for things and get them. Did they? Crispin had told her once to pray for a good husband. If she gave up Neale, would the good Lord let her marry Merry?

But Merry didn't want her. He wanted Hildegarde. Life was like that. One had to take what one could get. Not what one wanted.

When she got back to Round Hill she found a note from Merry. He said in it practically what he had said to Carew. "I am desperately disappointed. I feel like a peri outside the gates of Paradise. But I can't desert Uncle Buck."

Sally's eyes were stormy, "It is Hildegarde who would make it Paradise," she said to the doll, Sarah, who lay among the cushions of the couch, "it is I who am shut out."

It was still raining, and as she stood looking out of the window with Merry's letter in her hand, the dreariness of the day entered into Sally's soul, so that she seemed lost forever to youth and gayety.

Then suddenly, she found herself on her knees beside the couch, with her arms flung out across it. "Oh, good Lord deliver me," she whispered with a sobbing breath, "I'm afraid . . . all by myself . . . and nobody . . . cares. . . ."

Chapter XX

CAREW'S DAUGHTER

THE wild geese were flying north against a windy sky. To Crispin, contrasting this flight with the one he had watched with Hildegarde on the day of her mother's funeral, it seemed symbolic of the change which had taken place in his attitude towards the woman he loved. Then there had been that wide and radiant sky, the geese in majestic formation against its serenity. And he, too, had been serene. Hildegarde had promised nothing, but his faith in a future that would bring her to him had been infinite. He had seen always ahead a life which she would share.

And now, blown this way and that by doubts, he felt his fellowship with those straining birds above him. Up there among the flying clouds weakness would be fatal. The race was to the swift. The battle to the strong.

But could one use one's strength against indifference? It had come to that. Hildegarde wrote intermittently. Her letters were always charming, but the warmth of friendliness almost of affection, which had once been apparent was lacking. It was useless to try to read into those pleasant pages something which did not exist. He need deceive himself no longer. Hildegarde was drifting away from him. His interests were not her interests. He was separated from her by more than the sea which rolled between them.

For Hildegarde was in France!

He had her latest letter in his pocket. He was on his way to the farm to read it to the old aunts. Two things had come to be a part of his week-ends at home — supper on Saturday night at the farm, and a pilgrimage at sunset to the hill where he had sat with Hildegarde.

Tonight, from that hilltop, looking towards the south, he had seen the geese — faint as smoke at first; and now above him, flying low under the clouds, their big bodies tilted against the streaming air-currents.

Yet, though the wind blew cold, spring was on the way. The snow was gone, below him in the valley a row of small peach trees flaunted their pink bloom, and almost under his hand, in a sheltered place, violets were springing up.

He plucked three of the violets to send to Hildegarde. He remembered an old song about " love, and truth and valor." That was what the three blue flowers would say to her. . . .

Then, suddenly he cast them aside. What would three violets mean to Hildegarde, this new Hildegarde? What was it she had said in her last letter; " Bob buys great bunches of violets. He calls me ' Violetta ', and writes verses about me."

That sort of thing! How could he compete!

The geese had gone and the sun had set in a threatening purple haze. Rain before morning. He rose and standing there in the dim light tried to summon the gracious presence which had so often come to comfort him. But tonight it did not come. It was as if Hildegarde, in this new mood, had cast off the last link which bound her to her mother. And the shade of Elizabeth Musgrove had no brave words for the man who loved her daughter.

When he reached the farm, a few crocuses shone like dim stars along the borders of the stone walk. The windows of the house were open, and as Crispin entered the kitchen, he was aware of the difference it made. The dark rooms seemed, even on this gray day, to gather to themselves something of the glamour of the world's awakening.

The two old ladies welcomed him eagerly. This visit from him had become the best thing in their week. When it happened that he could not come they had a sense of frustration, and found it hard to wait until another seven days had passed.

They had a good supper ready for him, and were concerned when they found he had no appetite. They missed, too, the shining quality which had conquered their imaginations.

Aunt Catherine asked anxiously, " Aren't you well? "

" Oh, yes. Why? "

" You didn't eat your pudding."

" It is delicious. But I'm not hungry." He pushed his plate away. " I have a letter from Hildegarde. May I read it? "

Aunt Catherine stood up. " We might as well go in the other room where the chairs are comfortable."

As they went into the living-room there was no light

in it except the light of the moon which they could see sailing high through the clouds.

Aunt Olivia struck a match and the wind through an open window blew it out. She struck another, " That's a wet wind," she said, " there'll be rain before we know it."

Aunt Catherine sat down in a great rocking chair, "Elizabeth loved the rain in the spring."

Crispin, with the glow of the lamp encircling him, said tensely, " I wish she were here."

" Elizabeth? "

"Yes. I have a feeling that Hildegarde needs her."

" She will always need her," Aunt Olivia said, " as we do — as we always shall. . . ."

Crispin took Hildegarde's letter out of his pocket. " I have never had such a letter from her," he said, " I don't know what to make of it."

Hildegarde began with apologies for not writing sooner, then went on to a description of the voyage:

" And now we have been two weeks in Paris. I can't talk like a guide-book, Crispin, because we haven't done any sight-seeing in the tourist sense of the word. I get glimpses of everything, as it were on the wing. For Bobby Gresham came over with us and brought his big car. We ride everywhere, and Bobby's idea of a perfect day is to find some place to eat. Not that he cares so much for food, but he makes a cult of patronizing the unusual. He hates the obvious — and scorns the restaurants where the uninitiated flock. He ushers us triumphantly into some charmingly secluded dining-room in town, or we follow a winding road along the river until we come to some quaint and exquisite inn where we are served in a riot of spring bloom. It is delightfully adventuring and Bobby is a perfect host. Now and then I say something about seeing the art-galleries and old churches, but Bobby won't have it. He says such things are bromidic — " For heaven's sake, Hildegarde, leave the sight-seeing to the poor souls who don't know any better." Then off we go to some jewel of a place where they make an omelette with an incomparable sauce, or cook little birds on a spit in front of a fire — and Bob buys great bunches of violets, and makes me tie my hair with a purple ribbon and not wear any hat, and calls me ' Violetta ' and writes verses about me.

" Does all this sound silly? Well, perhaps it is. But it is gorgeously gay. And it goes to my head like wine. Daddy loves it, too. We are living very cheaply with a pair of old French aristocrats, who lost their money in the war, and lost their sons. Yet, in spite of the cheapness we are quite elegant, for the house has its lovely old furniture, long mirrors and little brocaded chairs, and gilt clocks. Aunt Anne is out a lot, she knows so many people. And Sally and her mother are shopping. So I have Daddy to myself. He seems as young as I, and I *adore* him, Crispin. I like the things he likes. He says I am part pagan, and part Puritan. That's why I understand both him and mother. Mother didn't understand . . . and so she was un-happy."

Crispin stopped there, " You see? Carew's got her."
" He talked that way once to Elizabeth," Aunt Olivia said, " and she listened and tried to learn his ways. But when he failed to keep faith with her, she turned

back to us. Some day that may happen to Hildegarde."

Crispin folded the letter, and went to the window and peered out. "It is raining hard," he said.

They waited, patiently. They knew there was more to come. But they asked no questions.

"It is hard to see ahead," Crispin said, with his back to the window. "Carew is taking her away from us — from me. He is obscuring the memory of her mother. He is giving her a new set of ideals. And the thing is hard to fight — when she's so far away. But I shall keep on fighting."

They were thrilled by his words. It was as if they were watching actual physical conflict — Louis and Crispin! Their sympathies were with him, yet their imaginations followed Hildegarde, and their feminine souls sensed the charm of it all — violets, verses, and lovers along the way. They had never had such things. They were old and ugly and without romance. But they had met it in books and in their own dreams.

But who would have thought that it would come to Hildegarde. They remembered her slim and defiant in her black. "I want to be gloomy," she had said.

And now she was no longer gloomy. And she was not wearing black. She adored her father. Liked the life she led with him. Wanted no other.

And against that, Crispin could set only the memory of the years they had spent together. Was it enough? Out of her thoughts, Aunt Catherine demanded: "What are you going to do when you leave college?"

"I shall go to Washington. In Rutledge's office. I

have talked with father and he has given me five thousand dollars. And that's enough to marry on."

Five thousand dollars against young Gresham's millions! Crispin's words were confident, but they were aware again of his lack of radiance — "She's so far away," he said, uncertainly, and sat down.

There were things in Hildegarde's letter which he hadn't read to the old aunts. Things so unlike her, that he had hated to have them know. The part about love-making for example. "I have met some charming Frenchmen. I am not quite so sure, perhaps, of their sincerity as of their artistry. But it is very interesting."

That wasn't the real Hildegarde speaking. That was why he hated it. He wanted her to be herself. To write to him as she really felt, not as an echo of the sophistication with which she was surrounded? She was putting up barriers of artificiality and affectation. It wasn't like her.

The old women tried to comfort him. "Louis Carew is not the kind to last long with anybody. He likes new toys."

Crispin leaned a little forward. "I have a feeling that Hildegarde's mother is with me in this battle. There are times when she seems very close."

"Elizabeth often said that love never dies," Aunt Catherine told him. "Perhaps it doesn't. Perhaps it lives and speaks. . . ."

Their voices were low in the quiet room. Only the rain was noisy against the panes. They talked for a long time of Hildegarde and her little girl days. They rehearsed Elizabeth's love story, and its unhappy end-ing. " She always said she had been too impetuous. She begged Hildegarde to know the man she married. . . ."

" She knows me better than anyone else." Crispin said.

He rose. " I've got to be going. It always helps me to come. You're such a part of the old life. And you love her."

They loved her and missed her. They said it with tears in their eyes.

And when Crispin was gone, they said to each other that they would miss him, too. They would lose him as they had lost the others — Elizabeth and Hildegarde, everybody they had loved.

Chapter XXI

MERRY PLAYS FAIR

THE bronze turtle had much company during the summer days. There were the bees and the birds and the butterflies, the lillies on the pond, the roses in the garden. The air was fragrant as it had been a thousand years ago in Japan. Perhaps the bronze turtle remembered.

But of human companionship there was none. The house on the hill was closed. Now and then Delia opened it and dusted and aired. But she and Sampson kept, otherwise, to their own quarters. And the crystal cat slept alone in the dark, on the lacquered cabinet.

Then one heavenly day in July, when the breeze blew cool from the Bay, a man stood by the pool and plucked a rose from a bush at its edge. It was a tiny rose, just big enough to go in a letter, and the letter was to go to Paris.

Crispin had not had many letters from Hildegarde. But he had doggedly kept on writing. He had steadily refused to believe she was fickle or shallow. If she did not love him, there were at least all the years of friendship for herself and for her mother. Some day she would remember.

On that faith he lived. He was working now in the Washington office, and had a small car of his own. He had motored over to Round Hill, and would return by moonlight.

As yet he had not visited the house. It was late and he wanted his dinner. He decided to come back later. When the dark had fallen, he would hold a tryst with memory. If Sampson was about, or Delia, they would let him in, and he would sit by the Blue Window, and look off over the Bay.

He rode on, therefore, to Christopher's. The big man welcomed him heartily, and set a table out of doors for him. The Bay had ruffles of silver across its blue, and the gulls were silver. Christopher's garden was full of old-fashioned flowers — larkspur, bleeding hearts, lady-slipper. Columbus, stretched flat on a green bench chattered his teeth at a humming-bird poised above the porch boxes of petunias.

There were crabs for dinner, devilled in their red shells. "We are catching such big ones," Christopher said, "rusty and sweet as a nut."

Crispin ate with an appetite. "Not so many people around," he said.

"No. The fall is my great season, when the hunting begins. Winslow was out here the other day to talk about it. Wants to get his sink-box license before he goes over to join the Round Hill party in Paris. There won't be a day after he comes back that he and Carew won't be out with their guns. Some men are natural-born hunters. Winslow's one. He'll follow anything until he gets it, whether it's a bird, or a business deal, or a woman. He wanted Sally Hulburt, and he got her, more's the pity."

Crispin nodded. "She's too good for him."

"Any girl is. He's as hard as nails. He told me Miss Sally is to be married at Round Hill. The Hulburts have rented their own house, and Sally doesn't want a town wedding." He brushed an imaginary crumb off of the table. "I'll bet her mother put her up to being married at Carew's."

Crispin, not much interested, repeatedly idly, "Her mother?"

"Ethel Hulburt. The next thing she'll be marrying Carew."

Crispin, electrified into attention, turned in his chair, "*Carew?*"

"Yes. The two of them lunched here a lot before they left for Paris. Anyone with half an eye could see how things were going —"

In a flash there came to Crispin a line in Hildegarde's last letter. "I am not seeing quite so much of Daddy. Sally has finished her shopping and plays around with me. And her Mother doesn't care for the things we do. So Aunt Anne goes with us. And that leaves Ethel for Daddy to take care of. He has to be polite — but I sometimes wish he wouldn't."

Did Hildegarde suspect? And was she afraid? Or did her words mean nothing?

When he left the Inn later, the moon was hanging low above the waters. He drove up the hill and got out of his car. The house lay wrapped in stillness. Then from the kennels he heard the yelping of the dogs.

And above him on the porch, a voice: "Is that you, Harlowe?"

It was Meriweather. "I thought nobody else could

look quite like such a sylvan god under the moon."
He descended a few steps and shook hands with Crispin. " I am staying down here for a few days getting some data for Carew."

Crispin was frank, " I came " he said, " to keep a tryst with Hildegarde — "

Merry stood very still.   " Memories? "

" Yes."

" I have a few myself," he stopped, and changed the subject. " Look here, why can't you stay all night. I'm dead lonesome, and there are enough beds for an army."

" There's nothing I'd like better."

So it was settled, and Meriweather called Sampson.

" They's plenty of baids," Sampson said, when he had greeted Crispin, " jes cryin' out for somebody to sleep in 'em.   Delia say this house am so empty, it rattle lak a locus' skin."

" Tell her to wait until fall and she'll have a house full.   Miss Sally's going to be married here."

" At Roun' Hill? " Sampson demanded.

" Yes."

" Glory be," Sampson said, and departed to tell the news to Delia who came out presently to discuss it. She was fresh as a black-eyed daisy in her yellow gingham, and carried a pile of clean towels.

" Who say Mis' Sally gwine be married heah? "

" Mr. Carew wrote this morning.   I intended to tell you but it slipped my mind."

" It won't slip my min'," Delia informed him, " effen they's anything I enjoys mor'n a weddin', I ain' yit *seen* it.   Lawsee, Mistuh Merry, Ise gwine sing ' Praise Gawd ' ev'y mawin' twel the weddin' day."

" I'm not exactly happy to see Miss Sally marry Mr. Winslow."

" I ain' caring who she marry.   Effen she do'an like 'im, nobody kin mek her have 'im.   Miss Sally got a min' of her own, ain't she?   I ain' feelin' sorry for 'er lessen she's sorry for huhse'f."

They laughed at that, and she went away.   They heard her voice presently as she made the bed up-stairs.

" *I'se reached the lan' of cawn and wine,*" sang Delia.   And meant it.   She hadn't a care in the world. With a wedding in prospect why worry?

The front door was wide open, the moonlight pour-ing down through the Blue Window illumined the steps and lower hall.   " Shall we sit on the landing," Merry said, " it's a wonderful night."

Crispin wished he were alone.   He didn't want to talk to anyone.   He wanted to look out quietly on infinite space and think of Hildegarde.

As if the other understood his mood, he talked little. There were long stretches of silence.   At last Merry said:

" This place speaks of her, doesn't it? "

" Hildegarde?   Yes."

" You know of course that I love her, Harlowe?   I might as well tell you.   I've been looking upon you as my rival in the field.   But one can't have a rival when one has given up — the fight."

He rose and stood looking out of the window.   " I'd have fought through to the end if there had been a ghost of a chance. But before she went to Paris, I told her how I felt. . . . And, well . . . I'm out of it."

"I shall never be out of it," Crispin said, "till some other fellow wins."

"I know when I'm beaten. You don't. Perhaps that's why you'll fight through. And — and if I can't have her, Harlowe — I want you to get her. Not Gresham. I know him and he'd kill her — dreams."

He drew a deep breath. "I want Hildegarde to be happy. I'm not sure that I am anything but a dawdler and a drone, but I have at least this virtue that I can see all that she is. And Bobby can't. . . ."

Crispin said huskily, "You're a good sport, Merry — "

"Not very. But I think I play fair. . . . And she told me once that when she thought of her future — you were in it, Harlowe. . . ."

Crispin found the other's hand and grasped it. "I wouldn't tell you, perhaps," Merry said, "if it hadn't been for Bobby. He mustn't have her. . . ."

It was late when the two men went to bed. They had talked long and intimately; had learned much of each other, and that knowledge had brought them close together. They found under the Blue Window, the beginning of a friendship which was to last throughout the years.

It was just as they parted before Crispin's door that Merry remarked; "Louis' letter this morning worried me. If he marries Ethel — " He caught himself up. . . .

"You, too?" Crispin said, "is it as certain as that?"

" As what? "

" Other people are talking about it."

" What other people? "

" Christopher spoke of it — and in Hildegarde's last letter, there was a sentence which made me wonder. . . ."

" You think then that she — knows? "

" I'm not sure."

" Well, if she does — God help her."

Chapter XXII

A TRIUMPHAL ENTRY

HILDEGARDE'S home-coming in September was in the nature of a triumphal entry. The papers made much of it. Her name was linked constantly with Sally's. A gossipy little society weekly linked her name also with Bobby Gresham's.

Crispin, seeing her for the first time at Anne Carew's house in Baltimore, found in her the changes her letters had foreshadowed. She had cut her hair, and had lopped off with it, apparently, a certain quality of ingenuousness which had always charmed him. She seemed restless, excited, eager, flinging the challenge of her gay loveliness to all who cared to look.

Yet it was the old Hildegarde who flashed out a greeting, " *Crispin,* how glad I am!" And when he had to give way to other arrivals: " Wait till the crowd thins out. I want to talk to you."

He was content after that to stand by Dickory, the parrot, and watch Hildegarde in her new rôle. He wondered how she did it — with that air of ease. Yet blood told in such matters, and she was, after all, a Carew, with a background of generations of graciously-bred women. And there was that native ease which had belonged to Elizabeth Musgrove.

Bobby Gresham breezed in with a bunch of violets. " Pin them on, Hilda," he insisted, " in memory of the night we danced at Ciro's."

She had a little blush for that, and Crispin's heart contracted.

" Oh, look here," Bobby was saying, " why can't a half-dozen of us motor out to the club for dinner? "

She shook her head. " Give me time to get rested."

" But you are going to Round Hill tomorrow. Why won't you dine with me, Hildegarde? "

" Because I've seen enough of you, Bobby." Her smile softened the words.

She wore his violets, however, and when at last he went away, she sat down beside Crispin on a little sofa and said:

" Purple's all the rage in Paris."

She knew it was a silly thing to say after all the months of separation. Yet she found herself suddenly and strangely self-conscious. It had come to her with something of a shock, as she saw Crispin towering above the others, that there was no one in the room to compare with him. She had weighed him against Bobby and his friends as a year ago she had weighed his attractions against those of the farmers at her mother's funeral, and now, as then, she felt that he outranked all the men in strength and good looks.

" What do I care what is the rage in Paris? " Crispin was demanding. " Is that all you have to say to me? "

" What do you want me to talk about? "

" Anything but Paris fashions. And I wish you wouldn't wear Gresham's violets."

She laughed and relaxed. " It is good to have you

laying down the law again." She unpinned the violets and put them on the table. " Is that better? "

" You know it is. You are not in the least in love with Gresham. Why do you let him think you are? "

" I don't let him think it."

" You blushed when he spoke of Ciro's."

" Oh, that? I didn't blush because it was romantic, but because Bobby made me so conspicuous. He bought a basketful of violets, and everybody was look‹ ing at me . . . and I didn't like it."

" I should think not," Crispin said hotly.

" But I'm not going to talk about Bobby. Tell me about yourself, Crispin."

" There's nothing to tell except that I want to see you soon. A real visit — not just a snatched moment like this."

" Can you motor out with us tomorrow to Round Hill? "

He was radiant. " I'll say I can."

" Well, Sally and her mother are staying in town. There'll be just Aunt Anne and Daddy, and plenty of room in the car. We can have all Sunday to ourselves, with a ride on our horses and tea at Christopher's."

The invitation was not premeditated. But now that she had given it, Hildegarde had a sense of elation. " I'll tell Daddy not to ask any one else. I'm so tired of crowds."

He said boyishly, " You haven't changed a bit, although I thought so when I first saw you."

" What made you think that? "

" Oh, well, all the frills you took on in Paris, and your bobbed hair."

" Do you like my hair? "

" I miss the braids."

She nodded. " I know. I cried all night after I
had them cut. I felt as if I ought to put them in an
urn like the ashes of the dead."

" If you felt that way, why did you do it? "

" Daddy wanted it. I did it to please him."

He wondered what had become of her old independence of action. A year ago she would not have cut
her hair to please Louis Carew.

" There's Daddy now," she said, and rose.

Carew came in with Merry, and with Merry's uncle,
old Buchanan Meriweather.

Old Meriweather, having greeted the others, sat in
a corner and talked to Sally.

" My dear child, I knew your father. And Merry
has told me about you. I feel as if we were old
friends."

" What did Merry tell you? "

He smiled. " How pretty you are."

" What else? "

" And how gay."

" What else? "

" That you walked in a wood and that a Wolf ate
you up!"

" Oh . . . and what else? "

" That you are his little friend, and that he has this
marriage of yours much on his mind."

" Has he? Well, I have it a bit on my own mind.
But what's the use? It's too late to draw back."

He laid his thin old hand over her slender one. " My
dear, Merry read to me parts of your letters from

Paris. And I fell quite in love with Merry's friend. You don't object to my saying that, do you? And if those letters told me anything, it was that your marriage is a — mistake."

Their eyes met. Suddenly Sally found herself confessing. "Oh, it is. But I've got to go on with it."

"Why?"

"Because I'm not the kind to wait and wait for something I want, and then perhaps lose it."

"It is better to follow a dream forever than to wake up to a dreadful reality."

She shook her head. "Neale isn't such a dreadful reality."

"Isn't that rather casual praise of your future husband?"

She started to speak, and stopped as Merry came to present Hildegarde to his uncle.

"Sally's going to give me a cup of tea, Uncle Buck. I haven't seen her alone for two seconds since she arrived."

He carried Sally off. "Have you talked to Hildegarde?" she probed jealously.

"Yes. But she didn't have her mind on me. Not after her father came. What's up between Carew and your mother, Sally?"

"Romance and roses at their ages! At first Hildegarde was as blind as a bat. But I am beginning to think she suspects."

Merry, frowning, said, "It will break her heart."

"Hearts don't break," said little Sally, "but something will die within her when it happens. Something alive and bright."

It occurred to him that something had died in Sally since he last saw her. He spoke of it.

" You are as thin as a sheet of paper. And your eyes are tired."

" Flatterer."

" Don't be flippant, Sally. Aren't you well? "

" Bored stiff."

" Thank you."

" Oh, I don't mean with you, Merry. With life."

" I saw something of that in your letters from Paris. They struck a deeper note. I felt that I had never before known the real Sally."

She shrugged her shoulders. " There isn't any real Sally. I am four-sided like a painted wooden block — and every side different — "

She broke off as her mother joined them: " What is it, mother? "

" I've told Louis we'd go back to Round Hill to-night. There's really nothing we can do in town over Sunday."

" That's what I said."

" I know. But I thought we'd be ready to start fresh and early on Monday morning. But Louis wants to drive us in."

Hildegarde heard of the change of plan when she told her father, " I've asked Crispin to motor out with us."

" Harlowe? To Round Hill? "

" Yes! "

" Is he here? "

" He left a few moments ago. It is all right, isn't it? "

"No. There won't be room for him, Hildegarde. Ethel and Sally have decided not to stay in town."

Hildegarde's throat seemed suddenly dry, but she managed to say, "Crispin can come on the train."

"My dear child, I'd rather he didn't. Isn't this as good a time as any to let him drop out of your life?"

With a touch of her old fire, Hildegarde asked, "Why should I let him drop out of my life?"

"Oh, he isn't exactly our kind, is he?"

Her head went up. "I'm afraid I can't see it quite that way, Daddy."

He was proud of her grace and charm. Yet he would not yield. "I met Gresham a few moments ago, and he said he had asked if he could come out to Round Hill, and you had refused to do everything he had planned for you. What will he think when he finds you have given all tomorrow to Harlowe?"

"I don't care what Bobby thinks."

He shrugged. "You say that, but I wonder if you really mean it, Hildegarde."

Her eyes met his squarely. "Do you want me to marry Bobby?"

"I don't want you to marry anybody." His tone was emphatic, but he did not look at her. She stood for a moment without speaking, then she said, "I'll call up Crispin as soon as I can reach him at his hotel, and tell him not to come."

Her conversation with Crispin over the wire was brief. She knew he felt the lack of room in the car an insufficient excuse for her withdrawal of the invitation. Yet what could she say? Her father's words had been in effect a prohibition. There had been a time when she would have fought the thing out with him. But that time was past. She cared so much more for him than in those first days when she had come to Round Hill. And loving him, she was afraid. The very weapon of her defiance, which had once been so effective, she dared not use, lest she find him less tractable.

When Crispin demanded, " But how soon am I to see you? " she said.

" Some day in Baltimore."

She could, at least, she decided, have him at Miss Anne's. Or they could have tea somewhere together.

" I'll write, and let you know," she promised.

But it was not in Baltimore that she saw him next. For when she reached Round Hill there was a letter from Aunt Catherine. The two aunts wanted Hildegarde to visit them. It was nice now on the farm, and they were lonely. And they had some matters to talk over with her. Business. Of course, she must not come if it was not convenient, but they wished she might.

Hildegarde found herself longing suddenly for their homely faces, for their affection. For the little room where she had slept with her mother — her darling mother. And perhaps, if she went away from Daddy, he would miss her. He might not even want her to go. The things she had imagined might not be true, and he would beg her to stay.

But he did not beg her. When she told him that her aunts wanted her, " Why shouldn't they want you? " he asked gallantly.

" If you'd rather I didn't go, I'll stay at home."

" My dear, it is for you to do as you like. It's a God-forsaken place, I fancy. But you'll soon be coming back."

She ventured tremulously, " Will you be lonely without me? "

" Of course. What a silly question, Hildegarde! "

His tone was light, and his answer left her unsatisfied. Well, if he cared so little, why should she care? She would go and let him see how life seemed without her. And what was more, she would ask Crispin to come to the farm. He had spoken of an early visit to his parents. Why not make the two visits coincide? She wrote to him, and his answer was ecstatic:

" It will be quite the most perfect thing that has happened to me in a long time — to have you out there, all to myself."

Chapter XXIII

THE SILVER KEY

A WEEK later, Hildegarde left for the farm and
found Crispin at the train to meet her. He
took her out to her old home in his father's
car, and as they drove along, all her apprehensions left
her. The day was delightful, the air like wine, a
golden haze over the hills.

"It is good to be back again," Hildegarde said, and
thought that she meant it.

Aunt Olivia and Aunt Catherine welcomed her with
beaming faces. Tears were in Hildegarde's eyes as she
kissed them. She felt she had never before known
their real affection for her.

"Crispin will carry your bag upstairs," Aunt Catherine told her, "and when you come down, we will
have supper."

"We have killed the fatted calf," Aunt Olivia announced, "or rather it is a porker. There's a young
pig roasting in the oven."

Hildegarde, ascending the stairs, had a sudden vision of what that supper would be — roast pork and
a half-dozen hot things to go with it. What would
Bobby have said to that — Bobby with his ortolans,
his omelettes, his anchovies and artichokes?

As she entered her room, she was conscious of sudden
fright. Was it really so small? And so shabby? Had

she changed so much? She had thought she might find her mother's spirit waiting — the old sense of peace. But now she was aware only of the difference from her chintz-bright chamber at Round Hill, the tall ceilings and gilt garlands of her boudoir in Paris.

Crispin, coming up with the bags, set them down on the threshold. " Glad to get back? " he asked in his quick young voice.

" I don't know."

He glanced at her, saw the shadow on her face, and said the thing which was best for her.

" You won't know how you feel until you get your supper. Come on down and help us eat that young pig. I'll be ashamed of you if you don't have an appetite after your ride."

She found, as she sat at the table, that it wasn't so bad after all. The food was delicious, although there was too much of it, and it was heart-warming to have the three of them hanging on her words, eager to hear of her adventures.

" Crispin used to read us parts of your letters. We were always so glad when he came."

Hildegarde recalled with compunction the scantiness of her correspondence with the two old women. It seemed dreadful that neither of them had known anything but life on the farm. Her soul shuddered away from the thought of such an existence. As for herself, she couldn't stand it. She simply couldn't.

Her aunts insisted that while they washed the dishes, she should go for a walk with Crispin. So the two young people took their way along the familiar paths, through the grove, and up the hill where, almost a year ago, they had watched the flying geese.

They sat down at the foot of the great rock, and once more looked off together over the valley. Hildegarde wore a pansy-colored frock of a thin, fluttering material. As the darkness descended, she seemed a part of the purple night. The jewel on her finger matched the sparkle of the stars.

Crispin said out of the dark, " How often I have dreamed of you here like this!"

He told her then of the trysts he had kept on the hill, and of how her mother had seemed to come. " She was very real to me. Perhaps, as she used to say, ' Love never dies '."

" She was wonderful," Hildegarde told him. " Honor and courage were more to her than food and drink. I am not like that. Oh, Crispin, I could never have come back."

" How can you say that? When you haven't been tested? "

" I am like the Carews. They want beauty around them. They must have it. They can't live without it."

There was a new and stubborn note in his voice as he said, " Just what do you mean by beauty, Hildegarde? "

" Oh, having lovely things around you — nothing ugly, or sordid."

" Was it a lovely thing for your father to break your mother's heart? "

" *Crispin!* "

" Oh, there's beauty in moral and spiritual values,

Hildegarde. It isn't fashionable to talk about them. But I'll tell you this, that Elizabeth Musgrove found more beauty here on this old farm than Sally Hulburt will find in the whole of Winslow's house."

Crashing words! But with tonic in them. She found herself faltering an apology. "Of course, I don't approve of Sally, nor of the things that Daddy did. But mother forgave him, why shouldn't I?"

"Forgive him if you like — but don't talk of loveliness."

"Crispin, you know this farm is — unspeakable."

"Yes. I don't want you to live here — ever. But I know that nothing any Carew can ever do will match the life your mother made for herself. And for you. It was astounding that amid such surroundings she could hold herself above it all and make her child so sweet."

His voice broke on that. "Oh, Hildegarde, I'm not quarreling with you because you don't like all this. I am quarreling with you because you don't know yourself."

"Perhaps I do know myself."

"No. When the big thing comes, you'll meet it. And you won't meet it in your father's way, but your mother's. You are her child, Hildegarde."

In the momentary silence which followed, a light wind went whispering about them. Was Elizabeth there? Elizabeth Musgrove? In the purple dark?

Crispin's hand found Hildegarde's. "I have something for you."

"What?"

He pressed a small object into her palm, and as she
held it up, it caught the pale shine of the stars.

" What is it? " she asked.

" A key. A silver key."

" What is it for? "

" To unlock the door of a house.   Our house."

" But how perfectly absurd! "

" Why? "

" It can't be ' ours.' It may be yours, but it certainly isn't mine."

" It will be some day. I bought it because you are
to live in it. I may have to wait — a thousand years.
But in the end you'll come."

" In a thousand years there'll be no house."

" Yes. My dream of it will make it real forever,
and some day, even if we should be separated here,
your reincarnated spirit will find mine waiting on the
steps! "

" Don't," she said sharply. " I don't want to come
to you as a reincarnated spirit."

" Then come now."

" No. Please don't make love to me, Crispin . . .
Your will is so strong . . . And I don't want to be
won like that — because your will is stronger. If I
ever — care — I want my heart to run to meet you."

He caught both her hands in his. " Pray God that
time may come! " he said hoarsely, then flung her
hands away and stood up.

" It's time to go," he said, " if I'm to keep my
head."

As they walked along together, he told her of the
buying of the little house. " It is on the road to

Mount Vernon, so that we'll be neighbors of George Washington. I motored down and saw the sign For Sale — and it seemed so absolutely ours with a grove of pine trees back of it — and the river in front — and a garden. It isn't paid for, of course, only a part. But I shall work for the rest, and be glad to do it, and when I meet the shade of George Washington coming down the road, I shall say to him, ' It is all very well to be the father of your country, but I'd rather be the husband of Hildegarde Carew!' "

His mood of deep seriousness had passed. Hildegarde found herself talking to him in the old carefree fashion. When they walked through the grove, she tucked her arm in his and in the dark brushed her cheek against his coat. He was a dear and a darling, but she didn't want to marry him. She didn't want to marry anybody. She wanted things to be as they had once been with her father loving her and leaning on her for companionship. Perhaps, when she got back to Round Hill, she might find him like that. He might even let her be friends again with Crispin.

Crispin stayed over Sunday, and on Monday morning Hildegarde was left alone with her aunts. The routine of farm life began again. It had now to do with harvest-time — fruits and vegetables to be gathered and stored. It was a picturesque crop, and Hildegarde rather enjoyed the days. In the golden September light she stood on a ladder in the orchard and picked apples, or clipped grapes from the vines on the south hill.

The nights were the worst — deadly quiet settled down after supper. Her aunts did their best to stay

awake and be companionable, but the habit of years
was fixed. At half-past eight they would say apolo-
getically, " You won't mind if we go to bed? " and
Hildegarde, remembering that dinner at Round Hill
was just at its height, would feel desperately that she
must flap her wings and fly across the intervening
space.

Now and then, in the afternoons, she walked up the
hill where she had sat with Crispin. He wrote to her
every day, and she would read his letters, leaning
against the big rock.

She heard, too, from Bobby every day by wire or
telephone. He begged her to let him come and see her.
She was appalled by the fear that he might. She
couldn't imagine Bobby at the farm. He wouldn't
understand how once it had been glorified by her
mother's presence. He would see only its squalor.
Bobby belonged to dainty and delicate backgrounds.
She felt that if once he faced the big black stove in
the sitting room, he would dissolve with dismay.

There was, she discovered, one significant fact about
her so sojourn on the farm. She found herself missing *things*, not people. There was no one at Round
Hill, not even her father, whose companionship seemed
vital at the moment. The old aunts did very well indeed for company. She missed, as it were, the stage
properties — the crystal cat, the bronze turtle, the
silver pheasants on the table, Delia's crisp ginghams,
Sampson's delectable trays, the scarlet-coated ancestor
in the library.

It was Sally's wedding which took Hildegarde back
finally to Round Hill. Sally wrote that she wanted ad-

vice about the bridesmaids' costumes, and that it was
time things were getting under way.

On her last night at the farm, Hildegarde said farewell to that upper room in which she had spent so many
hours with her mother. Everything spoke of the past
— the little beds so close together, the books on the
shelves, the portraits on the wall. Here, after all the
tumult of her unhappy romance, Elizabeth Musgrove
had found peace. Here alone she had fought her
battles; here the baby Hildegarde had lain on her
arm, and here, in later years, the two had talked together. Hildegarde remembered that lovely face lighted
by the candle, and lighted, too, by the spirit which
burned within.

She knelt for a moment by her mother's bed. " Darling, darling," she said, " if you could only come back
to me! "

When she told her aunts " good-by," she cried a
little. She couldn't understand her emotion. She wasn't
really sorry to go. Her blood quickened, indeed, at
the thought of the good times that lay ahead of her.
But there was a touch of sadness in this second separation from the place which had so long sheltered her.

She met Sally in Baltimore. They were to stay at
Miss Anne's for a few days. Mrs. Hulburt was in New
York having some old jewels reset for her daughter's
wedding-present.

" Thank heaven, they're pearls," Sally said, as she
and Hildegarde sat in Miss Anne's sun-room an hour
after Hildegarde's arrival. " I hate anything else.
Those white jade ornaments of Neale's give me the
creeps."

Dickory, the parrot, preening her feathers, stopped for a moment to laugh sepulchrally.

"Listen to that," Sally said, "isn't she human? Well, I wish I could sit on a perch all day like a parrot, and have feathers for clothes. I am fed up on tailors and dressmakers."

She threw herself full-length on the couch, her hands over her head. "Everything is to be in the Spanish effect," she explained. "Madame says that I am the blonde Castilian type, whatever that may mean, and I'm to have a fan of lace in my hair, with the wedding veil in a mantilla drapery, and a short dress with lace flounces. Theatrical, I call it, but Madame says it will be *ravissante*.

She stuck her slippered feet up on the arm of the couch. "I wish I cared what I am going to wear." She turned and buried her face in a cushion.

Hildegarde went over and knelt beside her. "Sally!"

"Oh, I know I'm a fool. But I've got to go through with it."

"You haven't got to go through with it. Tell Neale."

"Do you think he'll give me up now? I'd have to fight him and fight mother, and I couldn't hold out."

"But if it means a life's unhappiness?"

"Oh, I shan't feel this way afterward. It's like taking a cold plunge. One gets hardened." She sat up, the tears still staining her cheeks. "You're a darling, Hildegarde, to care. Nobody else does."

In the days that followed, Mrs. Hulburt, Sally, and Hildegarde rushed hectically about town. Then, "worn to a frazzle," as Sally put it, they went back to Round Hill. They found there word from Meriweather. His uncle was very ill. There seemed to be little hope. Merry was afraid he would have to cancel all his plans for participation in the wedding. He was sorry, but it could not of course be helped.

The letter was written to Sally. She read it aloud at luncheon and listened, without joining in, to the various comments. When the meal was over, she mounted her horse and rode down to the inn.

" I want to use your telephone," she said to Christopher, " it is quite clandestine."

He smiled at her. " That sounds worse than it is, doesn't it? "

" Perhaps. I want to talk to Merry, and I don't want to shout it to the world. You know how the telephones are at Round Hill. One in the hall, with an echo like a foghorn, and the other in Louis' room with no chance for the rest of us to use it."

There was a booth at the inn, and Sally shut herself into it. When she got Merry on the wire, she said, " I am down at Christopher's, so I can say anything I please, but first, I want to ask about your uncle."

" I'm afraid he's very ill, Sally."

" He's such a dear. Will you give him my love? I liked him. He has eyes like yours. Please don't answer that, Merry. I couldn't say it at Round Hill, but down here it doesn't sound half bad. And shan't I see you before I am Mrs. Neale Winslow? The time is short, you know."

" Too short."

" Well, the sooner the better, as the man said when they put the noose around his neck. . . ."

" Sally! That sounds a bit tragical for a bride? "

" I'm not a bride. I am chief performer in a Spanish extravaganza. You should see my costume, Merry."

" Your wedding gown? "

" Call it that if you will.

" You ought to be married in sackcloth and ashes."

" Don't! " sharply. " I didn't call you up to be scolded."

" I'm sorry."

" I wonder if you are — really? Merry — try to come to my wedding . . . I want you."

" My dear, I will."

" Promise? "

" If it is humanly possible, Sally."

" Well, then ' good-by ' and ' God bless you.' "

As she rang off, he wondered if it was a little sob that he caught across the miles. He went back to his uncle, his mind in a turmoil.

" Sally sent her love to you."

" She probably meant it for you."

Merry shook his head and sat down. " She's going to marry Winslow."

" She wouldn't look at Winslow if you cared. I read that between the lines of every letter she wrote from Paris. And somebody ought to save her from that marriage."

" You mean, of course, that I should."

" I want you to be happy."

" I think I have put happiness behind me, Uncle Buck."

" We all think that, dear boy, when we are young. But there's more than one woman in the world — and this old house is lonely. . . ."

That was all they said about it. But that night, before old Buchanan Meriweather went to bed, he wrote a letter and gave it to his nurse. She was to mail it herself the first thing in the morning, and it was addressed to Sally Hulburt.

Chapter XXIV

SALLY SIGHTS A SAIL

THE open season for hunting was on. Not for duck and quail — the guns must wait for those until November. But yellow-legs, plover, reed-birds, the rails and waders, were legal prey. Flocks, wedge-shaped, crescent-shaped, or loosely scattered, flew low above the ruffled waters of the bay. Shadowy little companies flitted across the sands. On the wings of the wind came the clear whistles, the mellow cries, the musical pipings. The waves were dotted with tiny, floating forms which rose in startled flight at the approach of an intruder.

Christopher's place was full of men in canvas coats and caps, who talked a jargon, unintelligible to the un-initiated, of " sinkboxes " and " sneak boats," of " blinds " and " pushers." Prosperous, sophisticated gentlemen; some of them shooting because it was fashionable, but most of them from sheer love of it.

October came in with lowering clouds, and there was much rain, but the gunners made no complaint. The wet weather simply intensified their sense of sport, and the contrast between the chill without and the coziness of Christopher's hearthstone. They brought in after a day's hard exercise bags of dead birds, which Christopher broiled for them. And while they ate, Columbus, the cat, swung his black paws down from the mantel shelf and surveyed them with scornful eyes. When it came to killing, he needed no gun!

Winslow was among the hunters. His bags of dead birds were bigger than the others. He took them up to Round Hill to be cooked. He talked about them at the table. He seemed to think of nothing else, not even his wedding day, which was three weeks away. Sally made up a verse to fit the case and recited it at dinner:

> There was a little man,
> And he had a little gun,
> And his bullets were made of
> Lead, lead, lead!
> He went to the brook
> And shot a little duck,
> And forgot to go home
> To get mar-ri-ed —!

Winslow, glittering on the other side of the table, said, " I shall never forget — "

Bobby Gresham, who was dining with them, remarked: " Sally's rather a darling duck herself. Good enough to eat."

Winslow shot him a baleful glance. He was irritated, too, by Sally's mockery. He was thin-skinned, and there were times when her words stung him like the barb of a little bee. He wondered if, as his wife, she would irritate him. Yet it was too late to think of that. In three weeks she would marry him, and Gresham might save his flatteries. As for hunting, the season was on, and he intended to get all he could out of it. No one, not even Sally, could interfere with his sport.

Carew, too, hunted. Hildegarde rather hated it all. She didn't like to see things killed. Yet there was something to be said for the out-of-door aspect, the picturesqueness, the inherited love of sport which came to these men of English descent.

As for herself, she was tied up with engagements. Everybody was entertaining Sally, and Carew's daughter was, of course, included in the invitations. Back and forth the two girls swung between Round Hill and Baltimore, with Hildegarde troubled about the expense but enjoying it all none the less. Her father, when now and then she spoke to him about it, urged her not to worry. Winslow, he said, was putting him on to some good things which would soon be paying dividends.

Since their days at the farm together she had not seen Crispin, but his letters came regularly, whether she answered them or not.

" I haven't a bit of pride where you are concerned, Hildegarde. If you won't write, you won't, and that's the end of it. But I've got things to say, and if you don't want to read, you needn't. And the latest thing simply has to be told — I've bought a loveseat and a footstool for the house. They have crooked, carved legs and are done up in faded rose brocade, and they are, as you would say, ' adorable.' That's all the furniture so far, except the little photograph of you and your mother on the mantel. When I am feeling a bit down, I build a fire and sit on the seat and imagine you are beside me, with your little slippers on the

stool! I get a good deal of vicarious satisfaction out
of it. I hope that is the right word. I am never quite
sure about ' vicarious.' "

She wrote back that he must not. The idea of fur-
nishing a house for her! " It seems so complacent,
Crispin. As if you just had to crook your finger! "

His response to that was: " If crooking my finger
would do the trick, I'd have it permanently crippled.
But I am not complacent. There are nights when I
walk the floor in a deadly funk, my imagination playing with the idea that you are falling in love with somebody else. If that ever happens, Hildegarde, don't tell
me. Just send back the silver key. And I'll know you
are never going to sit by my fires, nor toast your
slippers at my hearth."

Hildegarde found her mind dwelling rather persist-
ently on the thought of that fireplace and Crispin in
front of it. She didn't want to think about it, but there
it was, popping up at the most unexpected moments in
the midst of Sally's chatter or of Bobby's jests.

Then one day, when, with a lot of others, she was
having tea in the art gallery of Winslow's house, she
came across a picture of George Washington! It had,
apparently, just been hung, and was unlike any other
portrait she had seen of the father of his country. It
gave him less the look of a graven image and more the
look of a human being. Here were the tired eyes, the
irritated frown of the harassed officer, the coarse skin
of the man whom the storms had beaten and the cold
hardened. He wore a shabby coat, his hair was wind-
blown, and there was something in his expression which
reminded her of Crispin as he had been that day under

the old oak. Washington had no laughter to light his
face, but one felt his youth and strength. Here was
not the statesman, but the soldier who was fighting the
battle of the moment with no idea of the honors ahead.

Bobby, coming up behind her, said, " Old George
needs a hair cut."

" I like him."

" You wouldn't in real life. Not with a coat like
that."

" One doesn't judge men by their coats."

" Dear child," Bobby surveyed her with a laughing
eye, " if I wore lace ruffles and ribbons, you'd adore
me."

" Not I."

" All women are like that. Caught by trappings —
men in khaki, men in scarlet, men in high boots. They
married thousands of 'em during the war. Coats, my
dear child, coats! "

Sally, joining them, was white as a sheet. " I have
such bad news. Merry's uncle is dead. Louis just
got the telegram."

" How dreadful! " Hildegarde said.

Bobby was more practical. " Good thing for Merry.
Nice estate, I understand."

Sally blazed at him. " Oh, that's like you, Bobby.
As if the money mattered! "

" Does, though," Bobby insisted. " Does with you.
Don't try to put it over on me, Sally."

Sally faced him squarely. " Do you mean I am
marrying Neale for his money? "

" What else? I wouldn't call him young or good-
looking."

" You're hateful, Bobby."

Hildegarde turned away. How could the two of them squabble like that with the thought of death so near? She wandered down the long room and stopped in front of the picture of the Chinese lady. Winslow, entering under the great archway, stopped beside her and said:

" That's one of the finest things in the collection."

" I don't like it half so well as your George Washington."

His cold eyes lighted. " Not many people have your discrimination. The Washington picture is extremely valuable, painted by an unknown artist. Undoubtedly an excellent likeness. I've had amazing offers for it."

" But you won't sell? "

" Perhaps. If I get my price."

" I wish I had money enough to buy it."

He was amused. " What would you do with it? "

A flush stained her cheeks. How could she tell him that in a flash she had seen the portrait over the fireplace of the little house?

She began to talk hurriedly about the lady with the butterflies. " I hate her face. There's something evil about it."

" Stand farther away," said Winslow. " If you'll sit in that chair, you'll get the best effect."

So Hildegarde sat in the king's chair and suited it so well that Winslow wished he might have her painted in an ermine cloak. She looked like a queen. If Crispin had seen her, his heart might have failed him. She was not in the least like the wife of a man with no furniture in his house but a loveseat and a footstool and a photograph in a frame!

When the party got back to Round Hill a few days later, Sally found the letter written by old Buck Meriweather. It had been waiting for a week or more and had not been forwarded. And so it happened that after he was dead, the old man spoke to Sally:

"Will you forgive one who is going very soon into a far country for writing as I am going to write? Sometimes we who are about to cross the border see things clearly. That is my only apology for what may seem to you an unwarrantable intrusion. I want Merry to be happy, and I have a feeling that you hold his happiness in your hands. Perhaps I haven't any right to say this. Perhaps it isn't true. But wrong or right, I wish that you would trust life for more than it will give you in the marriage you are contemplating. Won't you?

"That is all I have to say. To put it more definitely into words would be to confuse myself as well as you. I think you know what I mean. Shall we let it rest there, and again, will you forgive me?"

A strange letter, but one that stirred Sally's heart. "Won't you trust life for more than it will give you . . . ?" Wasn't he in effect asking her not to marry Neale?

How absurd! Why, the wedding was less than three weeks away! And her clothes were all made. Caterers were baking cakes, and florists planning decorations. Presents were pouring in. Even now Hildegarde was downstairs posting things in a note-book — the cosmetic boxes of old Irish silver which had come that morning, the table set of antique Italian lace, the *petit-point* bag with the jeweled clasp, the half-dozen duplicate pairs of Colonial candlesticks.

" It's preposterous," Sally said to the doll, Sarah, on the chiffonier.

Yet if she did not marry Neale? She would be free again! A great sense of relief surged over her. She found herself laughing hysterically, as one might who, hopeless on a desert island, sights a sail. She would be saved! She would own herself once more! She who had been bought with emeralds and frozen jade!

In a dream she dressed for dinner. She went downstairs outwardly composed but inwardly in a tumult. The men came in from their hunting. Winslow was in excellent spirits. His bag was big. He handed it to Sampson and stopped for a moment in the library to talk to Sally.

" It is raining hard outside," he said. " If it keeps it up in the morning I'll run into town. Would you like to go with me? "

She shook her head. " I don't believe I'm equal to it."

He glanced at her sharply. " What's the matter? Aren't you well? "

She tried to laugh. " Too much excitement, perhaps."

" I think we shall both be glad when the wedding is over." He stood, looking down at her. " You can rest as much as you like in my big house."

He went away then, and Sally sat thinking of the things he had said. The big house loomed in her imagination as grim and gruesome as a penitentiary, a prison with Winslow as a perpetual jailer. All her life she would be shut up with him!

No, she would not do it. She would tell Neale to-morrow. And her mother.

CHAPTER XXV

WINSLOW GOES A–HUNTING

IT was raining hard when, the next afternoon, a small, rubber-caped figure rode up to the inn. Entering the great room, where a half-dozen men in canvas coats lounged in front of the fire, a voice came from under the dripping rubber hat:

" I'm almost drowned."

The men jumped to their feet. " It's Sally Hulburt! "

They gathered about her.

With her hat off, her gold hair clung as close as a metal cap. She stood on the hearthstone and talked to them.

" Where's Winslow? " one of the men demanded.

" He's gone to town."

They teased her about that with shouting laughter. So this was the way the mouse played when the cat was away cutting coupons! Riding down alone in the rain. A rendezvous? They would have something to tell Neale when he came back!

Sally took their teasing good-naturedly. Her cheeks were red and her eyes bright. Her tongue had a pointed wit, and she was a match for the best of them.

But when at last she left the hearthstone and spoke alone with Christopher, she showed her agitation.

" I'm being clandestine again. Merry is coming here to meet me. Can you find us a quiet corner where we can talk? "

Christopher suggested the big pantry off the kitchen. " You can watch your chance and slip through the swinging door. I'll have one of the men keep an eye out for Mr. Meriweather."

Having executed this maneuver with success, Sally found herself presently in a small, square room with shelves along the sides on which were great china platters, covered silver dishes, and copper casseroles. There was another swinging door which led to the serving room where Christopher carved the meats. The place was secluded and cozy, with the driving rain making a gray curtain for the window, and a low-hung lamp bringing out the high lights on the silver and copper and showing the gay-colored designs on the china platters.

When Merry was ushered in by Christopher, and the big man had departed, Sally said:

" What did you think when you got my telegram? "

" I didn't stop to think. I came."

" After I had sent it, I was scared stiff."

" You needn't have been. I was coming anyhow. I had my bag packed. But why all this mystery, Sally? Meeting me like this? Not that I don't like it. I do. I feel like the hero of a swashbuckling novel. Riding post-haste through the rain! "

He laughed and drew out a chair for her at the small table which Christopher had set for them. " It is rather an adventure, little Sally."

Something in his voice made her turn and look up

at him as he stood behind her. The expression in his golden eyes as they met hers set her heart to beating wildly. The blood seemed to pound in her temples, as she said:

" I am not going to marry Neale."

" What! "

" I made up my mind yesterday."

" What happened? "

" Something that I'll tell you sometime. I feel now as if I had never intended to marry him. I was like a person in a nightmare and couldn't wake up."

He dropped into the chair opposite her and leaned across the table. Again that look in his eyes made her heart beat. " It's a remarkable thing, Sally, that I should have made up my mind before I got your telegram to come to you today. I had made up my mind to beg you not to marry Neale. I had made up my mind to ask you to marry me! "

From across the table Sally stared at him. " You are just saying that . . . as a joke. . . ." Her lips were dry.

" I'm not. I swear it. I've wanted it for a long time — ever since your letters began to come to me from Paris. But I didn't know positively until one night when I was talking with Uncle Buck — "

Christopher came in with tea and muffins and departed hastily. Any one with half an eye could see what was happening. Merry went on as if there had been no interruption.

" After he died, I was tied up with things I had to do. Yet I knew the time before your wedding was short. So last night I packed my bag . . . and now you tell

me you are free. It is more than a coincidence. It is
a miracle, Sally."

"But I'm not free, Merry."

"Why not?"

"I haven't told Neale or mother. I don't know
what they'll say to me. That's why I sent for you.
I felt that then they couldn't exactly throw me to the
lions! That you'd find some way to save me."

"Easy enough. We'll be married tomorrow without
telling them. You can meet me in Baltimore."

"Merry, I haven't said ' yes.' "

"Dear child, there's no time for formalities. You
can say ' yes ' when the clergyman asks you questions."
The golden eyes were dancing.

Sally found herself protesting with a quaver in her
voice. "But things like this don't happen to me,
Merry. I shall wake up presently and find myself in
the wood with the Wolf walking beside me."

"You'll wake up and find yourself in Harford
County, walking up the stairs of my old house with a
candle in your hand — which is much better. And
now — come over here and let me kiss you, Sally! "

It was the next night that Neale, arriving with his
bag of birds, found a note from Sally. She had written
it before she went to town. She would, she told him,
be married to Merry by the time he received it!

Winslow's world crashed! He crumpled the note in
his hand and went to look for Mrs. Hulburt. He met
her hurrying down from the upper floor to the first
landing.

"You've heard?" he demanded.

"Sampson just gave me a note. He said Sally's orders were that they were not to be delivered until you came in. Neale, the child must be mad — "

"Sit down," he said in a hard tone. "Speculation doesn't get us anywhere. We've got to talk it over."

She dropped on a seat under the Blue Window, but none of its peace entered into her soul. "Go on."

"Meriweather ought to be shot. He's a hound." Winslow still wore his shooting jacket; his bag of birds was in the hall below. "Does Carew know?" he asked. "Or any one?"

"No. Sally says in her note she will leave it to you to tell the world whatever you will."

He was savage. "What can I tell?"

He was thinking with sensitive agony how the world would laugh at him! Young beauty, it would say, had scorned him. Merry's golden eyes and golden youth had outweighed the moneybags of the old man. He should have known better than to believe in the love of May for December.

He made a quick decision. "I don't want the reporters down here until I have something to talk about. Just keep your mouth shut, Ethel, until after dinner."

He was not polite. He didn't want to be. He felt that in some way Ethel must be culpable. She should have brought Sally up better. To be obedient.

"I don't see how I can face them all." Ethel was struggling with a touch of hysteria. "They'll be sure to ask about Sally."

He considered that. "Very well. I'll send you off to town in my motor. You can say Sally wanted you to join her. What reason did she give for going in?"

"Hats. Another one. I told her she had enough. But she wouldn't listen."

"You might have suspected." He caught himself up. No use to quarrel with Ethel. "Of course, every one will know the truth eventually. But I've got to have time. . . . Get on your wraps. I'll have the car around as soon as you are ready."

Thus, protesting a little, but half-glad to be out of it, Mrs. Hulburt was spirited away to Baltimore to spend a lonely night in a hotel. And so it happened that at the Round Hill dinner table were just four of them — Carew and Winslow, Miss Anne and Hildegarde. Winslow, perfectly groomed, apparently at his ease, glittering, seemed to reflect the shine of the silver. He might almost have been hung with prisms like the candelabra. He beamed on them all, told scintillating stories, laughed in that crackling way of his at Carew's jokes.

Hildegarde, listening, told herself that Neale's manner was too perfect. Something had happened. She was sure of it. Mystery was in the air. Sally had taken an early train that morning and had asked no one to go with her. And now Ethel gone, with no reason at all. For why shouldn't Sally have come back for the night? And then, added to that, had been a scene with Sally in the morning, when the bride-to-be had come into Hildegarde's room and had asked:

"Do you believe that the good Lord answers prayers, Hilda?"

"Of course."

"Did you ever pray for a husband?"

"Sally!"

" I'm not joking. I got that from Crispin. He told me if I ever wanted a good husband, I should ask for one."

Hildegarde, sitting up in bed, had demanded: " Aren't you being a bit flippant? I am sure Crispin wouldn't make light of such matters."

" He was in dead earnest. He said if I wanted one, I must ask. And I've been asking for weeks."

She stopped there, radiant. " *Darling,* I can't tell you. But a lovely thing has happened."

After dinner Neale went up to use Carew's telephone. He had, he said, some important messages. Miss Anne motored out to the Country Club for a promised game of bridge. Hildegarde and her father sat on the porch alone, while Carew smoked his after-dinner cigar.

It was an enchanting night. There was a bit of chill in the air, and Hildegarde was wrapped in a Spanish shawl which she had brought back with her from abroad. Carew wore an old army cloak of his father's. The wind ruffled his hair so that it stood up like an eagle's crest. By the light of the moon he resembled more than ever the red-coated grandfather in the library. He was indeed as much a part of the background as the white columns, the fan-lighted door, and the coat-of-arms above the portico.

Hildegarde spoke of the moon. " Christopher calls it the hunter's moon. And it is wonderful."

" It will be even more wonderful later. There's something weird about it as the night wanes."

They sat in silence watching the gold creep across the waters of the bay. Carew was in a chair, and

Hildegarde on the step below him. She laid her cheek against his knee. " Love me, Daddy? "

" You know I do."

" Sometimes . . . I like to think when we are together that mother . . . is with us."

His hand was on her hair. " Hildegarde . . . I want you to know that she was the dearest. . . . Yet I never made her happy."

Hildegarde looked up at him. " You've made me happy."

" Have I? I am afraid I wasn't born to make people happy. And some day you'll leave me."

" What do you mean? "

" You'll marry. All girls do."

Out of the content of the moment she laughed. " Why look so far ahead? "

A cloud darkened the moon, but the dead gold of it still illumined the scene, and in that dead-gold light they saw a figure moving among the trees.

" It's Winslow," Carew said. " He must have come out of the side door."

Neither of them called, although Neale in the stillness could easily have heard their voices. They watched him go in and out, threading his way along the sable trunks until he was lost to view.

" He has some important matters pending," Carew remarked. " He says exercise makes his mind work. The thing he is interested in just now interests me. If it goes through our fortunes are assured. If it doesn't, we are done for."

" What do you mean by ' done for,' Daddy? "

" It's our last hope. I've practically no assets. I'd have to sell the house."

Hildegarde wished he wouldn't talk about unpleasant things. She didn't want to think about finances. She wanted to think how wonderful it was to sit here with her hand in her father's, and to know that he loved her.

The cloud which had darkened the moon was gone. The trees once more caught the light — and up through that shining world, transmuted by its radiance into something hard and gleaming like a golden statue, came Winslow.

He walked straight toward them and stopped at the steps. " On such a night as this one ought to ride. What do you say to my ordering the horses for us, Hildegarde? "

She was speechless with surprise. Recovering herself, she asked, " Is Daddy invited? "

Winslow's laugh crackled. " No."

" Then I'm not going."

Again he laughed. " Carew, tell your daughter to come with me."

" Why not include me in the party, Neale? "

" I want Hildegarde's advice about Sally. Does that satisfy you? "

" Oh, well, run along with him, Hildegarde."

She rose with some reluctance. " Of course, if it's about Sally. I'll get into my riding-clothes. . . ."

When she again joined them, the horses were ready, and Winslow, too, had changed. Presently the two of them were riding down toward the Bay, with the world like gold lacquer in that strange, still light.

Hildegarde spoke of it. " The valley looks like a Japanese tray. I feel if the moon should drop, it would clink."

" I didn't bring you out here to talk about the

moon." Winslow stopped his horse, and her horse, too, stopped. "I am in the dickens of a mess, Hildegarde. Sally has run away with Merry."

So that was it! Sally's radiance!

"They were married this afternoon," Winslow went on with a touch of violence in his tone, "in Baltimore. I had a note, and Ethel had one. I sent Ethel into town because I didn't want her telling the world. The reporters will be after me presently like dogs after a fox. I've held them off temporarily, but by morning I must have a story for them."

Hildegarde said with a touch of sharpness, "What have I to do with it?"

"A great deal, I hope. You can help me out of a most embarrassing situation." He leaned toward her and said without further preamble, "I want you to marry me, Hildegarde. . . ."

She gave a startled exclamation and drew back from him, then she set her horse in a mad gallop toward home.

He galloped after her and caught at her bridle. "Listen to me," he said. "This isn't a new thing. For a long time I've known I made a mistake in choosing Sally. It came into my mind first at the ball and afterward in Paris. But it was too late to draw back. And now she has taken it into her own hands, and I can tell you. The other day, when you sat in the king's chair, you were like a queen — I wanted you — "

She was beating her heel against her horse's flanks. "Let me go," she said wildly. "Oh, what would Daddy say if he knew you were talking to me like this?"

" I think he would be reasonable."

" He wouldn't. He wouldn't be reasonable. He would be furious. . . ."

" I can make or break him, Hildegarde. And he knows it. He won't go against me."

His voice was at a flat level. It was as if by some trick of ventriloquism the golden statue had been made to speak.

Hildegarde struggled desperately with a sense of fright. Her lips were dry. " You know I can't marry you."

" Why not? If you say ' no,' I shall wash my hands of your father's affairs."

" It is ' no,' of course."

" With your father taking the consequences? "

" He'll be glad to take them."

" Will he? Well, we'll ask him. This thing has got to be settled tonight, Hildegarde. We'll ride now to the house and find Carew and put the question before him."

Chapter XXVI

THREE SHADOWS TALK IN THE MOONLIGHT

LOUIS CAREW, watching Winslow ride off with his daughter, had a humorous sense of his own inadequacy to meet the situation. Why hadn't he told Neale if he had anything to talk over to do it here? Why such secrecy about his affairs with Sally? And why bring Hildegarde into it?

But Neale was Neale. When he wanted his way, he got it. Carew, shrugging his shoulders, rose and walked down to the garden. He sat for a long time on the stone bench, the smoke from his cigar mingling with the scent of the few late roses. It was an enchanting night. He remembered another night under a hunter's moon. Elizabeth had sat beside him on the stone bench and he had spoken of the effect of this strange and spectral light. " There's no other moon like it. I've followed a fox under it, with a feeling that all the time the scene wasn't real. It is almost uncanny, the sense it gives of doing things in a dream."

She had asked about the fox-hunt, and he had described it. " All that seems a bit cruel, doesn't it? " she had said.

" There's the sport."

" Not for the poor little fox."

He had kissed her and had loved her for her tenderheartedness. Women should be like that. Yes, she had been the dearest. . . . And Hildegarde was like her. . . . He wasn't good enough for either of them. . . . The Carew blood . . . galloping . . . rackety . . . wild for adventure!

He was waked from his meditation by the sound of hoof-beats. Hildegarde and Winslow were coming up the drive. Carew called, and they turned towards him. As Hildegarde reached him, she spoke with an effect of breathlessness, " Neale has something to say to you, Daddy. That's why we're back so soon." She jumped from her horse and stood beside him.

Winslow also dismounted. " There's no reason to get excited, Hildegarde. That's the trouble with women. They go off half-cocked."

Carew did not like his tone. But then Neale was Neale. And not a gentleman.

He tried to take the situation lightly. " Have you two been quarrelling? "

" No," Winslow wasted no time. " Sally's married. Ran away with Merry. This afternoon. I want Hildegarde to marry me in Sally's place."

Carew gave a short laugh. " Are you out of your mind, Neale? "

" No. But I've been put in an intolerable position. Everybody will be laughing at me. Saying I'm jilted. If I marry Hildegarde the world can't laugh. It can guess at things, but it won't know."

" You'll have to face it. When you come to your senses, you'll realize the utter absurdity of trying to substitute Hildegarde. Things like that simply aren't done, my dear fellow."

His arm went round his daughter. " Daddy, *dar-*

ling," she whispered, and laid her cheek against his sleeve.

" Aren't you being," Winslow's cold voice questioned, " a bit up-stage? "

" If you choose to call it that. . . ."

" If you'll come down to earth you'll realize that I can make or break you, Louis."

" What do you mean? "

" Not a share of the stock I bought for you is in your name. And my money bought it. If I don't choose to turn it over to you, who can force me? And what could you tell the court? That you pulled wires — for pay? "

Carew's arm dropped from his daughter's shoulder. " Are you threatening me? "

" It depends upon what you call it. But without the stock there's nothing left. Round Hill will have to go, and all the rest of it. Hildegarde said you'd think my proposition to her an insult. I told her you'd have too much sense to quarrel with me. So we rode back to see which of us — knows you best." His hesitation gave to his last words a touch of insolence.

Carew spoke to his daughter. " Go up to the house, Hildegarde. I want to have this out alone with Neale."

" No. What is there to discuss with him, Daddy? Let him do his worst. Why should we mind? We shall have each other."

Neale's laugh was disagreeable. " Will you? What about Ethel Hulburt? "

As he saw Hildegarde shrink from him, her hand up as if to ward off a blow, Carew had a feeling that had more than once assailed him under the hunter's moon — that the scene was not real. That he was a shadow, facing shadows.

And the shadow called Winslow was saying: " If Louis marries Ethel, what will you do, Hildegarde? "

And the shadow which was Hildegarde was saying: " Oh, I'm done with both of you. I didn't know there were such men in the world!"

And the shadow which was himself was saying: " I am not going to marry Ethel, Hildegarde. I loved your mother."

The spell of his memories was still upon him. Ethel Hulburt had, for the moment, no meaning in his life. He was exalted, careless of consequences. " Do your worst," he told Winslow. " Hildegarde and I will stick it out together."

She came to him then, and they stood confronting Winslow triumphantly. " Oh, have it your way," he said with violence, " but I have a feeling that you'll see it differently in the morning. Shall we say at nine? In the library? You can — dream over it."

He mounted and rode off, taking Hildegarde's horse with him. When he was gone, Hildegarde cried in her father's arms and Louis swore that nothing else mattered if only they might be together. His mood was, he realized later, the madness of the hunter's moon. Subconsciously he knew, even while he made his earnest asseverations to his daughter, that the matter would have to be settled in some less emotional way with Winslow.

They sat on the stone bench, and he told her of the things he had been thinking of her mother. The moon waned, and the bronze turtle, afloat on the gilded pool, became at last a shadow among the shadows.

"It has been wonderful to talk like this," Hildegarde said, as she and her father went finally up the hill. She bade him "good-night" at the library door, and turned as she ascended the stairs to wave a hand to him. He waved back, blew a kiss from the tips of his fingers. He had doffed his great cloak but still carried it over his arm. Dark and debonair, he gave her a glance from his laughing eyes which seemed to light her world. Always afterwards she was to carry in her heart the picture of her father as he stood laughing up at her.

She slept well that night. She was not afraid of poverty, and she had no doubts as to the outcome of the interview with Neale Winslow. She and Daddy would stand together. And now that Ethel was out of it. . . ! She pictured a future in which she and her father surmounted every obstacle. A sort of fairy-tale existence. Material things did not matter. One's happiness came from something higher. Half-awake, she saw a little house . . . a loveseat . . . a footstool . . . they must buy one more chair . . . for Daddy!

Carew, sitting late before the library fire, was less sanguine than his daughter. As the reaction set in against those earlier high moments, he weighed the difficulties ahead. One could not easily defy Winslow, and the results of defiance wculd be — the Deluge! There was, of course, Anne. What she had might help. But he was not going to drag her down in the wreck of his fortunes. He rose, got out his account books, studied them, and flung them from him. Everything was in a hopeless muddle. He stirred the dying fire and stared into it. If Neale took the house he would claim all there was in it — he had always wanted the crystal cat, and the lacquered cabinet, the silver pheasants which had for three generations trailed their shining feathers down the dining tables of convivial Carews. Neale was an insatiable collector. Next to his ambition for social prominence was his passion for rare and beautiful objects. One need hope for little with such a man. He was capable of setting Hildegarde and her father with their few remaining effects out on the front lawn, as poor tenants were set out in the streets in the old melodramas.

With his imagination now actively at work, Louis saw pictures in the fire of himself and Hildegarde squeezed into a squalid apartment. Of Hildegarde washing dishes, of himself going forth to seek a job. No Carew had ever lived in an apartment! No Carew had ever washed dishes! No Carew had ever sought a job! There was, of course, a chance for super-economies in Paris! But even Paris might prove too much for their pocket-books.

Paris! Another picture in the fire. Of Hildegarde in Bobby Gresham's big car, with her arms full of violets, purple ribbons in her hair, gay, laughing, lovely.

By Jove, that was the solution! Bobby! Louis laughed with relief. Why hadn't it come to him before? Bobby's millions matched Winslow's. He was young, good-looking, and Hildegarde liked him. If she could only be brought to see the advantages.

Gresham would be glad to retrieve the family fortunes.
With Hildegarde married — well, Ethel and he might
make a go of it. One couldn't live on the heights forever!

He went to the writing table and dashed off a note
to his daughter. He would see that she got it the first
thing in the morning. With Bobby up her sleeve, she
could face Neale with serenity. It would be like a
scene in a comedy. The villain foiled . . . ! He
leaned back in his chair and laughed. Old Neale
wasn't so bad. They had been great friends. But
nobody could put it over like that on Hildegarde.

It was characteristic of Carew that with his change
of mood he should find himself forgiving his enemy.
Poor old chap . . . the blow to his pride had been
shattering. Neale was thin-skinned — and Sally had
flouted him! And the world would laugh!

So, when on his way to his room a little later, he
passed Neale's door, he knocked. Neale, opening it,
showed himself wrapped in a gorgeous Eastern gown.
" Well? " he asked.

" Look here," Louis said, " What about that engagement we have for tomorrow morning — to shoot on
Flat Island? "

" It's off, of course."

" But why? Why not call a truce temporarily?
There are always women to marry, Neale. But there
aren't always birds to shoot."

Winslow stared at him. " Do you mean you'll go
out with me? "

" Why not? We'll have from five-thirty to nine.
Breakfast at Christopher's before sunrise and the re-

porters at bay until you've talked to Hildegarde. What do you say? "

" I'll say this — that you ought to be blowing a reed pipe among the rushes. You've got no more sense of responsibility than a — goat."

" So Ethel tells me," there was a glint of laughter in Carew's eyes, " only she puts it more poetically as — Pan."

Winslow meditated a moment, then agreed, " I'll go. As you say it will be one way to avoid the newspaper men. I don't see why I didn't insist on settling the thing tonight. Then I'd have had a story ready."

Louis shrugged his shoulders. " You'll probably have a better one by waiting until morning. But I suggest we don't talk about it. Hildegarde will make the final decision. And until we have it out with her, we won't discuss it. It would be a pity to spoil a perfectly good morning's shooting with an argument."

It was typical of the sporting attitude of the two men that they started off before daylight with what seemed on the surface the utmost friendliness. They had a hearty breakfast at the Inn, with a great fire on the hearth, with Christopher serving ham and eggs and hot cakes, and with other hunters coming in to eat other hearty breakfasts at other tables.

Through it all, the light-heartedness of Louis was a matter of amazement to Winslow. He had, apparently, not a care in the world. He cracked jokes with Christopher, and with the men at the surrounding tables laughed a great deal, and when at last he stood for a moment with his back to the blaze he gave an effect of youth which was astounding.

It was, Winslow decided, as they rode away, the reaction from the high emotionalism of the night before. The chances were that since their talk in the moonlight, Louis had come to see the advantages of having a rich son-in-law. " He knows what I can do for him," Neale told himself, and began to breathe more freely than at any time since the news had come to him of Sally's flight.

Louis kept, however, strictly to his resolution not to talk about his daughter. He talked of everything else as they drove in Winslow's car to the Flat Island pier. It was a long, low pier used only by the hunters at this season, and by the fishermen all the year round. Reeds and rushes grew high on each side of it, and at the far end a small motor boat was tied. It was this boat which they took, leaving Winslow's car by the side of the road.

It was a wonderful morning. Even in the midst of his mental disturbance Winslow was aware of the beauty of the dawn — faint pearl at first like one of his Japanese prints, then with the light stealing in and washing the world with silver. The teal, at rest upon the waves, dotted the shore-line with black. Other birds flew up from the sedge. The boat slipped through water so still that their progress scarcely rocked the rushes. They left behind them a thin triangular wake, as sharp as an etching on steel.

They found great numbers of birds on the Island — yellow-legs, rail and reed-birds — lovely piping things, all of them, flitting like shadows over the sand. Even Winslow had to admit that it was a pity to spoil the charm of the scene by killing — but it was birds they had come for and they took full toll.

On their way back, Louis steered the boat, standing up, and singing under his breath an inconsequential tune. Neale watching him, asked, " Aren't you ever serious? "

" Why should I be? "

" But — with all there is ahead of you . . . Hildegarde's future. . . ."

" I thought we weren't going to talk about Hildegarde."

" But, why not?   Sensibly? "

" Because — I'm not sensible."

Winslow flushed with irritation.   " Oh, well, if you want to act like a — fool — "

" My dear fellow — why not act like a fool, when acting like a wise man brings worries? "

" But we all have worries — "

" Not — this morning.   Neale, did you ever see anything more enchanting than that steamer rising up like Venus above the water — white as milk? "

Thus he shelved further discussion, and it was only at the last, quite surprisingly, as they tied up at the pier that he introduced Hildegarde's name.

He got out his flask and proposed a toast.

" I drink," he said, with cup upraised, " to my adorable daughter."

" To our marriage? "

Louis laughed.   " As you please," he said, " the first part of the toast is the only one for which I am responsible."

"You may find yourself responsible for all of it," Winslow flung back, his face darkened by a frown. "I wish you'd stop being mysterious. You know what I want, and you've got to give it to me!"

"I know what you want," Louis said, "but I'm not going to talk about it." He leaped out of the boat, gathered up his traps and went on ahead whistling, while Winslow, his lips in a thin line, followed him.

CHAPTER XXVII

ELIZABETH'S DAUGHTER FIGHTS THROUGH

WHEN Hildegarde woke, after a night of dreamless sleep, she found the sun streaming in and Delia standing by the bed. " Yo' Daddy lef' a note for you, honey," she said, and delivered it.

Hildegarde sat up and opened the envelope. Delia went on to light the fire and draw the water for her mistress' bath. When she came back, Hildegarde was at the window, looking out.

" How 'ull you have yo' aigs, honey? "

" I don't want any eggs. I don't want any breakfast, Delia."

The colored woman's quick ear caught a note of distress. " Somepin happened? " she demanded.

" Yes."

" Is it yo' Daddy? "

" It's everything. . . ."

Her tone was final. Delia retiring discreetly to the threshold urged, " Won't you have jes' a leetle cup o' choc'lit? "

" Nothing now," as she turned she showed her troubled face, her tear-wet eyes, " I'll let you know."

Delia, entering the kitchen a few moments later, expressed herself tumultuously to Sampson. " You needn' tell *me*. I tole you yistiddy things was queer. Miss Sally goin' off in a rush in the mornin' and Miss Ethel goin' off in a rush in the evenin'. And Mistuh Neale givin' orders we ain' to say where he is, effen anybody 'phones."

Sampson agreed. " An' nobody havin' breakfus' this mornin' ceptin' Miss Anne. And she never eats nothin' but orange juice, lessen she git fat."

Delia came close to him. " Mis' Ethel's at the bottom of it. You lissen to me. . . . I calls her a snake, wormin' herself in. That's what I calls her."

Sampson was gloomy. " Effen Mistuh Louis marries Mis' Ethel, I goes."

" An' you won't go alone. I packs my trunk and shakes the dus' f'om my feet. Miss Ethel kaint give me no orders."

For once however in her life, Delia's intuitions had failed her. The note to Hildegarde was not about Ethel Hulburt. It was about Bobby.

Carew had written: " I've been thinking it all out, Hildegarde, and it looks as if our hope is in Bobby Gresham. You like him, don't you? And he's a gentleman. He loves you, and with him as your husband we could laugh at Neale. It is hard for you to understand what Neale can do to me. I am utterly in his power financially, and I am not used to poverty. But Bobby would be the solution. Think about it, Hildegarde, and let me know. I'll see you in the morning. You are my dear child, and I want you to be happy. It would be intolerable for me to see you suffer. And this seems to be the way out. Let's try it."

Hildegarde having read the note, had crushed it in her hand. So much for a dream! Shattered. She had thought last night there was full understanding between herself and her father.

And now he offered her — Bobby!

Bobby was a clown — Pierrot, Harlequin, almost fantastically funny. A man to play around with, but not to marry. Why, all the world knew Bobby's inconstancies. One did not want a husband like that, swearing love on his knees at one moment, and at the next swearing devotion at other slippered feet.

Last night she had felt so safe. She had thought she and her father stood shoulder to shoulder in their defiance of Winslow, their acceptance of the future. And now. . . ? Never with her mother had she had these devastating experiences with a weathercock mind. Her mother had faced things strongly. She would not have dreamed of Gresham as a husband for her daughter. She would not have been afraid of Neale. But her father was afraid. And he was weak. It was weakness which had kept him in Winslow's power; and which had made possible his dalliance with Ethel when he really didn't want her.

Or did he want her? Might he not even at this moment be changing his mind? There was nothing stable in him. He was blown by the wind. . . .

After Delia left her, she dressed slowly. She would go down and have a moment with her father before Winslow came. She didn't quite know what she would say to him. She only knew that she was going to tell him what she thought of him. He deserved it. After

that she would go away. Back to the farm. As her
mother had done. . . .

When at last she was ready, she opened her door.
Delia was in the hall ostensibly busy, but with an eye
to interesting developments.

" Yo' Daddy's gone a-huntin'," she said, as Hildegarde appeared, " with Mr. Neale."

" Not this morning," incredulously.

" Yes, honey."

" When did they go? "

" Befo' sun-up."

In Hildegarde's state of mind this seemed the final
affront — that he could go off with their enemy, while
destinies hung in the balance!

" What time are they coming back, Delia? "

" Mistuh Neale he tole Sampson they'd git here by
nine. They's been a lot of men calling up, but Mistuh
Neale gave orders we wasn't to ax no questions or
answer none."

Reporters, probably, on the track of Sally's jilted
suitor. The telephone rang again and Delia went to
answer it. Hildegarde following the maid down the
stairs moved automatically. She was beyond sensation. Numb.

She came to the first landing, and stopped. The
lattices of the great window were flung wide, framing
an expanse of deep unbroken blue. Hildegarde stared,
fascinated. Back of her was her father's house,
haunted by shadows, darkened by the dreadfulness of
strife and misunderstanding — ahead of her was that
cloudless azure curtain, hiding what one felt must be
ineffable light.

She leaned on the sill and looked out — blue sky, blue bay, a fresh breeze blowing. The peace of it entered into her soul. She seemed to hear her lover's voice. " I think if you called I should hear you."

Her heart called to him now, " *Crispin, Crispin.*" In this crisis she felt the need of his strength and sanity. . . . " *Crispin, Crispin.*"

For the first time since she had read her father's letter her mind worked clearly. It was working, indeed, clearly, for the first time since the night of Winslow's ball. She had been proud to be called " Carew's daughter." Had fashioned herself after his pattern. Had preened herself when she had heard other people say: " She's like him."

Yet it was her mother after whom she should have patterned. And it was the daughter of Elizabeth Musgrove who must act in this emergency. Her mother had said so many times, " Our souls are lamps to guide us." Hildegarde reflected that the light within her own soul was a flickering taper. Would it serve to show the way?

She had no other guide. There was, of course, Aunt Anne. But Aunt Anne must not be brought into this. She loved her brother, blamed him, forgave him. Hildegarde must settle this thing herself.

And settling it meant going away!

To the farm!

Well, why not? The old aunts seemed like rocks of steadfastness in this sea of change. And there was the steadfastness of Crispin. And, above all, the memory of the serenity and steadfastness of her mother.

Oh, she belonged to all that — not to this life of

greed and shallowness. And she would tell them so —
Neale and her father. She hated the thought of it.
But the thing had to be done. In a few minutes she
would be facing them in the library, and their argu-
ments would swing back and forth. But nothing they
could say would alter her decision. The spirit which
had sustained her mother would sustain her now.
There was no bondage like that of being chained to
weakness. The only freedom was in the strength of
one's soul.

How often her mother had said these things to her
in their candle-lighted room, and they had meant little
because life had not taught her their truth. But
now the truth of them seemed to blaze down on her
from those blue heavens. As if again her mother
spoke.

She turned from the window and went upstairs again.
She packed a small bag, put on a straight dark frock,
and laid her hat and coat beside the bag. Then she
made her way to the library.

The minutes passed. The clock in the hall chimed
the hour. Nine thin notes that left a silvery echo.
She rose restlessly, and went to the window which
overlooked the front drive. Two automobiles were
parked by the side of the road, and on the steps of the
house between the white pillars a half dozen newspaper
men were waiting.

When at last Winslow drove up, Hildegarde saw him
stop and parley with the men. Her father came on,
hurrying a bit.

" Here we are at last," he said, as he entered the
library. " You and I will have to talk fast, Hildegarde.

Neale's right at my heels. I had hoped to have a little time alone with you to discuss my letter. You got it? "

" Yes."

" And we are both for Bobby? "

" No."

She saw his frown, his impatience. " Surely we are going to stand together, Hildegarde."

" I thought we stood together last night."

" Too impractical. I knew that as soon as I left you. Neither one of us could live in poverty and be happy. Hildegarde, do you know what you'll be letting me in for if you refuse to marry Gresham? For years Neale has been my old man of the sea. I've carried him on my back. And now that you have a chance to save me, you say coolly that you won't. I didn't dream you'd take this attitude. I thought it was settled. If I hadn't, I'd have stayed at home this morning, to try to make you see it."

" You can never make me see it."

There was no time for further argument. Winslow's voice sounded in the hall. " Give me a half-hour, gentlemen, and I'll have something to tell you."

He came in and shut the door. " They are like hounds at a kill," he said, with bitterness. Then, " Sorry we're late, Hildegarde. But we had tire trouble."

As she faced the two men they seemed to Hildegarde more than ever formidable. She was aware, suddenly, of the weakness of her defenses. Slight, unshielded, she was alone in this clash of arms.

Yet was she alone? Back of her was all the courage of the men and women of her mother's blood. For

them there had been no white flag. Fearlessness. It
was to them that she must look for help in this tense
moment, not to the red-coated grandfather above the
fireplace.

Spiritual strength! The sword and buckler of her
belief in herself! She had an almost physical sense of
contest and of clamour, although until Winslow spoke
there was not a sound.

" Well? " that was all. Just that sinister mono-
syllable without a trace of emotion.

" I can't marry you, Neale."

His face did not change. " Have you considered the
advantages? "

" I can't see any advantages."

" I am offering you everything."

" You are offering me your — pocketbook."

It seemed to her that the words went off with a sharp
report like a gun, hitting the walls and reverberating
up to the ceiling. She had a sense of exhilaration,
hot blood was in her cheeks, her eyes held leaping
fires.

She was a gallant little figure. Fighting. With her
back to the wall. Winslow, even in the midst of his
exasperation, was keenly aware of her warmth and
ardor. What a fool he had been from the first not to
choose Hildegarde. The child was enchanting!

His voice was persuasive. " I am offering you more
than my pocketbook."

" Yet if I married you it would be because of your
money. You know that, Neale."

He did know it, and raged because of the truth of it.
Was there nothing in him that would win what he

wanted? Would youth and beauty turn always from him?

He demanded savagely of Carew. " Are you with Hildegarde in this? "

" No."

" You want her to marry me? "

Louis said with sullenness, " I can see the advantages."

" And you have advised her to do it? "

" I haven't advised her."

" Why not? "

" Because she prefers not to take my advice."

Winslow looked at Hildegarde. " You are willing if you refuse to marry me that your father shall pay the price."

Her breath was quick: " Why shouldn't he pay it as well as I? "

" You mean that marriage with me would be worse for you than financial ruin for your father? "

" I mean that for a woman, marriage without love is the greatest price she can pay."

" Which is, of course, nonsense."

" No," she leaned forward, speaking in a passion of earnestness, " marriage doesn't mean to me what you two make of it. It isn't a thing of barter and sale. It is a sacred thing — so sacred that when I go to my husband, I shall go with a flame in my heart . . . like the fire . . . on an altar. And . . . I shall pray that all my life the flame may burn clear and bright. . . ."

She stopped and they sat there, staring at her with a touch of terror. It was as if in her high defense of her dreams she had shown them an Eden where they too, once had dwelt, but from which they were now eternally shut out.

She rose, " That's all, I think. I am going away from Round Hill. It was a mistake for me to come. I am not a Carew. I belong to my mother's kind and class. And I shall be happier among them."

Winslow, also on his feet, gave a last rapier-thrust: " If you go, you know what will happen. Louis will marry Ethel."

Hildegarde said, steadily, " He must do as he thinks best."

Her father was standing beside the lacquered cabinet, his frowning gaze bent upon the floor. " So you are going to desert me — as your mother did? "

" What else could she do? "

" She might have given me — another chance. But she was hard, as you are. She didn't understand me. You don't."

Once upon a time that break in his voice would have brought her to his feet. But not now. " I am not hard. I am simply trying to hold on to my self-respect."

" I thought you loved me."

" Love doesn't mean being weak because others ask it. It means being hard because one is right."

He flung up his head, " It means nothing of the kind. It means that you have made up your mind to leave me because you want to marry that clodhopper — Crispin."

Dead silence. Then Hildegarde blazed: " I am going back to do as I please. You can marry Ethel if you want to, and Neale can keep his mansion and his money. I've got to live my own life. I'm going to be free. I'm done with this — forever."

Before they could stop her, she had left them. Out in the hall, she caught a glimpse through the open door of the newspaper men still waiting. She sped up the stairs. The light from the Blue Window streamed down on her. *Oh, heavenly light, help me now. . . . Oh, Blue Window shine upon my way. . . . I am never coming back. . . . I am never coming back. . . . I am never coming back. . . ."*

Chapter XXVIII

FIVE SAINTS WATCH TOGETHER

THE old farmhouse was dark with the gloom of a rainy October day. The two aunts went about their tasks drearily. There wasn't much to look forward to. Ahead of them were other rainy days, and the snows of winter. Monotony. Old age closing in upon them. Loneliness.

At noon they ate a silent meal. Still raining. Drearily. Aunt Olivia had an inspiration. " I'll bake this afternoon instead of tomorrow. If it clears I'll want to be working out-of-doors in the morning."

Aunt Catherine, cheered by a break in the weekly program, said, " Make some spice cake, and we'll send a box to Hildegarde."

Aunt Olivia had a feeling that sending cake to Hildegarde was carrying coals to Newcastle. Yet such things were the only expression they could make of their affection for their niece. " I'll frost it and put nuts on it."

They washed the dishes and built a great fire in the range. The kitchen glowed with it. The rain streamed against the windows. The old women beat eggs, creamed butter and sugar, and found a certain excitement in testing the boiling syrup for the frosting until it showed thread-like filaments on the spoon.

" They'll be having plenty of cake for Sally's wedding," Aunt Catherine said, out of her thoughts of Hildegarde.

" Not like this." In some things Aunt Olivia was dogmatic. This cake recipe had been handed down in her family. She was sure that nothing baked at Round Hill could measure up to it.

Their last letter from their niece had given an account of the spectacular wedding preparations. She had sent samples of Sally's dress and of her own. The old aunts had never heard anything like it. They wished they might see Hildegarde in her bridesmaid's gown. They were sure she would outshine Sally.

" Perhaps she'll be getting married some day," Miss Catherine said, " and we can be there."

" If she marries Crispin, she won't have all that fuss and feathers."

" She won't marry him if Louis has his way."

" I don't know as I blame him — when you think of all his friends can do for her."

They went on beating their eggs and cracking their nuts for the frosting. The cakes were out of the oven now, and the room was rich with fragrance.

" Let's have some for our supper," Aunt Catherine said, " it's all I'll want with a cup of tea."

" We are getting so we eat less and less," her sister told her.

" Well, most old people get that way, don't they? "

They were beginning to call themselves old. It was a sign of disintegration. They needed youth about them and high spirits. They had no initiative when it came to making new interests. In the death of Elizabeth and in the departure of her daughter they had lost all which had given zest to their lives.

Aunt Olivia smoothed the frosting in snowy layers over the dark cakes. Aunt Catherine placed the nuts in prim rows on top. When they finished, they looked at the clock. " It's after five," Aunt Olivia said, " we'll go out and feed the chickens, and then come in and have our tea."

They wore rubber coats, and carried a lantern. It was dark enough for that, and they had to visit the barns and outhouses. Of late they had hired a man to help with the heavy work. But he left at four and they made their rounds after he had gone to be sure that everything was safe and snug.

As they came back to the house they heard the whistle of the five-fifteen train — a whistle made hoarse tonight, and faint, by the thickness of the atmosphere.

The five-fifteen was the most important train that stopped at the town — an express which went on to the far west. On clear nights as it came out of the cut, trailing a long line of lighted windows, it was a challenge to their imaginations. Who sat at those windows? And where were they going? And how did they look? And what did they say? And what did they eat at this hour in the dining-car?

But tonight the rain shut the train from them, so they went on into the kitchen and closed the door. There they found warmth and the rich fragrance which still lingered from the baking of the cakes. The room was very still. Not a sound but the streaming rain, and the singing kettle. It was very cosy, but they were conscious of a need of company. On nights like this they felt the loneliness.

They set two plates on the red table-cloth, and made the tea. They had brought in the daily paper from the mail box. After supper they would wash the dishes, and Aunt Olivia would read aloud to Aunt Catherine. And that would be their evening.

The storm increased. The rain was noisier than ever, so noisy that when Aunt Olivia said, " Did you hear a car stop, Catherine? " her sister said, " It was the wind."

But it was not the wind. Presently there was the unmistakable sound of footsteps on the porch. Then a voice that made their hearts jump. *Hildegarde's!* "*Such* a night . . . if you'll hold my umbrella."

She came in, the man who had driven her from the station just behind her. "*Such a night,*" she said again, " oh, you *darlings.* . . ."

The wind literally blew her into their arms. The man who had brought her bag closed the door with difficulty. " If this keeps up," he stated, " it 'ull be doing some damage."

But what cared those two old women if the wind blew or if the storm raged? Youth had entered their lonely house and had lighted it. Hildegarde's cheeks were red with the bluster of the night, her eyes were bright with happiness. " Oh, you *darlings, darlings, darlings!* " she said over and over again, and the reiteration was like a song.

She paid the man and he went out. Hildegarde wore a raincoat of thin red oilskin. She had a red umbrella and a red hat. Her vividness was amazing. " You're

like a redbird, like a redbird," the old women said to
her. " Come and get warm, come and get warm. . . .
Have you had your supper . . . have you had your
supper? . . ." they kept saying these things over and
over again in their excitement. It was a perfect babel
of sound, and out of it Hildegarde's voice emerged,
with laughter in it. " I'm not in the least chilled, but
I'm hungry enough to eat a house."

They helped her strip off the shimmering coat, they
took the red hat from her, and opened the red umbrella
that it might dry. They did these things in a sort of
dream. It seemed incredible that she was here when
they had wanted her so much. Usually the things they
had wanted had been withheld. But here she was, and
she was saying: " I am never going back. Never."

" Why not? " they asked, breathlessly.

" Oh, it's a long story. I'll tell you while we're having supper. I'm starved. Aunt Olivia, you've baked a
spice cake. What a heavenly thing to do. The minute
I opened the door I smelled the dee-liciousness. . . ."

They felt it was delightful the way she said " dee-
licious." They laughed with her. " You run along
upstairs," Aunt Olivia urged, " and make yourself comfortable, and we'll cook something hot. There's everything in the pantry. . . ."

After that they rushed back and forth excitedly,
getting things ready. " We'll have coffee," Aunt
Catherine said, " I'll drink a cup if it keeps me awake
all night."

Aunt Olivia felt that it would be a great adventure
to keep awake. She wanted coffee, and she wanted
more than that. She wanted a good supper. She

wanted to eat with Hildegarde. She wanted something of everything they would cook. " We'll have cream toast enough for all of us, and poach enough eggs."

Because of the lack of warmth, they decided not to eat in the dining-room. But they put a white cloth in place of the red one on the kitchen table, and they set on it glass dishes of pickled peaches, and other pickles and red plum jelly, and strawberry preserves, and when Hildegarde came down, and beheld the steaming dishes, she said, " Is this the fatted calf? "

And Aunt Olivia said, " This is your welcome home."

But there was another welcome. Hildegarde had found it in that upper room where she had slept with her mother. This time the room had not seemed small, it had not seemed squalid. It had seemed like a calm and beautiful island in a sea of strife. With the rain beating around it, it was safe and still. All the clamour she had left at Round Hill seemed far away. Blessedly far. She could not even catch the echo.

And so as she sat at her aunts' table, and they bent their heads in their usual silent grace, she lifted her own, " Oh, dear Lord," she said, " I am so — thankful. . . ." That was all. But it seemed to the old aunts, listening, that their sister, Elizabeth, spoke.

While Hildegarde ate, she talked to them. She told them everything. They had a right to know. Summing it all up, it came to this — that Louis had asked things of her which were impossible. There had been no other way but to leave him.

" If I had stayed, I should have given up my self-respect — my freedom."

Aunt Olivia, pouring a third reckless cup of coffee, said: " It won't be easy after you have lived in luxury."

" There's the luxury of a mind at ease," Hildegarde said staunchly.

They gazed at her with admiration. She seemed so strong and sure. Yet she was slender as a willow, a slip of a thing, almost a child.

It was significant that, throughout the whole conversation there had been no mention of Crispin. They had not seemed to avoid it. But they had avoided it.

And now out of a silence in which they heard the beating of the rain, the howling of the wind, Aunt Catherine said, " Does Crispin know that you've left your father? "

" No. I am going to write to him tonight."

It was a simple statement, but something in her voice seemed to open to the two old women the gate of romance, as Crispin had opened it when he had talked to them. And as they listened they did not feel barred out of her paradise as those two dark men had felt on the morning she had left Round Hill. They had rather a sense of being included in this miracle which was happening before their eyes.

After Hildegarde went upstairs, they talked of it in low tones. " She's found out that she cares," they told each other, as they made the house fast for the night.

They could hear Hildegarde moving about in her room. It was wonderful how those little echoes of her footsteps broke the loneliness which had bound them for so long.

Longing to hear again that lovely voice, Aunt Olivia called up the stairs: " Have you any ink? "

" My fountain pen is filled."

" Are you warm enough? "

" Yes."

" You might write your letter by the kitchen fire."

" I shall sit up in bed with a pillow for a desk. I've done it a thousand times, and with the blankets I shall be toasting."

She was standing now at the head of the stairs with a faint light behind her. She wore a pale blue robe — a thing of silky texture and wing-like sleeves.

" It's like having an angel in the house," Aunt Olivia remarked as she rejoined her sister in the kitchen.

" I wonder if she'd like her breakfast upstairs."

" You might ask her."

Aunt Catherine trotted into the narrow hall, and had presently, her glimpse of the angel-visitant shining above her. " Shall we bring your breakfast up to you? "

" Darling . . . of course not. I want to come down. I want to run out in the rain if it is raining. I want to run out in the sun if it is shining. And oh, Aunt Catherine, if we could have hot cakes. . . ."

They would, they planned ecstatically, have sausage with the cakes. They found their own appetites returning. They no longer felt old. " We'll set the table in the dining-room. We might as well begin to have a fire in there, now that Hildegarde's back."

It was amazing to be swept along like this on a tide of anticipation. Whether it rained or shone in the morning, Hildegarde would be going in and out, she would eat with her young girl's appetite. They would hear her lovely laughter.

After they went to bed, the reckless cup of coffee kept them awake. But little cared they! The wind blew and the rain washed unceasingly against the windows, but, upstairs, snug as a bird in a nest, Hildegarde was writing a letter. They had a vision of her propped up on her pillows, the blue gown about her, the sweep of dark hair across her forehead, the candle on her bedside table, her pen flying.

But Hildegarde's pen was not flying. She was finding her letter hard to write. She began bravely, stopped, went on, tore up what she had written. For how was she ever going to tell Crispin what was in her mind? That she loved him? That her heart beat high with the thought of it? That against all the shams and shallowness his strength and sincerity shone like a star? And that she had known it all in that moment when her father had said: " You are going back to marry that clodhopper — Crispin."

She would, of course, never tell Crispin that her father had called him a clodhopper. But she would tell him the rest. How her heart had called to him. How she had wanted to take the train at once to his little house, and unlock the door with her silver key. How her sorrow at leaving her father had been swallowed up in her joy that at last she knew her love.

Yet how could she write it? What words were adequate? What pen could flame with the fire that burned her soul?

Another attempt. Failure! She lay back on her pillows, dreams in her eyes. How still it was, how heavenly still, with a sudden break in the storm. . . .

Matthew, Mark, Luke and *John* . . . all the saints

had come back. And another saint . . . Elizabeth, leaning close, with wings folded about the bed. . . .

The wind again, shaking the shutters, the rain splashing. Hildegarde roused herself, picked up her pen, wrote her letter, sealed it. Then she blew out her candle, settled herself for the night . . . slept.

The five saints guarded her — the four at the posts and the one with folded wings. Peace was there in the midst of the storm. And promise for the future.

Chapter XXIX

A GOLDEN MORNING

THE papers made the most of the sensation with which Sally had provided them. Winslow's sensitive soul squirmed as he read the headlines. He suffered tortures. Hildegarde's flight had been the final blow. Yet he had faced the newspaper men with an impassive front, and had told his story artfully. He had hinted at his own dissatisfaction with the engagement before Sally ran away. One gained the impression that it had been he and not Sally who had first wanted to break the bonds, but that a sense of honor had restrained him.

Sally was furious. "It isn't true. That's why I hate it," she told her young husband. "I deserve punishment. But not this."

"The man's a cheap cad. If you say so, I'll go down and make him eat his words."

Sally shook her head. "No, it would simply be nuts for the newspapers and beastly for me. But if you want a chastened wife, you have her. Henceforth I shall be a Griselda. As meek as they make 'em."

Merry kissed her. "I don't want you meek. You know that."

He had just come back from Round Hill. Louis had sent for him. "I need you," he had said, "I don't want to break in on your honeymoon."

Sally had protested, " But he *is* breaking in."

" That's Louis. Selfish."

" I thought you loved him."

" I do. But there's somebody I love better," his golden eyes were close to hers.

She sighed with delight. " You aren't sorry then that you married me? "

" Sorry? " he held her close. " I wish I could make you feel the gladness."

It was due finally to Sally's insistence that he went to Round Hill. " There's something back of Hildegarde's leaving Louis. I want you to find out."

So Merry had gone, and had returned with the whole story. Louis had admitted that he and Winslow between them had driven Hildegarde to the wall. " We had common sense on our side, of course. Money makes for happiness in the long run. But perhaps we went the wrong way about it."

Carew's complaining voice had gone on and on justifying himself, wailing over Winslow's demands on him. " He doesn't dare put the screws on too tight. I've told him if he pushes me too far, I'll broadcast the whole story! That he wanted Sally and couldn't get her, and that Hildegarde wouldn't have him. He hates having fun made of him. And he'd be the laughing stock of our world if they knew. I've got him on the hip . . . but of course that doesn't pay my debts. I'll have to give up some of the antiques, and Anne and I will go again to Paris."

Merry, relating all this to his wife, had added, " Louis' affairs are in a dreadful mess. Winslow will straighten them out, I think, and there will be no open break between him and Louis. Neale has changed a lot. Do you remember when we saw ' The Gods of the Mountain,' Sally? Well, he makes me think of that — only it's the other way around — as if something alive had turned to stone."

Sally shivered. " Think if I had married him."

" I refuse to think of it."

He described the house at Round Hill as he had found it. " Everything is in confusion. It gave me a queer feeling to see your wedding presents. Winslow is having them repacked, and your mother is superintending the job."

" She blames everything on me," his young wife informed him, " she told me so over the telephone yesterday. She says that her heart is broken and that I've done it." Sally was silent for a moment. " Louis will mend her heart for her," she went on presently, " it's inevitable. They will console each other for the sins of their rebellious daughters. The situation would be tragic for me, if I hadn't had it all my life to contend with." The red blood came up into Sally's cheeks. " Merry, if ever I . . . have a daughter . . . help me to show her how to grasp at the fine things, not at the shoddy and tawdry ones. . . ."

" Please God . . ." his voice broke, he swept her into his arms.

Late that night as they started upstairs, Sally said, " Do you thing she will marry Crispin? "

" Hildegarde? "

" Yes."

" I hope so."

She was smiling down at him. There was no shadow

between them of the past. Her candle was lighted, and it illumined his world. Following her up the stairs, he forgot that in his dreams there had ever been any other woman carrying a candle.

CHAPTER XXX

CRISPIN HEARS A CRY

THE news of Sally's elopement came late to Crispin. There were things to be done to the little house on the Potomac, and he had snatched at the lovely fall days in which to do them, taking a short vacation from his office. He left instructions that no mail except his personal letters should be forwarded. He liked the thought of the detachment. There was no telephone. He would be alone to think of Hildegarde. That was enough. He wanted nothing more.

Totally unaware of the emotional hurricane which had swept Round Hill, he cooked three meals a day with the assured technic of a man who has lived much out of doors. He washed his dishes, swept and garnished his own quarters, and moved about the house deftly, fitting in open shelves for books, putting a last coat of paint on a garden bench, making everything ready for the woman who would promise him nothing, but who would come some day walking up the path to open the door with her silver key. And he would find her sitting by his fire! He would admit no doubts. She was his to the end of the world!

The emptiness of the house disturbed him not a bit! He peopled it with future occupants and found much content. He saw Hildegarde in every room, but most often by the fireplace. His hearth was for her delight. Somebody else had said that, and the phrase pleased him. And the hearth would be for the delight, too, of their friends. Hospitality was such a wonderful thing! There would be his family and Hildegarde's old aunts, the people from Round Hill.

And up from Mount Vernon would come the shades of their distinguished neighbors — riding along the road in a big barouche, walking in the garden. How Hildegarde would love the make-believe on this historic soil!

And far away in the future . . . around the hearth . . . a small and shining troop . . . flitting back and forth in the firelight . . . finding fairy tales in the coals. Far away in the future, yes, but with the door flung wide for them when they came. . . .

It was on the night of the fifth day that he rode to Mount Vernon — a wonderful night with a hunter's moon. The river, stretched inertly like a great golden monster, slept between the low hills. When he came to the great mansion he saw that the windows were dark, yet in imagination he saw them lighted, with strains of music drifting out on the tides of moonlight. Once upon a time, under other moons, boats had come up to this landing place with freight of belles and beaux. Carriages galloping over the rough roads had deposited other loads of beauty and gallantry. In the shadows of the great trees had been this *rendezvous* and that — he seemed even now to glimpse the flutter of a scarf, the shine of a buckle, to catch a note of low laughter, the throbbing cadence of a passionate avowal.

The thought did not sadden him. Great passions were of the soul, and lasted throughout eternity. He would adore Hildegarde until the sun grew cold. Somewhere in some celestial sphere those other lovers lived out their spiritual destinies.

The youth in him would listen to no doctrine of annihilation. His blood was warm. Hope was his heritage. He felt that if Hildegarde were there, he could make her see things as he saw them. That nothing mattered in the whole wide world but youth and love and faith in life.

On the way home, he stopped at a neighbor's to get the cream for his mornings coffee. As he stood in the kitchen, an old newspaper was spread out on the table. His eye caught the headlines. . . . Sally's name! Winslow's! The whole thing was there in great black lines — little Sally had run away with Meriweather!

He asked for the paper and got it. He read the details sitting by his fire. Good work! Winslow had got what was coming to him!

He wondered what Hildegarde thought of it. He'd call her up in the morning. She must have thought his silence strange under the circumstances. And he'd wire to Merry.

When he went to bed he found it hard to sleep. He had set up a cot in the screened porch, and the moonlight washed over him.

When at last he drifted into slumber, he began to dream. At first the thing was nebulous, vague. He saw forms floating as in a fog. Then, all at once, as if a strong wind had blown the forms away, he was aware of a vast blue space, and of a voice crying, "*Crispin,*

Crispin." And the space seemed marked by a lattice, as if a great window stretched from horizon to horizon and from the sky above to the earth that was under it, and out from the window the voice kept crying, *" Crispin! "* And all through the night he caught the echo of that cry. And the voice was Hildegarde's!

When he waked in the morning he found himself restless, unhappy. He could not shake off the impression of his dream. Yet it was a peach of a morning! The hills were red and green and gold in the autumn sun — there was the incessant chatter of flocking birds, the chrysanthemums in the garden were like bobbing balloons as the breeze swept through them, and up the river came the Norfolk boat, with its hoarse whistle of salutation to passing craft.

He went down to the river for a bath, and came back wrapped in his mackintosh and with his hair tight-curled to find the neighbor from whom he had borrowed the paper at his gate. The neighbor, returning from the cross-roads store which was also the post-office, had brought a special delivery letter for Crispin.

" They asked me to give it to you," he said, " I signed for it."

Crispin said, " Thank you." Tore it open. Read it.

Then he spoke of the beauty of the morning. He said that his bath in the river had been cold but corking. He said . . . *" Darling, darling, may I open your door with my silver key? "* . . . he said he was going to cook a big breakfast and eat every bit of it. He said that it was kind of the neighbor to invite him over but . . . *" Darling, darling, may I open your door with my silver key? "* . . . but he thought he wouldn't. . . . Yes, on second thought he *would* accept the invitation to breakfast. He wanted to telephone a telegram. If they would promise not to do anything but put on an extra plate . . . " *Darling, darling. . . !* "

As he talked, Crispin seemed to the neighbor calm and coherent. The neighbor could not know, of course, the tumult of Crispin's thoughts, the ecstacy which thrilled to the hastily-scrawled words which he had read. He wished the neighbor would go.

The neighbor went.

Crispin had held the letter crushed in his hand. He opened it now, read again the few lines, read them aloud: " *Darling, darling, may I open your door with my silver key?* "

He laid the letter against his lips, waved it aloft Laughed. Why, the thing had come! The incredible thing! She loved him!

" *Darling, darling. . . .* "

The address she had given was that of the farm She had offered no explanations. He wanted none They would have hours henceforth for explanations.

And now, " *May I open your door with my silve, key?* "

The wonderfulness of her. The dearness. Elizabeth's daughter. His wife.

Chapter XXXI

JUST HILDEGARDE

IT HAD rained drearily all the week, but there was nothing dreary in the atmosphere of the old farmhouse. The glow of Hildegarde's presence lighted it. It seemed astounding to the two aunts that her coming should have made such a difference. They waked in the morning to hear her singing, and all day long there was her laughter. Her youth and buoyancy made of every act an amazing adventure — of going through the nests for eggs, of setting the table, of gathering armfuls of autumn leaves, of foraging in the garden for the best of the wind-blown chrysanthemums, or of going down to the box for the mail.

" You'll take cold," her aunts warned her on a certain joyous morning when she came in with the newspapers and letters, her hair wet, her red raincoat glistening.

She shone upon them. " The gods will keep me until Crispin comes."

She was utterly frank about it, including them in her ecstasies. She had had Crispin's telegram and had lived since then on the heights. He was coming this very afternoon. Having made up her mind, Hildegarde's surrender was complete. The old aunts were almost afraid of such happiness. Her mother had been like that when she married Louis.

Hildegarde rarely spoke of her father. " I've pigeonholed him," she said once when his name was mentioned.

" Do you mean you don't think of him? "

" It hurts me to think of him, and I don't want anything to spoil my happiness with Crispin."

There was a strength in thus shelving the disagreeable which reminded them of her mother.

Olivia, probing a bit, asked, " Don't you miss the luxuries? "

Then Hildegarde voiced a great truth. "Luxuries don't count when people fail you. It is like sailing on a fine ship with a hole in its bottom. You don't care for the fineness — you just want — a raft — "

Aunt Catherine spoke with dry amusement, " I suppose Olivia and I are two planks in the raft? "

" You are two white sails on a lonely sea."

" And Crispin is your rudder? "

" Crispin! " Hildegarde flung a kiss upward from the tips of her fingers. " Crispin is the captain, the crew and the bo'sun, too! Aunt Olivia, do you think I am very silly? "

They did not think her silly. They thought her wonderful, although they did not express it that way. They never used superlatives.

In the mail which Hildegarde had brought was a letter from Sally. Hildegarde, sitting on the edge of the kitchen table, read it to the two aunts, who, each in a red-cushioned rocking chair, listened as if it were a message from a strange country. Never, never, had they lived as Sally was living in a world of high and romantic experiences. She spoke a new language, but they loved it.

Hildegarde, *you angel:* Crispin has just telephoned, and I am so thrilled I can hardly hold my pen. But I *must* write. To think that you, too, have run away from Round Hill! And you are going to be married! Crispin didn't tell me all that in words, but his voice told me. He was so happy that he was incoherent. And he had a train to make.

Precious child, may you never regret it! I don't. I am as care-free as a summer cloud, and as domestic as my doll, Sarah. Nothing matters in my young life but Merry. And each day I am falling more in love with him. Which sounds as brazen as a brass band, but it isn't. A wife should love her husband — and I am as meek as they make 'em. Old-fashioned. I really feel that I shouldn't in the least mind Merry's foot on my neck, but I know it will never be there, for he is so gallant and gay and generous — a gentleman, thank God. I've never been quite a lady, mother's daughter couldn't be — not even with my birth and background.

I tell Merry that I'm going to grow old like Sarah — part my hair in the middle and wear caps. He says he doesn't care what I wear, and that he'd rather have me in caps than with my face lifted. But that's a long time off, isn't it? And there are the long years of youth between, and Merry and I are going to make the best of them. Merry thinks he'll go into politics, and I am perfectly sure that I shall make a fortune in raising geese. There are loads of them now on the place — as plump as dumplings and as dignified as dowagers.

But this isn't to advertise myself as a goose-girl. So I shall stop at once. And you will have your wedding here, won't you? And as soon as possible? Write that you will. Or let Crispin wire. We can hardly wait to hear.

Ever rapturously,

SALLY.

Hildegarde, red as a rose, folded the letter. " Sally is taking a great deal for granted."

But not too much! The old aunts knew that.

" If we could have you until spring," Aunt Catherine ventured, " we should like it. But we want you to do as you think best."

Looking at the wistful old faces, Hildegarde said: " Don't worry. I'll stay with you through the winter. I'd like a wedding in May — " She caught herself up. " I am talking as if it were settled."

It was settled. In her mind and in theirs, as it had been in Sally's!

Hildegarde went to the train to meet her lover. The two of them returned in a heavy downpour. After the greetings were over, one of the aunts said:

" I am sorry it rains."

" Why be sorry? We love it, Hildegarde and I. With the leaves blowing."

Crispin had his arm about Hildegarde. It was beautiful to see them. They shed a rosy light over the dark old house.

From her shelter Hildegarde announced, " We are going for a walk."

" In this storm? "

" Why not? It is heavenly outside. And we'll be home in time for supper."

Well, if heaven for these two meant facing the elements there was no reason why they shouldn't. The old aunts watched the lovers go down the path. A sweep of wind buffeted them, swirled around them an eddy of leaves, lifted their umbrella. They turned their backs to the blast, saw the watchers at the window, and waved. They seemed to the two old creatures as vivid as a burst of sunshine against the dun dreariness of the day.

" Were we ever like that, Olivia? "

" Never, but Elizabeth was."

They had supper to cook and went about it. The rooms were dark, and they lighted the lamps.

" I hope they're not getting wet," Aunt Catherine said, as she drew the curtains.

Aunt Olivia was arranging flowers in a bowl. Crispin had brought roses to Hildegarde — little saffron ones.

" Merry gave you violets, and so did Bobby," he had said, " but I remembered the old yellow rosebush by the gate."

" They were always Hildegarde's favorites," Aunt Catherine remarked now as she set the bowl in the center of the table, " and they were Elizabeth's. She liked them in this bowl, because it was blue."

The table looked really very festive. There were, to be sure, no silver pheasants, no Florentine lace, but the linen was spick and span, and the roses helped. The two aunts surveyed it with satisfaction. Then they went into the kitchen.

It was some time after that a knock came on the front door. The old women had little company, and most people entered by the back way. Aunt Olivia took off her apron and went through the living-room. She stopped to light the lamp in the front hall, then she opened the door.

Louis Carew stood there. He said at once: " May I see Hildegarde? I am her father."

" Hildegarde is out. Will you come in and wait? "

He came in and seemed very elegant and out of place in the plain room. Miss Olivia didn't know what to say to him; it was usually Catherine who took the initiative in conversation. She stammered, " I'll get my sister," and fled.

In the kitchen she spoke breathlessly, " It's Louis Carew."

" What does he want? "

" He asked for Hildegarde."

For a moment Aunt Catherine did not speak. Then she said, " Why should he come now to spoil her happiness? " She was untying her apron. " You watch the supper, Olivia."

Louis Carew was still standing when Aunt Catherine entered. In her old-fashioned way she said, " Won't you sit down? " but he waited for her to be seated.

She took a rocking chair, but she did not rock, and in spite of her clumsy plumpness there was something of dignity and distinction in her repose.

She began, " You want to see Hildegarde? "

" Yes."

" She has gone for a walk. It will be some time

before she comes in. Is there anything you can say
to me? "

" Has she told you she left Round Hill? "

" Yes."

" I am here to reason with her. I had common-
sense on my side, but not tact. I want her to return
with me."

" Why should she return? "

" Because she was precipitate, and because the farm
is no place for her."

She knew what he meant. She knew that this house
must seem to him crude, cheap and uncomfortable.
That she and Olivia must seem common and stupid
old creatures, that he shrank from the thought of such
a home and such associates for his daughter. So she
said at once:

" Hildegarde will not live on the farm. She is going
to marry Crispin Harlowe."

Carew's hands clutched at the arms of his chair.
" Has she promised? "

" Yes."

" Is he here? "

She nodded. " They are out now together."

" In the rain? "

" They don't know that it rains."

" Why not? "

" They are in love."

He laughed harshly. " They think they are."

" Put it any way you like," Aunt Catherine told him,
" but there's this about it, they don't care whether the
sun shines or the storm beats. They are young, life
is before them, they are happy."

She spoke with a restrained force that startled him. She was not, he perceived, as colorless as he had thought. There was, indeed, something about her which, in spite of her clumsiness and lack of comeliness, reminded him of Elizabeth. It was, if he had known it, a spiritual quality which linked her with her sister. If she had not Elizabeth's vision, she had at least a sane sense of values. And she knew nothing of weakness. Her life had been hard, and it had made her strong.

He jumped to his feet and stood looking down at her: " Do you think I am going to let her marry Harlowe? What kind of future will she have with him? "

" What kind of future will she have with you? "

It was a fierce challenge. He met it almost with violence. " She will have the things which belong to girls of her class. Elizabeth wanted her to have them. She sent the child to me."

" She hoped for better things, and they have not come. And Hildegarde is glad to be with us again. She feels that her mother's spirit still lingers in this house."

He cast a half-fearful look about him. " Here? "

" Yes. The peace of her. The beauty of her mind and soul. She gave these to her child. You gave nothing but handsome clothes and a trip to Paris."

When he answered her, there was a touch of contempt in his voice. What did she know of life? This drab old dame! Shut within her narrow acres! " I can't expect you to understand. I am practical, and you are not. If Hildegarde marries Harlowe, she may have regrets. It isn't always wise to spurn the flesh-pots."

"She doesn't spurn them," the old woman assured him. "I think there are times when she longs for them. But they would never satisfy her."

He dropped into a chair. "It is useless for us to discuss it. When Hildegarde comes, she can say what she wants to do."

"You mean to see her?"

"Yes."

There was silence for a moment, then the old woman said, "I am going to ask you, for the love you once bore the mother, to let the child alone."

The wistfulness in her voice disturbed him. He began to wish that he had not pushed this thing. This dark old house oppressed him. The thought of Elizabeth's spirit there to challenge him for his stewardship of her child gave him a shivering sense of uneasiness.

And this old woman with her hard strength made him feel a weakling. She made him feel that he had pulled the roof of his fortunes down on his head, when, as a matter of fact, the roof had fallen.

He wanted to escape. There were people who made him feel strong. Ethel, for example! She might be shallow, and her methods were obvious. But she was comforting — and she had none of these fantastic ideas about conscience.

Yet — there had been a loveliness about Elizabeth. There was a loveliness about Hildegarde!

With a real emotion in his voice, he said: "The best I have ever given to any one, I have given to

Elizabeth and to her daughter. And I have — lost them — ”

His haggard eyes met hers. She said gently:

“ Some day — I think, Hildegarde’s heart will come back to you.”

But he knew that it would not come back. Not if he married Ethel. . . . He took his hat and coat from the chair where he had laid them. “ Will you tell her I was here? ”

“ Tomorrow, perhaps. Not tonight. I should hate to cast a shadow on our little feast.”

Through the open door he could see the homely preparations, the table with its clean white cloth and its saffron roses. Here there would be no men in dinner coats, no women in shimmering gowns. Just Hildegarde in her simple dress. *Just Hildegarde.* . . .

He bade the old aunt an abrupt “ Good-night.”

She heard his retreating footsteps in the hall. The outer door opened and shut, and presently the taxi coughed and sputtered on its way to the station.

The rain had stopped and there was a stiff breeze blowing — it blew so hard, indeed, on the hilltop where Crispin stood with Hildegarde, that only the great rock at their backs saved them from being swept before it like leaves from a tree.

The night had come, and the sky above them was an inverted sapphire bowl. The valley curving up to meet it was blue with shadows. The lovers on their hilltop seemed thus enclosed in a limitless sphere studded overhead with the brightness of the stars, and below with the lights of the countryside. They had a sense of the infinite, the eternal. They had walked in the rain, had taken refuge in the church, and had come at last in the clearing weather to the place which was dedicated to their meetings with the serene spirit which watched over them. They were young and ardent, and they had been wildly and humanly happy, yet now, for the moment, their happiness was glorified by the ethereal, the exquisite.

"Our marriage shall be forever," Crispin whispered. "I shall love you to the end of the world."

Perhaps because he believed it, it might come true. To Louis Carew love had been always the adventure of the moment. To Crispin it meant allegiance to an ideal. Thus the two starting from different points would arrive at last at different goals. As a man thinks shapes, in the main, his destiny.

"I shall love you to the end of the world," said Crispin therefore, and held Hildegarde close, and took the kiss for which he had asked when he stood by the gate a year ago.

Around them swept the murmuring breeze, and it seemed to Crispin that Elizabeth's voice said low in his ear:

"Hold her to your heart as I have held her."

When it was time for them to go, they raced hand in hand down the hill. Up the road they went, passing a taxi whose lights cast them into the shadow so that they were not seen by the occupant. Hildegarde did not know that her father was in the taxi. If she had known, she would have let him go. Her happiness did not include him. The time might come when she would forgive, but today she had forgotten him.

The two young people laughed as they ran. They

came to the old oak under which Crispin had stood when he had first known that he loved Hildegarde. He stopped her there and kissed her. He kissed her again before they entered the warm little house. Life was wonderful. Everything was wonderful!

They opened the door and went in.

" Where have you been? " the old aunts asked them.

And Hildegarde said, " In heaven " — and opened her arms to them.

THE END

TEMPLE BAILEY

An Autobiography

ALTHOUGH my ancestry is all of New England, I was born in the old town of Petersburg, Virginia. I went later to Richmond, and finally at the age of five to Washington, D. C., returning to Richmond for a few years in a girls' school, which was picturesquely quartered in General Lee's mansion, now the home of the Virginia Historical Association.

I think it was, perhaps, because of my life in cities that I learned in early years to appreciate the romance of them, the picturesqueness, the charm. It was, indeed, one reason for my adoration of Dickens, that he made London a place of dear delights, finding in crowded squares and quiet streets the human stories.

I was not a strong child, and my school-life was somewhat intermittent, but my father in my out-of-school days supervised my English as carefully as my mother supervised my manners. I had to write themes which my father blue-penciled, and so I came to girlhood and finally to womanhood with a rather easy gift of writing. But I really did not want to write. I was not in the least ambitious for a career. I was tremendously interested in people. I have, in fact, been always an intensely social person, liking my kind, and clinging somewhat stubbornly to old ideals of democracy and the doctrine that " a man's a man for a' that."

There came, however, a season of stress and sorrow which drove me to self-expression. I scribbled a story or two, and found, eventually, that editors liked them. A prize came to me from a love-story contest in the Ladies' Home Journal, and I was much encouraged. After that, I wrote children's stories, a child's book, love stories; appearing at last in the pages of Harper's, Scribner's, the Saturday Evening Post, the Outlook, Collier's, and most of the women's magazines.

A series of novels followed. The first was " Glory of Youth," then " Contrary Mary," " Mistress Anne," " The Tin Soldier," " The Trumpeter Swan," " The Gay Cockade," " The Dim Lantern," and " Peacock Feathers."

Many of my books have Washington as a background, because I know it best, but whether I range from Boston and Nantucket to Maryland and the Chesapeake, or on to the Rockies and the Pacific Coast, I find that while people are modified by environment, they are fundamentally alike, and that the drama of life is as ancient as Genesis, and as modern as an airship.